I0626731

HUNTED

AN ARA CLASSEN NOVEL

LYNN TYLER

Lynn Tyler
Kitchener, Ontario, Canada
www.lynntylerbooks.com

Book Layout © 2015 BookDesignTemplates.com

Hunted by Lynn Tyler. -- 1st ed.
ISBN 978-0-9951899-0-4

To Andrew, because you named her.

CHAPTER ONE

There was nothing Ara Classen hated more than arrogant vampires. Unless they happened to be arrogant vampires with a thing for committing blood rape.

Which meant the man sitting at the table in their interrogation room didn't have to do anything else to make her hate him.

Her partner, Fen Blair, cracked his knuckles and hovered over the suspect. "The victim made a positive identification. She picked your picture out of the lineup we provided her. And the DNA from the scene is going to nail your ass to the wall."

"I fail to see the problem. Since when is drinking from a live donor against the law?" Their suspect had the nerve to inspect his nails and brush a non-existent piece of lint off the shoulder of his black blazer.

"Since the first world war," Ara said, resisting the urge to smack the guy upside the head. He had been a member of the Vampire Elder Council for decades. Her grandfather, another elder, would be mortified if she attacked a fellow vampire just because he was stupid. "We have used donated *bagged* blood since then, as mandated by law."

The suspect scoffed. "There are circumstances where having a live donor is perfectly legal, and even encouraged."

Some older vampires detested the very thought of bagged blood. Bagged blood severely limited vampire strength and senses. She didn't notice the loss very much, given that she'd been raised on the stuff, but the transition had been hard for the old vampires. "So you admit you took blood from an unwilling human then." Fen leaned down and braced his weight on the tabletop so only an inch of space remained between their faces.

She appreciated the way Fen made it a statement instead of a question. She also appreciated the way he loomed over the suspect, forcing the man to tilt his head back to look him in the face.

Fen would like the show of submission. His wolf drove him to show his dominance and there was nothing her partner liked better than to intimidate suspects, especially if they were guilty. Particularly if the suspects were pricks, like the guy sitting before them.

The suspect flinched just a little before gathering himself together again. "I fail to see the problem. I needed blood and the human was nearby. The law states I am allowed to use a human if I am in need of blood."

"In an emergency, yes," Ara said, making a show of flipping through the man's file. "However, I have a delivery slip here that proves you accepted a delivery of blood just yesterday morning. With access to that much blood, your situation would hardly be classified as an emergency. Besides, the law also states you must have the express permission of the human donor before you take blood."

She didn't mention the fact that he'd nearly drained the young human woman to death. Nor did she point out that the young woman had tried desperately to fight him off, if her injuries were anything to go by.

Ara had promised the girl she would make sure her attacker received the stiffest punishment there was. She wasn't about to let one tiny little loophole in the law stop her from keeping that promise.

The vampire drummed his fingers on the table. "Really, Arabella Classen. Has your grandfather been completely remiss about teaching you to respect your elders?"

"He taught me to use my brain and only respect those who deserve it." It wasn't a lie. He *had* taught her that respect had to be earned. The suspect didn't need to know how Ara's grand-father lectured her on how to be a proper vampire daughter every time they got together.

He continued to drum his fingers. He shifted in his chair and re-crossed his legs.

"Something wrong?" Ara asked pleasantly, pleased to get some type of reaction from the suspect.

"I need some blood."

"Really?" Fen drawled. "You attacked the victim only three days ago. The amount of blood you took from that girl should have satisfied you for a week at the very least."

The suspect clamped his mouth shut. A spark of something familiar rippled through her. The way he held himself, the way he clenched his fingers together until his knuckles whitened all screamed at her. A fine sheen of sweat glistened on his upper lip and his leg twitched as if he were trying to stop himself from bouncing it.

Next to her, Fen pushed his face even closer to the suspect's and peeled his lips away from his teeth. They weren't his wolf fangs; those only came out when he was in his animal form. Still, Fen's human teeth were no joke. His pitch-black hair and eerie pale-green eyes made him look sinister and more than a little unbalanced. She almost felt sorry for the suspect.

Almost.

Then she remembered the young woman they'd visited in the hospital. Her throat had been practically torn out. It was a miracle she'd survived and even more of a miracle she'd been with it enough to point to a photo.

The girl would carry the scars of her attack for the rest of her life, both physical and emotional. No amount of therapy would ever erase the fear the girl would carry of vampires, and probably of all paranormals for the rest of her life.

Fen snarled and gripped the edge of the table. For a split second, she wondered if his beast would charge to the surface

He took a breath and closed his eyes. She'd seen him do this often enough to know he was pushing the wolf back, forcing the creature further into his mind.

Too bad. She wouldn't have minded if he tore this guy to pieces.

Her partner's next words didn't surprise her one bit. "You're addicted."

The suspect licked his lips. A manic light sparkled in his eyes. "Yes," he hissed.

A snarl of her own slipped from her lips. She'd seen this situation dozens of times before. Suspects thought they could get out of their punishment if they played the addict card. It grated on her nerves. "The fact that you confessed to an addiction to live blood won't help you."

"I'm sure you can see I wasn't in full control of my impulses. Surely, you can understand, Inspector Classen. You must have had live blood at some point in your life. The last time I checked, they still taught vampire young how to hunt in case of emergencies. And you are not so young to have been raised completely on bagged blood. I knew you when you were mere hours old."

She brushed aside his words. She remembered the taste of live blood, the power that rushed through her veins and the strength that invaded her muscles, how acute her senses had been. The memory of the intense craving for human blood also stood out in her brain. "My experiences and self-control are not being investigated. Yours are. And while I have no doubt you are addicted, addiction does not happen overnight. It takes a series of experiences with live human donors to become addicted."

The suspect's expression hardened. "We should be returning to the old ways and you know it. We outnumber and outpower humans. Why are we bending to their will?"

There was no point trying to talk sense into this man. "Human lives matter."

In the end, it didn't matter if he was addicted or not—blood rape was against the law. Her gut curdled. How many people had this man attacked? How many had he killed before the human woman in the hospital survived to identify him?

The man curled his lip. "Humans are nothing more than paid labor for our industries and a food source. Their lives are worthless. Tell me, how does your grandfather feel about you lowering yourself to protect humans? Humans, especially their females, are only good for their blood. The adrenaline they pump into their blood during an attack is delicious. You should try it."

His words brought her back to that hospital room, back to the young woman, barely out of her teenage years, pale, injured and terrified. She had been in that girl's position before. She remembered the pain and the fear, remembered the decades it took to trust a male again. This girl didn't have all those decades to rebuild her life.

And this vampire scum didn't even care.

Shame welled within her. Once upon a time, she'd had plenty of human friends. Her mother had warned her of the pitfalls, but she hadn't listened. Until her friends grew up and questioned why she wasn't aging with them. She'd distanced herself from humans then. It had been difficult to separate herself from people she'd truly cared about because she couldn't confess she was a vampire.

The 1950s had come along, ushering in a new era with both shifters and vampires revealing their existence. Suddenly, the need to hide her true nature was no longer required. By that time, she'd realized she would outlive any human she befriended. It didn't seem worth the heartache, so the wall she built between herself and humans had remained intact.

Something in her snapped. Her gut boiled, blood thundered through her veins and sharp pain seared her mouth as her fangs exploded through her gums. She drew back her fist and punched him in the face.

His nose cracked under her knuckles, and blood, warm and wet, flowed over her hand. "You're a bastard. And my grandfather will be happy to find out we're getting rid of the likes of you."

The man cupped his nose and looked up at her, his eyes wide. "You broke my nose."

Fen laughed, low and rough. "You had it coming."

The suspect was out of his chair and over the table before she could even process what was happening, scattering paper and notes everywhere.

Luckily, Fen was on the ball. Her partner gripped the crazed vampire by the neck and swung him sideways, slamming him into the wall.

The interview room door opened and Bo strolled in. "Got ourselves a lively one today, do we?"

"I'll say," Fen said, shaking the suspect a little.

"What happened to him?"

Fen laughed again. "Ara broke his nose for a little quip about human females not being worth more than a convenient meal."

Bo shook his head. "When will they learn? What's he in for?"

Ara spared him a look, confident in Fen's control of the situation. "Blood rape."

Her brother's face darkened. "The girl in the hospital?"

She nodded.

If there was one thing Bo couldn't stand, it was violence against females, of any race or species. "Well then, I'll have to think things through. Should I prolong it? Then again, why would I want to waste my time on the likes of him?"

The assailant gurgled, clearly trying to say something. Fen loosened his grip. He smiled at the man. It would have been polite but for the flash of his teeth, the incisors sharp and deadly. "What was that?" Fen asked.

"Who the fuck is he?"

Swearing from a former Elder. Now they were getting somewhere.

She flashed the slime a sweet smile. "Meet my brother, Bo Classen. He will take things from here."

The vampire struggled in earnest, stark terror replacing the faint fear. His face drained of color. Even his lips paled. "No. No. *Nooo*."

Bo grinned, his expression so dark and twisted, she would have pulled back if she hadn't known her brother reserved it for the criminals they worked with on a daily basis. "I see my reputation precedes me. And I don't appreciate scum like you trying to harm my sister."

Her brother grabbed the man and dragged him out of the room, the suspect's screams echoing off the surrounding walls.

CHAPTER TWO

"So, did it feel good?" Fen smirked.

Ara shook her hand out. She could pretend ignorance, but he'd call her bluff. Besides, it wasn't like she regretted it. "Breaking his nose? Yeah. It felt good."

"Lucky. I would have loved to do something like that. Or bite him, give him a taste of his own medicine."

Her partner couldn't rough up a suspect. His beast always simmered just below the surface, and giving in to one moment of spontaneous violence could unleash a furious wolf in the station. She'd seen it happen once, and only once, and it wasn't something she was keen to see again.

"You have plans for tonight?" Fen asked.

"Nope. Just a couple chocolate bars and a television marathon. What about you?"

"Well, Colin's invited everyone over for a drink. So you know how that goes. I'll probably end up breaking up a few fights, maybe discipline a pup or two. The last time Colin threw a party, one of the younger wolves took it upon himself to mark his territory. It got kind of messy."

She snorted. "He pissed on a tree? Is that what you're telling me?"

"Actually, he pissed on Colin's car. He was in the dog house for two weeks for that one."

"That's a bad joke," she said, though a smile stretched her mouth anyway.

He continued to prattle on about the pack's antics. She nodded every once in a while to show she was listening, grateful for his voice. The guy knew her too well. He knew how badly her loss of control affected her, just as he knew how well the endless stream of babble gave her something to concentrate on.

She collected the scattered papers as she listened, stuffing it back into the file. The suspect's screaming had died away. "Shall we?"

She was still unsettled when they left the interview room. Rage and shame battled for dominance in the pit of her stomach. She held her body as stiffly as possible, determined to regain some sense of control over her emotions.

Their shared office was at the end of the hall, well away from the rest of the officers. In order to get there, they had to pass Bo's room. And, if the silence was anything to go by, he'd decided not to play with his food.

Bo didn't actually eat criminals. He didn't truly enjoy his job either. Someone had to do it, and Grandfather pushed Bo toward the position from the second Bo entered the police academy. Once Grandfather set his mind on something, one needed an iron will to resist him.

Luckily, she was iron to the core.

"Just a second." She paused by Bo's door. "I just want to check on Bo. He's been too quiet recently."

Even though her senses were dulled by the lack of live blood, she heard the hiss of a blade swinging through the air, followed by a dull thud. Something heavy hit the door and she backed away quickly.

The blood rapist's head had most likely just been separated from his body.

She shuddered and picked up her pace, eager to get away from the suddenly stifling hall. "I'll check on him later. After he's cleaned up."

"Does it still bother you? The executions, I mean," Fen asked. "Even after all this time?"

"It doesn't bother you?" she shot back. "Not even a little?"

"Shifters are different. We'll do anything to keep our pack

safe, even if that means killing." He shrugged and held their office door open.

'Office' was a rather generous term for the room they'd been assigned. It had been a broom closet before they'd joined the force. It had just enough room for a long table they liked to call their desk, two chairs and two filing cabinets. The mini fridge where she stored her blood—when she remembered to bring any—and Fen's meat was jammed under the desk, and their coats always hung on the back of the door.

She turned her back to him as she jammed the suspect's file into their filing cabinet. She'd already known his answer before he said anything. He'd told her hundreds of times that shifters valued the pack over the individual.

"It's okay, you know?" he whispered. "It's all right that killing bothers you. A good thing, even."

Plastic crinkled and the scent of smoked meat filled the room. She wrinkled her nose. Fen wasn't as unaffected as he liked everyone to believe. He ate when he was upset, and it was usually some kind of animal product. Lately, he'd been chowing down on beef jerky. At least it was better than raw meat. Not that he'd actually ever brought beef tartare into the office.

She sighed and pushed away from the table. "I worry more about Bo. He's not as psycho as he comes across. This has to be screwing with him in some way."

"Bo's not a baby anymore. He can handle himself."

She knew that. She really did. It didn't stop her heart from sinking when she thought about the innocent little boy he used to be.

She pulled her shoulders back and tilted her chin at an angle her mother had always called stubborn. The only thing wallowing in misery would accomplish was to highlight her vulnerability.

"Can I have some?" She held out her hand and wiggled her fingers.

"Why should I? You don't even like it. You told me it was gross."

"Sharing is caring," she quipped, holding out a hand for some of his stash.

If Fen saw through her attempt at changing the subject, he didn't mention it. "The last time you looked at my jerky, you told me it was so full of nitrates and fat, no one in their right mind would touch it. Now you want some?"

"It's not like I have to worry about clogged arteries or high blood pressure." She wiggled her fingers.

"Have a bag of blood or something."

"I drank my last one this morning. I would go raid Bo's stash but, you know, he has a severed head to deal with."

Fen let out a long suffering sigh and held the bag out to her.

Grinning, she dipped her fingers in and grabbed a piece of the dried meat. Flavor exploded on her tongue, rich, earthy and slightly spicy. "Thanks."

"Ew, sick," Fen said. "Don't talk with your mouth full."

"Like you care."

He smiled. "I know. It made you smile though."

They chewed in silence for a couple of seconds. "I still remember the look on your face when you first saw me eating food. You looked like you thought I was going to die or something," she said when she'd swallowed.

"Be nice," he answered. "I can't help it if everyone thinks all vampires do is suck blood like leeches. How was I supposed to know you could eat and drink whatever the hell you want? Not to mention the fact that you actually have a heartbeat and working lungs. And that you can walk around in full sunlight."

"It's not like shifters are forthcoming about their physiology. I didn't know you could shift into your wolf form whenever you wanted instead of getting all furry only on the full moon," she responded.

She grabbed another strip of jerky. "I am in for one hell of a lecture from the chief tomorrow. I can't believe I lost control like that. Why did they even bother installing cameras in the paranormal interrogation room?"

"They just want to cover their asses. They can't do anything to us, not really. We're employed by the Council for Paranormal Affairs, not the police board."

Her partner was right. Technically, the police didn't employ them. They just shared space with them. It wouldn't stop the human police chief from making himself known in the morning though.

"Relax, Ara. Why don't you come over tonight? Grab a drink and unwind."

If it were anyone but Fen asking, she would've thought she was getting hit on. She and Fen had been partners for the last five years and she'd met his pack plenty of times. "I'm not in the mood."

"Come on. Mandy will be there. And I'm pretty sure Colin invited Bo for a poker game tonight if you want to watch over him for a while."

He looked at her with a grin. He knew exactly what to say to convince her. It was a hazard of working with a wolf shifter; they always scented when their prey was weakening.

Maybe spending time with Mandy, Fen's sister—and, more recently, her best friend—would shake her out of her funk. She could soothe her worries over her brother's mental state at the same time.

"Fine. Let's do the paperwork in the morning and go."

"Jeez, don't sound so enthusiastic. It's not like I'm dragging you out of here by your hair."

The words forced a small shudder out of her. Fen had no way of knowing what those words triggered. She swallowed past the sudden nausea gathered in her throat and concentrated on keeping her face blank.

Apparently she'd failed because Fen was at her side in the

span of a second. "I'm sorry. I shouldn't have said that, especially with what went down a few minutes ago. Mandy is forever quizzing me on your dating habits. You should go so she can ask you herself, take the pressure off me a little."

She forced a smile. "Well, that settles it then. I'll go to get Mandy out of your hair. I'm not sure if she's interested because she wants to set me up with someone or if she's hoping for me to set her up."

"Thank you. Come on, I'll drive. You look like death warmed over."

"Gee, thanks."

Fen looked over at her, his sunny smile back in place. The average person would never know there was a dangerous wolf constantly fighting for dominance with his human side. "You're welcome. How fast do you think we can get there?"

She grinned, remembering Fen's driving habits. There was a reason she always worried about him getting arrested while driving.

"What do you think the chances are that we can sneak past the chief's office without him noticing?" she shot back.

"Pretty good. That man's not very observant."

"He had to have been a good officer at some point," she argued. Although, why she was sticking up for the guy, she really didn't know. "Otherwise, how would he have become chief?"

"Police corruption."

She pointed her finger at his chest. "I always knew something was fishy."

Ara didn't really think the chief was a corrupt officer. Just a poor one. "Let's chance it. I don't want to wait around until he decides to leave. Might be all night. I heard he had a fight with his wife, so it might be a while."

Luck was not on their side. The chief's office door was wide open and he looked up when they tiptoed by. "Don't think I don't know what happened. We'll talk in the morning," The chief snarled.

The man looked troubled, scared even. She could scent his blood, rich with adrenaline, and her stomach growled, reminding her she hadn't had her normal ration of blood that morning. The meat had some protein in it and would tide her over until she got to the Alpha House, but she'd need to raid the fridge for the blood Colin kept on hand for her and Bo.

Fen frowned, a concerned expression etched onto his face. As a shifter, he smelled so much more than blood. He scented emotion. He'd told her fear smelled like clean, sharp steel and copper.

It was how she would have described the scent of blood if anyone bothered to ask.

"What happened?" her partner asked. "Something isn't right."

"There's been an attack." The chief scowled at them like they had committed the crime.

She went on instant alert. There was something the chief wasn't telling them. "Do you need our help?"

"Perhaps."

Forgetting about her need for blood, Ara stepped into the room. She could count on one hand how many times she'd entered the office willingly. The number of times the Toronto chief of police had asked them to help with a case was even fewer. "We can go right now if you need us to."

The chief shook his head. "I need my guys to finish up before I send the two of you out."

"Are you sure?" Fen asked. "I can go over to the scene and see if I can scent anything."

"You know how I feel about the two of you working with my guys," the chief said.

Ara let out a grim laugh. "You do know we're not going to eat them, right?"

The chief glared at her. She glared right back. She was so

sick of the humans in this station. They were disgusted by paranormals. Most humans were. The only reason there wasn't
more discrimination was because vampires owned most of the
large companies in the world.

It was easy to build a successful company when one lived
for hundreds of years.

The chief backed down first, breaking eye contact and
standing so quickly that his chair rolled back and hit the wall
with a crash. He pushed past them into the hall, muttering about
how his job would be so much better if certain upstart vampires
really did have to stay in the dark, like the Dracula stories suggested.

Fen stopped her from following the man by placing a hand
on her wrist. He shook his head. "Come on. There's no point
talking to him right now. You'd probably break his arm or
something."

"Not funny," she grumbled.

"Never underestimate a woman when she's angry," he commented. He tapped his nose. "Besides, he's too pissed off to talk
properly anyway."

"I didn't need any special scent power to see he was pissed,"
she mumbled.

"Let's go," he said. "There's an entire bottle of scotch with
my name on it at home. And I don't want to have to battle with
Colin over it."

Despite her anger, she gave a grudging smile. So many people came and went at the Alpha House that Fen really did label
his stuff, including his alcohol.

She followed him out to his car, still fuming over the chief's
reaction. He didn't like paranormals and expressed that to them
numerous times.

There was no use fretting over the chief, not when he refused to tell them what was going on. Pushing it from her mind,
she slid into the passenger seat next to Fen and buckled her seatbelt.

CHAPTER THREE

She gripped the arm rest and rolled down the window, letting the late summer wind rush over her face.

Summer in Canada was a wonderful thing. Late August was especially beautiful. There was a hint of something crisp floating on the breeze. If she closed her eyes and concentrated, she could almost smell autumn coming.

The engine purred as Fen pushed it harder. The hum was soothing, and her eyes fluttered open. A part of her wanted to laugh with exhilaration at the speed. Another part of her, the more rational part, cautioned her as the scenery began to blur.

"You're going to get arrested," she pointed out. The words didn't come out as harsh as she meant them to. She was having far too much fun.

There were advantages to being nearly indestructible. Not having to worry too much about dying in a car accident was one of them. Still, the idea of trying to talk one of their own out of writing Fen a ticket wasn't very palatable.

"Relax," the man in question said from beside her. "I know what I'm doing."

"Right. Do you have any sway with the local traffic cops? Because I don't."

The car swerved and he cursed. She stared hard at his profile. He was normally an aggressive driver, but he didn't usually drive like he was *trying* to hit something.

Unless he needed an outlet for his wolf.

"What's going on? I know it's not only the murders."

"Caught on to that, did you?"

Ara shrugged. "I know you."

Fen rubbed the back of his neck with one hand before gripping the steering wheel hard enough to leave dents. "It's been a rough couple of weeks with the pack. I've had to dole out a lot more discipline lately. It worries me."

His confession surprised her; she'd always thought the local wolf shifter pack was relatively stable. Colin, Fen's littermate, was an exceptional alpha. He was widely known in the paranormal community. Every time she'd been to pack grounds, everyone had seemed content. "Have there been challenges to his leadership?"

"Not to his leadership, exactly. Everyone is more on edge than usual. Little things become big issues. It's normal around a full moon, but this has gone on far too long. It's always the same thing, no matter who it is."

That piqued her interest. "What's the problem?"

"Territory disputes. Everyone wants to shift their homes away from the forest. Of course, that puts everyone in very close quarters. And while we are pack animals, we all want our own space. Let's just say, one of the teenagers taking a leak on Colin's car has been the least of my worries."

"You're being very detailed about what's going on," she commented. Normally, members of the paranormal community were pretty secretive. She had been alive long enough to have gleaned most of the details about shifter packs, but Fen generally kept his mouth shut about pack matters.

He shrugged, staring forward. She scented the rush of blood before the flush rose up his neck. "You're my partner and my sister's best friend. I trust you not to go blabbing about our troubles to everyone and their mother."

She stared at him. It always amazed her how much he trusted her. Wolf shifters, as a rule, didn't normally trust anyone outside their pack structure.

Then again, maybe he needed someone outside his pack to

talk things over with. She knew most of his pack and they always spoke to him in hushed tones, as if they were afraid he would punish them for talking too loudly.

"Why did you get stuck being the big bad wolf anyway?" she blurted.

He gave her a half smile. "Just my destiny, I guess. Like Colin was destined to be the alpha."

She snorted. "I don't believe in destiny. If I did, I would say it royally screwed you over. Aren't you the oldest of your litter? Doesn't the oldest usually become alpha?"

"I wasn't screwed over. I think it's the other way around, actually," Fen answered. "I get my own wing in the Alpha House, and I don't have to make any of the big decisions. All I have to do is slap sense into people once in a while."

She got the feeling there was something else behind his words, something he wasn't telling her.

Suddenly, her phone chirped. She groaned, recognizing her mother's ringtone.

"Aren't you going to answer that?" Fen asked when the ringing continued.

"No. My mom's got this uncanny ability. She always knows when I've had a bad day. If I dismiss the call, she'll know I sent it right to voicemail and she'll just keep trying until I pick up."

Fen nodded and faced forward again. She caught the amused expression and rushed to explain. "She tried to set me up on a blind date last week. Can you imagine?"

"You say that like dating someone would be a bad thing."

"I'm not much of the domestic type. Men always expect women to know how to cook and clean and all that stuff. They generally don't want to hear about the five different ways to incapacitate a raging shifter."

"Remind me to stay on your good side," he quipped.

She rolled her eyes. "You know what I mean. Anyway,

she's bound and determined to see me married off and pregnant."

"Really? I didn't get that impression when I met her."

Ara shrugged. "She seems to think I would be more fulfilled if I had someone to share my life with."

He pulled up to an iron gate and waved to the young woman manning the booth. She'd always admired Colin's setup. He'd had a long, high wall installed along the perimeter of his land. The only way on or off pack territory was to go through the gate.

It reminded her of a gated community, only more beautiful.

The gate swung open and Fen eased up the long drive. He slowed to a near crawl. He was always careful on pack land. Pups ran around freely, and many weren't exactly careful around the road.

"Your mother's got a point, you know?" Fen said.

"What?" Surprise colored her voice.

"You have to admit, having someone to come home to sounds pretty nice."

A small spark of jealousy lit in her belly. Who did Fen want to come home to? "I guess," she said slowly. "If I could find a good guy. Not that I think there are very many out there."

They pulled to a stop in front of the huge Alpha House. She unbuckled her seat belt and reached for the handle. Gentle fingers closed around her wrist just as her hand brushed the metal. Startled, she looked over at Fen. "What's up?"

"Do *you* believe it?"

Well, color her confused. "Believe what?"

"That there are good men out there?"

"Sure. You're a good guy. Colin's decent. Bo's a passable little brother."

Fen tugged her gently back into the seat. "I know about your father, Ara."

CHAPTER FOUR

She froze, her heart pounding. Fen would be able to scent her distress.

Still, she struggled to keep her voice even. "What do you know about that man?"

"Bo told me and Colin what your father did." Fen's voice was soft, and full of sympathy.

Fury buffeted against her. His reaction—the softening, the pity—had been exactly what she'd wanted to avoid. "How dare he!"

"If it helps, he'd had quite a lot to drink."

Closing her eyes, she attempted to calm down. "Ten, nine, eight…"

She wasn't quite calm enough by the time she got to zero, so she continued. "Negative one, negative two…"

By negative fifteen, she felt in control again. "What happened with my father doesn't affect me. Not anymore."

She wouldn't let it.

Still, Fen held her wrist. "It must be hard trusting me, trusting any man after what happened."

"If Bo has told you everything, then you already know how he used to hit my mother on a regular basis. And how he beat me so severely, it nearly killed me. Which is pretty hard to do considering I'm a vampire."

The grip on her arm softened, and his thumb rubbed soothingly against the sensitive skin of her inner wrist. "I'm sorry. He said you were very young. I wish I could kill him for you."

She huffed and tugged on her arm. "I don't need your pity.

It made me stronger. It made me who I am today."

He let go of her arm only to cup her jaw, forcing her to look him in the eye. She stared at him, pushing as much nonchalance into her expression as she could.

His hand was so big it spanned most of her face. She flinched, a sudden memory of another hand against her head, one shattering her cheekbone and breaking her jaw, and then cursed. The visit to the young woman in the hospital and all this talk about her father unearthed her carefully buried memories.

"Shh," he whispered. He stroked her cheek, his eyes fastened on hers. Shifters used touch as a means of comfort, in both their animal and human forms. She'd seen Fen play with Mandy's hair countless times. Hell, she'd even seen him cuddle up to Colin a time or two when he was really stressed.

"I won't let you down. Ever. I want you to know that."

The sincerity reflected in his eyes caused her breath to catch slightly. She nodded, dislodging his hand. "I know. I trust you."

"Not fully," he said. "That's okay. I just needed to tell you the truth. No one will hurt you when I'm around."

She stared at him until someone knocked on the window. "You guys plan on coming in, or are you just going to sit in there and be all melancholy for the rest of the night?"

She sucked in a deep breath and turned to greet her best friend. "Hey, Mandy. We're coming. We were just talking about the case we were working today."

Mandy opened the door for her and tossed her brother a look Ara couldn't interpret. Eager to change the subject, she hooked her arm through her friend's. "I could use a cocktail."

"She needs blood too," Fen said.

Mandy laughed and pulled her along. "We'll get you hooked up."

She followed the woman into the house, smiling at everyone as best she could. She could fake it with the best of them.

The house never failed to impress her. House was probably not the best word for the building where Fen lived with his brother and sister. Mansion definitely fit better.

It was huge but not pretentious. The alpha tried hard to make sure the house was comfortable. While the kitchen had every conceivable gadget known to mankind, and maybe a few that humans didn't know existed yet, it also sported a large scrubbed pine table.

She cracked open the fridge, helped herself to a bag of blood then turned her back to the door. She let her teeth extend and popped her fangs through the plastic, grimacing around the bag. Cold blood wasn't bad, but bagged blood did carry a faintly chemically taste.

"Want a cocktail?" Mandy asked.

She pulled the bag away from her mouth and licked any stray streaks of blood off her teeth. Shifters wouldn't care if there was still blood in her mouth, but she'd been conditioned early on to make sure she didn't showcase the fact that she was a vampire.

"Cranberry and vodka."

It was waiting for her by the time she and Mandy made it to Colin's wet bar. The alpha grinned. "I heard you needed some liquid gold."

She accepted the drink. The first sip was heaven. It slid down her throat smoothly, warming her belly without burning on the way down. "Thanks."

"No worries. Tough day?"

"You have no idea."

Colin looked at her, suddenly grave. "Actually, I do. Fen disappeared upstairs as soon as he came in. Said he needed a few minutes alone. He only does that when it's been a hard shift."

The alpha turned and greeted another newcomer while Mandy made her own drink.

Ara wandered into the hall and stopped at the foot of a wide, curved staircase. Mandy and Fen shared the right wing while

Colin had the entire left wing. She'd been up in Mandy's rooms before, when the two of them were getting ready for a night out.

Fen's rooms had always remained a mystery.

"Ara?"

Mandy's voice startled her out of her reverie. Damn those shifters for being able to move around so quietly.

"Want another one?" Mandy asked, holding her hand out for Ara's empty glass.

She hadn't even been aware she'd finished. "Thanks."

Mandy smiled and patted her arm. "I'll keep them coming, huh?"

True to her word, her friend kept her well supplied. Two hours, one bag of blood and four cocktails later, Bo finally walked in, his ever-present sword strapped to his back. He went straight to the bar and helped himself to Colin's finest vodka. Her brother tossed it back as if it were water and immediately poured another glass.

She pushed to her feet, intent on going over to soothe him, but the room started spinning.

A warm hand cupped her elbow, steadying her. "Don't worry about him. Colin will make sure he's okay."

Slowly, her eyes focused on Fen. "I know. He's still my baby brother. You know, I was the first one to hold him. Even before Mama. The doctor put him in my arms and he looked up at me. It was love at first sight."

That was what she meant to say, anyway. Instead, the words came out jumbled and slurred.

Her partner nudged her back into her seat. "I've never seen you this drunk. What's going on?"

"I may have had too much. I don't know. Every time I turn around, my glass is full. I think Mandy might be on a mission to get me drunk."

Again, the words were hardly intelligible, but Fen seemed to work out what she was saying. "Mandy? How much has she had?"

Her best friend appeared out of nowhere. She shot them a mischievous smile. "A few."

The room spun again and Ara reached out for the first solid thing to keep her upright—Fen's arm. "How many?"

Mandy's smile fell as she looked closer at Ara. "You've probably had three quarters of a bottle of vodka. I've seen you put back a lot more without it affecting you. Are you sure you've had enough blood?"

Oh. Right. She hadn't had enough blood. Mandy had offered her a second bag, one she'd declined. Probably not her best idea. The more alcohol a vampire drank, the faster their bodies used the blood they'd ingested. If she didn't have some blood soon, she'd probably end up with alcohol poisoning.

She wobbled to the kitchen, found a bag and slapped it to her teeth, ignoring the feeling of her fangs punching through the plastic. She waited until the bag had drained before rooting around in the fridge for another one.

She stared at it for a moment, thinking she should probably make sure Bo had had enough. He was a lot bigger than her, and he was all tightly-packed muscle. He needed a heck of a lot more blood than she did.

She only stumbled once when she spun around to march out, and shook off Fen's hand.

He simply gripped her elbow instead. "Are you sure you've had enough blood?"

"Enough that I don't have to worry about alcohol poisoning." Which was true. She could already feel the enzymes running through her veins.

"Ara, I really think you should have another bag."

"I need to check on Bo first."

Fen didn't seem satisfied with her answer but he didn't say anything. He tightened his hold on her arm.

"I'm fine," she said, pleased when she didn't slur the words.

She couldn't fool her partner. He steered her in the right direction, never taking his hand off her elbow.

"What's up with you?"

She blinked up at her brother's voice. "I've maybe had a little too much to drink."

Bo tossed back another shot before staring at her. "It's hard for a vampire to get drunk."

She waved her hand. "Hard day. I just wanted to know if you're all right."

Colin appeared at her brother's shoulder with another shot glass. He collapsed into an armchair and handed the drink to Bo. "Why wouldn't he be all right?"

She eyed her brother, though her words were for the wolf shifter. "You know, he's not as crazy as everyone thinks."

The alpha raised an eyebrow at her. "I know he's not psychotic. I happen to think he would make an excellent shifter."

She spun around, about to make a derisive comment, and wobbled. The next second, she found herself sitting on Colin's lap.

Her brother's voice floated above her. "Maybe I should take her home."

Those words were the last thing she remembered.

****

Everything hurt. The sun was too bright, and Ara wondered if the cab driver was making a conscious effort to hit every single pothole along the way.

Her car had been in her parking spot when she'd staggered outside, though how it had gotten there was anyone's guess.

She rubbed her throbbing temples and groaned when the car lurched again. She wanted to ask if the taxi had any suspension, but she was afraid to open her mouth.

"Listen, lady," the cabby called from the front. "If you puke in my car, there's an extra charge. And you're cleaning it up."

She shot the man her best glare. He stared back at her, unimpressed, until he hit another pothole that had even him swearing. She'd managed to get down a bag of blood when she'd first woken up. She probably needed more, but she didn't know if she could keep it down. Damn Mandy for giving her so much to drink.

She conveniently brushed aside the fact that, if she'd paced herself and asked for blood instead, she wouldn't be suffering.

Finally, the cab screeched to a halt in front of the precinct.

"Oh, thank God," she murmured as she passed a wad of cash to the driver.

The walk into the station was only marginally better. At least Ara managed to walk in a straight line, and she only stumbled once on the way to the office.

Good Lord, when had the hall become so damn long? By the time she pushed the office door open, she was sweating.

Fen chuckled as she collapsed into her chair. "Guess you overdid it big time last night, didn't you?"

She cracked open one eye and glared at him. "Why didn't you stop me?"

"I thought you needed to relax, and honestly, I didn't realize how much you'd had until you ended up in my brother's lap."

"Oh, crap. That actually happened?" She dropped her head into her hands and groaned. She'd hoped that little incident had been some kind of weird dream.

"Sure did. You also called him a few choice words for telling you Bo would make a better shifter than vampire. Don't worry. He's not upset."

She groaned again and her stomach churned. She tried to decide if she was hungry, in need of blood, or nauseated. She settled on nauseated. "How did I get home?"

"Bo made sure you got home safely."

She made a mental note to call her brother and gestured toward the pile of files perched on the table in front of her partner.

"Slide some of those over."

"Are you sure you feel up to it?" Fen asked, even as he moved a few toward her. "I can do it."

"I'll be fine. Besides, maybe it will take my mind off my current misery. Has there been any word on when the chief is going to want to talk to us?"

"Nope."

She would bet her entire paycheck that the chief would be calling in the next few seconds. She hadn't made much of an attempt to sneak past his office on the way down the hall. There was no way the man would have missed her arrival.

She'd no sooner flipped open the file and put her pen to the paper when their phone rang.

Fen picked up the receiver. She didn't need a shifter's enhanced senses to hear the chief yelling into the phone.

"We've been summoned?" she asked when her partner hung up.

"Yep."

It was time to pay the piper for her loss of control. She rose from her seat and steeled herself. "Let's go."

CHAPTER FIVE

The room reeked of sweat, heavy cologne and stale donuts. Ara caught Fen scrunching his nose and wondered how bad the smell was for him.

She sat in one of the straight-backed chairs in front of the chief's massive desk. She was fairly sure he reserved these seats specifically for his chats with her and Fen. They reminded her of the chairs her mother forced her to sit in when she had her annual photo taken. Photography in the early 1900s had been a long and uncomfortable ordeal.

"I assume the two of you know why you're here?" the chief said without even looking up from his computer screen.

She expected Fen to say something witty, but he sat next to her in silence. As much as she always told him to keep his smart-ass remarks to himself when they spoke with the chief, she missed them now.

"Well?" their boss said, finally looking up at them.

Ara clamped her mouth shut and stared back at him. Answering questions like this one never did them any good anyway. Besides, as soon as one of them started talking, he would cut them off.

He glowered at them for a full minute before speaking. "It is unacceptable to rough up a suspect."

"What exactly are you referring to?" Fen interjected. "We did no such thing."

The chief turned his laptop around. It was playing the footage of her breaking the guy's nose in a constant loop. "What do you call this then?"

"With all due respect," Fen said, though the tone of his voice hinted that he had very little respect at all, "the vampire in question had already confessed to his crime. He was no longer a suspect."

"Technicalities. You're still not allowed to rough them up."

Her temper flared to life. This man had little to no care for the suspects she and Fen interrogated. There was no doubt in her mind he'd called them out on her loss of control because they were paranormals. If the inspectors had been human, she would bet her life they wouldn't be in here now.

"Why does it matter that I broke his nose? He was executed anyway," she asked.

The human's eyes narrowed and a small smirk played at the corners of his lips. He tapped his pen against the desk as he observed her. She could tell right away her words were exactly what the chief was waiting for, and she cursed herself for playing right into his hand.

"Tell me, Ms. Classen, are all vampires as heartless as you and your brother, or is it a family trait?"

Fen surged to his feet. "We were brought on to this force to deal with paranormal offenders. We have our own set of rules and our own procedures. And we do not tolerate the vile crimes among our people that humans seem to think others can be rehabilitated from."

A sour expression settled on the chief's face, his brow wrinkling and his mouth puckering. "I'm well aware of how very little respect for life you creatures have in your communities."

"Did you hear what he said?" Ara asked, jabbing a finger toward the screen. "Did you hear how he had no remorse for violating that young woman? A young *human* woman, by the way. Once a vampire is addicted to live blood, there's no going back. You can't cure that. You're a father, aren't you? Don't you have three daughters? Do you think her father will care that I broke his nose?"

His expression darkened. She braced herself for the tirade

that was sure to come. Normally, the chief's shouting wouldn't bother her, but her head pounded harder than ever.

Instead, the man sat back again and raked his gaze across her face. "You look a little worse for wear. In fact, you look hungover. Hard night drinking?"

Tilting her chin, she stared the chief right in the eye. She refused to lie. She also refused to give him the satisfaction of being right.

The human took her silence as agreement. "You creatures are unbelievable. So you break a guy's nose, hand him over to be executed and go out and celebrate?"

Next to her, Fen sneered. "You really see us as that heartless, do you? Did you ever once think about all the shit we see? I know you go home and crack open a beer or two. Don't bother to deny it, I can scent it the morning after."

As discreetly as she could, she reached over and pressed her fingertips to his wrist. To her surprise, her partner shut up and sat down.

"I apologize," she said, not taking her hand from Fen's arm. "I lost control of my temper. It won't happen again."

She saw the man's lips move, heard his voice rising, and promptly tuned him out. There was no point in listening. He always said the same thing.

Her stomach churned and a light sweat bloomed on her skin. Her gums itched, her eyelids twitched and her muscles cramped. The blood she'd ingested at home was a distant memory. She definitely needed at least one more bag. Unfortunately, she hadn't remembered to bring any with her in her early morning misery. To make matters worse, the chief's pulse thumping in his neck and the sweet smell of adrenaline rising off him were making him look more appetizing by the minute.

"Ms. Classen? Are you listening?"

She refocused her attention. "I'm sorry?"

Blood rushed to the chief's face, turning it brick-red. It thundered through his veins, adrenaline, anger and the slight edge of fear calling to her most basic nature. She concentrated on breathing as normally as possible, even as everything within her tugged toward the man's pulsing jugular.

"I said you and Mr. Blair have been reassigned. Neither of you will be interrogating any suspects until further notice."

Fen ground his teeth. It was never a good sign when Fen started grinding his teeth.

She pulled herself together, gathering the last of her reserves, and took over. "You don't have the authority to reassign us. Our job descriptions are very clear. We are to interrogate paranormal criminals, extract confessions and hand them over to the council executioner."

The sneer on the chief's face was triumphant. "You see, I combed through your contracts. Unfortunately, I'm not allowed to fire you. I *am*, however, allowed to reassign you to another case if there are paranormal elements."

"Who will interview the paranormal suspects you bring in?" she asked.

"You don't need to worry about that. For now, you're in the field." He slid a folder across the desk.

"Are you insane?" Fen spat. "You can't put a human in a room alone with a crazed shifter or an addicted vampire. And the agreements between your governments and ours are very clear. Bo cannot work with humans. You will have no way to send the paranormal criminals to execution."

"I still can't believe how brutal your legal system is. Execution is not a humane way to deal with criminals."

She restrained herself from pointing out that humans had the death penalty around the world. And while facing the executioner was terrifying, their deaths were always quick. There was no death row for paranormals.

Her hand still rested on Fen's forearm, and she felt the muscles ripple under his skin. He always kept rigid control over his wolf, even when letting a little of his beast show would probably make their jobs easier. He wasn't always so in control of his human side. His tongue could lash a person to pieces.

When she looked up, she was surprised to see his eyes caught halfway between human and wolf. The chief didn't seem to notice the way his irises had expanded. The change was so slight, so minute, even she wouldn't have noticed it if she weren't sitting so close to him.

Making sure her partner didn't get fired, or become Bo's next client, became her priority. "Fine. I assume our first case will be the one you were talking about last night?"

The chief pursed his lips as if he smelled something distasteful. "Yes. I arranged to have the files delivered to your office while we were meeting."

She gritted her teeth against the impulse to bare her fangs at him. "We'll get right to it."

Hoping Fen had enough control of himself, she rose and stalked to the door, head high and back straight.

CHAPTER SIX

Fen walked so close behind her, she felt the heat of his body. "Better?" she asked her partner.

"Yeah. Thanks. I shouldn't have let him affect me."

"What happened? You usually have far more control over your wolf."

"The pack bond is unsettled. It's disconcerting. Colin had hoped that yesterday's get-together would ease some of the tension." Fen rubbed the back of his neck.

"Let me guess. It didn't get better."

"It got worse overnight."

"How close were you to losing control?" It would be mad to have a half-crazed wolf in the field.

"I was in full control. I was just adding a little might to Colin's authority. Sometimes being the 'big bad wolf,' as you put it, gives me just enough influence to convince people to listen to the alpha without complaint." His irises were still slightly enlarged. She sniffed the air, testing the hormones that pumped through her partner's body, but she didn't detect anything out of the ordinary.

"How are you feeling, sis? Whoa. You look like you've seen better days." Bo strolled toward them, grinning like a fool.

She would have rolled her eyes, but she was pretty sure it would result in her head falling off. "Good morning to you too, Boris."

"Aw, what did I ever do to you? Using the full first name is so wrong."

"Older-sister privilege."

He grinned at her, and she couldn't help her own smile.

They'd often commiserated over the awful names their fool mother had given them.

Bo shifted his glance to her partner. "Hey, Fen. How goes it?"

The shifter growled and walked into their office.

Her brother stared at Fen's back. "What's his problem?"

"We've been reassigned. We're out in the field now."

"Can the chief do that?"

"Apparently. You know what that means, don't you?"

She saw the exact second when Bo realized how much the chief had screwed them all over. "Well, fuck me blind."

"Ew, no thanks. Anyway, I have no idea how long this will be."

Bo drew his eyebrows together. "Let me get this straight. He's reassigned you, thereby holding up the whole process and allowing dangerous paranormals to roam the streets that much longer, all because you broke some criminal's nose before I beheaded him?"

"Right. The thing is, we would have been more than happy to help out. He didn't have to reassign us for that."

Bo scowled. "Don't kid yourself, sis. He reassigned you because he's a prick, not because he wanted to make sure he had your help."

Silence stretched between them, the long, awkward kind that had most people squirming and searching for something to say. Eventually, Bo lifted his hands and massaged his temples.

She kicked into big-sister mode with an enthusiasm she hadn't felt since Bo turned sixteen. Placing her palm against his forehead, she peered at him closely. "Are you feeling okay? What's wrong?"

He batted her hand away from his head and grimaced. "I'm fine. I just had too much to drink last night."

"You drank after you dropped me off?" She frowned. She didn't like the idea of her baby brother sitting alone in his empty kitchen, drinking his stress away.

"Are you kidding? Colin wouldn't let me drive after I'd had that much to drink." He stared at her as if she'd lost her mind.

Bo had crashed at her apartment more than once. She couldn't remember how she got home, but she knew without a doubt that she'd been alone when she'd woken up. "So, you went back to Colin's after you dropped me off?"

Bo's lips twitched as if he were trying to hide a smile. "I didn't drive you home. By the time you fell all over Colin, I was half in the bag. Fen drove you home."

Inside the office, her partner swore. Loudly and with extreme creativity.

Her brother smiled after Fen muttered something about being thrown under the goddamn bus. "See if I ever let you get out of a speeding ticket again!" Fen yelled.

Bo just snorted. "When have you ever written a ticket?"

"I'm going to start. And I'm going to tail your car with my ticket pad ready. Honestly, you'd better never go even a kilometer over the speed limit."

Bo laughed at the irritation in Fen's voice. "Get out of here." She ushered him down the hall, pushing him when he didn't move fast enough. "He's cranky because the chief was an asshole when he reassigned us. Don't pick at him."

"Yeah, yeah. Well, I guess I'll just sharpen my blades or something. It's not like I'll have any business in my office until you guys get back to interrogation. And Ara?"

"Yeah?"

"I think he's worked up over more than the chief." He turned on his heel and waved at her over his shoulder.

She didn't answer, anxious to get back to the office and soothe her partner's ruffled feathers. And to ask why he'd lied to her.

Fen was already sitting at their shared desk, his head bent and his gaze fastened resolutely on the file in front of him.

"So," she said when she walked in. "Want to tell me why

you lied about Bo taking me home?"

He didn't even look up at her when he answered. "I said Bo made sure you got home safe. Not that he drove you home."

"Semantics. You knew what I would think when you said it."

He blew out a dramatic sigh and pursed his lips. "Bo was going to drive you, but there was no way I would let you get in a car with someone who'd been drinking. Besides, he realized pretty quickly that he shouldn't get behind the wheel. So I took you home. Then I picked up Mandy, and we swung by work to get your car. She dropped it off and we went back home together."

She considered him for a moment. He'd never lied to her before. "What was the big deal about you taking me home? Did I puke all over your car? Oh God, I did, didn't I?"

Before she could offer to pay to have his car detailed, Fen interrupted her. "No. It's just that you've never invited me in before, and I didn't want you to feel awkward with me now."

She should have known Bo hadn't taken her home. When she'd woken up, she'd been under her covers, though still fully clothed; her brother would have just dumped her on her bed. Plus, there was a glass of water and two painkillers on her nightstand. Bo probably would have raided her fridge instead of thinking about how shitty she would feel the next morning.

"Thank you," she said after a moment. "You could have just left me on the couch, you know."

He shrugged, but the sudden warm, coppery scent rising from him told her his heart had started pumping hard. He cleared his throat twice and tapped his pen on the table.

The idea of seeing Fen flustered seemed rather intimate, like something only a lover should witness. And she was definitely not his lover.

"What did I do?" Her voice was a little higher than normal. In her mind's eye, she saw herself pinning Fen against the wall and kissing him.

Fen's eyes snapped to hers and widened. "Nothing. Nothing."

"Are you sure?"

"Yeah. It's just that I've never been inside your place before. It felt like I was invading your private space or something."

She shook out the tingle in her fingers and stared at him. Could things get any more awkward?

Coughing to break the sudden silence, she reached across the desk and pulled the folder closer. "How about we split the reports? It will be faster to get through them that way."

She didn't wait for him to answer. Instead, she grabbed half the stack and pushed the rest back toward him.

The words almost floated off the page, screaming for her attention. What she read surprised her.

Something had happened.

Something that ended with human injuries.

And it was terrifying.

CHAPTER SEVEN

Normally, sifting through paperwork was the most boring part of her job. She dreaded reading it almost as much as she dreaded filling it out.

The events described on the pages in front of her were anything but boring.

"Does your half of the file talk about something attacking shifters?" she asked.

"Yes." Fen's voice was a cross between disbelieving and incredulous. What in their right mind would attack a shifter, let alone a building full of them?

Only other paranormals would even contemplate the idea, but they'd have to be completely crazy to attempt something like this.

Or suicidal.

"I can't decide if the descriptions are a result of rumors and mob mentality or if they're real," Fen muttered. "They keep insisting whatever attacked them was a shifter. I don't get it though. No one can agree on what kind of shifter it was."

Ara glanced down at her paper again. Words like 'enormous,' 'beast,' and 'terrifying' were not typically something a shifter would say. Not when they were the top of the food chain. And yet, multiple witnesses talked about how utterly terrified they'd been when the unknown creature had crashed through the door.

She latched on to one particular fact she'd noticed throughout the witness statements. "Yeah. Some say it was a wolf, others some kind of cat shifter, and there's even a few who swear the shifter was a bear. And the smell. No one can seem to describe it, yet they all agree the smell was terrifying."

She tried to think of a smell that terrified her. The closest she could come up with was the memory of the time she'd passed a burning building when she was just a child. The fire had been out of control, and she'd gagged on the smell of the burning flesh of the humans trapped inside.

It had been horrifying, and it still filled her with intense grief. But though it had inspired many emotions, terror hadn't been one of them.

Fen jabbed his pen at his own pile. "Mine say that too. And everyone mentions the size. Yes, shifters are typically larger than our normal animal counterparts, but only slightly. I've never met a shifter whose animal is as big as these descriptions. Even Colin, who is one of the more powerful alphas in the country, isn't *that* big."

She pursed her lips and thought back to the last time she'd watched him shift. She'd seen him in animal form numerous times. She often pulled babysitting duty during pack runs, watching the pups who were too young to shift. "Alphas are bigger than normal shifters?"

Fen nodded absently, still rifling through his papers. "Generally."

"You're bigger than Colin. Quite a bit, actually."

He finally looked at her, watching her in a way that made her think about being stalked, overpowered, and consumed. "Size doesn't always dictate who becomes alpha, just like age."

She'd never really thought about how he'd ended up as the pack beta when he'd been the firstborn in his litter. She wanted to know what made him tick. They'd been working together for years. She knew his family—hell, his sister was her best friend. She'd been to his house, and he apparently knew her well enough to find the painkillers in her bathroom cabinet. It didn't matter how well she knew him though; he always kept the wilder side of his nature hidden.

There was something in his gaze that told her she might not like the consequences if she pushed, so she kept her mouth shut. "You done with your pile?"

"Yeah." He pushed the papers across the table. She copied the movement, giving him her half to read.

Another hour passed before she looked up, more than a little frustrated. "No forensic reports."

"Nope. But forensic reports take time. And the department is seriously backlogged. It will probably be weeks before those reports will be available, and that's assuming the team even knows what they're looking at."

Logically, she knew he was right, but it didn't lessen her irritation. Especially after she read the report from the lead officers. "How in the world did they manage to get lost in the woods?"

Fen smirked. "They're humans."

She huffed and went back to the report. It started off well enough—for humans investigating a paranormal incident, anyway. They'd taken some measurements, although they hadn't noted what kind of paw prints they were measuring. There was documentation of evidence they'd collected. And then it stopped. It seemed like they quit investigating the second they got lost. She and Fen would have to inspect the woods themselves.

She shook her head and withdrew a plain manila envelope from the folder. "Think the crime scene photos are any good?"

Fen shrugged and motioned for her to get on with it.

Photos of victims were always hard for her to look at. All those wasted lives, all those innocents lost. These humans' only sin was to keep an open mind and frequent a restaurant owned by a shifter.

Her chest ached as she gazed at the empty eyes of the people in the photos. Her body quivered as she thought about the sense-lessness of it all.

Fen drummed his finger on the table. "The human deaths are not our concern."

Her mouth dropped open. "Are you insane?"

She'd never heard him so cold before. She knew he had very little reason to like humans. Most paranormals barely tolerated humans and vice versa. But even with the mutual dislike, Fen had never been so bloody disconnected before.

He tapped his pen on the table again. She wanted to grab it and snap it in half. Her nails bit into her palms as she waited for his explanation.

"I will go insane if I think too much about what's already been lost. I'm not heartless, Ara. I mourn for them too. The hu-man part of this investigation is being handled by the police."

Her irritation drained in one fell swoop, leaving her limp and exhausted. "You're right. I'm sorry."

He sighed. "I get it. I really do. Life, of any kind, is precious to shifters. The best thing we can do for everyone right now is figure out what happened."

The photos were clear and there were plenty of them, but they'd obviously been taken from a human point of view. They focused on things like blood spatter and body positions.

The photos of the actual damage, the ones that could have helped them narrow down the type of shifter they were looking for, were too far away to see details. "I wish whoever took the photos would have gotten a little closer to the gouges in the wall. There are so many of them, I can't determine which ones belong to the creature and which belong to known shifters."

She slid them back into the envelope when they were done. "I take back what I said to the chief about this not being in our job description. This is clearly not a lone wolf attack. We should have been brought in from the beginning."

"There were human deaths. The rules are a little gray in

cases where both humans and paranormals are involved. Either side can investigate. Of course the chief wasn't going to let us investigate if he thought he could do it himself. He hates the fact that he can't really control us."

She blew out a breath, ruffling her bangs. "Our best bet is to go over to the scene as soon as possible and see if we can get a better idea of what we're dealing with."

"The attack was about a week ago," Fen said. "Let's hope it hasn't degraded too much. Do you want to drive this time?"

"I took a cab, so I guess I'll pray you won't get us arrested on the way there."

Fen smirked and headed to the small safe the chief had grudgingly allowed them to install their first week of service. Neither of them made a habit of carrying a duty weapon. Most of the time, the paranormals were delivered to them and they simply needed to carry out the interrogations. At the time, they'd both thought that making a show of locking their weapons in a safe would put the human officers at ease. Then it had become a habit.

He handed her the pistol and she measured its weight in her palm. Its cool smoothness felt right against her skin. She slipped the gun into the harness he handed her and clipped it to her waistband.

"Let's go."

The chief wasn't in his office when they passed but Bo leaned against the wall outside his own office, evidently waiting for them. "Where are you guys going?"

"Out to the scene." Fen's tone was sharp, cutting. Apparently, he was still upset about Bo spilling the beans.

Bo stared blankly at Fen then turned his back on the irate shifter. "Ara, come with me a sec."

Quirking her eyebrow at her brother's demand, she followed him into the room. She always hesitated to call the room his office. There was an easy chair in the corner facing a small television. A mini fridge stood on the other side of the room.

The rest of the office stored weapons. Lots of them. Swords gleamed from the walls, a couple of crossbows lay on a table and one wicked-looking device—a long, wooden handle with three chained and spiked balls attached, which he'd once told her was a war flail—hung above the door. His own duty pistol was hanging from a nail in the wall. She knew he never used it; he had never even loaded it. He hung it there just to piss off the chief.

The room always creeped her out. She knew most of the weapons Bo kept were ceremonial. The only one he really used was the custom, silver-laced steel broadsword. It had been commissioned by the vampire elders when he'd taken the job. She hadn't seen him without it since and was pretty sure he slept snuggled up to it.

He closed the door on a spluttering Fen and handed her a bag of blood from his fridge. "Go sit down before you fall down," he ordered.

She smiled gratefully as she obeyed and accepted the bag of blood. "Thanks."

"You're pale and drawn. Even as drunk as you were last night, you still should look better. Why didn't you have any this morning?"

She shrugged. "I had some. I wasn't sure I could keep anymore down."

He sat on the arm of the chair while she popped her fangs through the plastic and drained the bag. "You really shouldn't let it get that bad. And you forgot to stock your fridge, didn't you?"

She shivered as the last of the blood entered her system. Closing her eyes, she felt the strength rush back into her body. The ache in her head eased, her stomach unclenched and her muscles relaxed. "Thanks," she said again.

He looked her over critically before nodding. "You'll do.

You do know you'll need to replace that bag, right?"

His cheeky tone reminded her of the little five-year-old version of himself she sometimes struggled to remember. She forcefully put the thought aside. It wouldn't do her any good to think about what she would eventually forget during her long life. It only made her melancholy.

"I'll bring some tomorrow. I should go before Fen has a stroke or something. Stay out of trouble."

He smirked. "Most women tell me I'm the best kind of trouble."

"I need brain bleach," she groaned, covering her eyes with one hand. She got to her feet, already feeling better.

"Whatever," Bo answered. "Listen, stay safe, okay?"

"I'm pretty hard to kill."

"True. You're the toughest girl I know, and that's saying something. You're not immortal though. I'll be an only child if you kick the bucket. Which means I'll be the only target when our grandparents or mom decide they need a new heir."

She stroked his hair back once, ignoring his deep rumble of protest. Despite being nearly a century old himself, she knew he still liked the small gestures of affection, even if he acted like he didn't. He was actually a giant softie, as hard as he tried to hide it.

The door banged open, slamming hard against the wall before bouncing back. The flail mounted above the door clattered to the ground, the steel bludgeons bouncing hard. Startled, she spun around and ended up in front of her brother.

"What is going on in here?" Fen growled.

Growling wasn't an exaggeration either. He sounded like he was caught halfway between wolf and man.

"Bo was just making sure I got some blood before we left. What is your problem?" she asked.

"I heard him snarling at you," Fen insisted, stepping closer.

"You need to calm down, man," Bo said, gently moving her

aside. "There is no way you're going to drive around God only knows where with my sister when you can barely control your shift."

For the span of five seconds, Ara thought her partner was going to tear her brother to shreds, or at least try to. The aggression abruptly drained out of Fen's body, taking with it the scent of adrenaline. "Sorry. You ready to go?"

She followed him out the door, a little unsure if getting in the car with a visibly unstable wolf shifter was the best idea she'd ever had. One of them might be a little bloody by the time they got to the scene, and she would be damned if it would be her.

CHAPTER EIGHT

They arrived at the crime scene without killing each other. She released the rigid hold she had on her muscles and wriggled her chin. Thankfully, she hadn't bitten through her lip in her frustration with her partner. The whole drive to the restaurant, she'd had to listen to Fen lecture her about putting herself between an angry wolf shifter and his target. Sometimes it was easier to let him vent his irritation.

She was never one to take the easy way, however. "Stop being a dick. He's my baby brother. It was an accident this time, but I will always stand between him and. He would do the same for me."

"He is a fully-grown male vampire, and an executioner. He doesn't need your protection," Fen shot back.

"So you wouldn't help Mandy if she needed it?"

Fen leaned so close she could feel his breath on her face. "Mandy is mine."

Mine. As in pack. She'd heard him say similar things before.

"Well, Bo is *mine*. He's my pack. So step off."

He growled and backed away, slamming his hands onto the steering wheel.

"What is really going on?" she burst out.

Her partner's chest expanded as he sucked in a lungful of air. "Don't freak out."

"Don't freak out? You've been growling at me for twenty minutes and I haven't jumped out of the car screaming. What makes you think I'm going to freak out now?"

"You're mine too."

She almost forgot to breathe. She wasn't freaking out. A little poleaxed, maybe. What would this mean for their partnership?

Fen cursed under his breath. "See, I knew you would freak. We—our pack, I mean—consider you and Bo ours. Like honorary wolf shifters."

She was thoroughly bewildered. "If you consider both of us *yours*, why did you get upset with Bo?"

"You're my partner."

"So?"

He rolled his eyes. "God save us from oblivious females."

She was far from oblivious. She'd known from day one by the strong scent of testosterone and norepinephrine rising from his skin that he was attracted to her. She'd gone about her business, talking shop and busting noses, and he'd followed her lead.

His reaction to Bo's posturing made her wonder if there was something deeper than just attraction.

And if she was inclined to do anything about it.

It was definitely not the time to think about their relationship, professional or otherwise.

Fen sighed. "We'll talk about it later."

A whole flock of birds took up residence in her stomach. "We should go," she said, proud when her voice remained even.

He opened his car door and wrinkled his nose.

"What?" she asked, getting out on her own side, hauling out their crime scene kit from the backseat. She was used to her partner reacting to whatever he scented in the environment. "What do you smell?"

"Something stinks. It's pretty bad, actually. Can't you smell it?"

She lifted her face and attempted to catch what had disgusted him, but her heightened sense of smell only applied to blood and the body's chemicals. While she could pick up on hormones in the bloodstream, she didn't always know what they meant.

Adrenaline saturated the air, clogging her nose and tripling her heartbeat. She closed her eyes and sorted through the mess of old scents.

Something faint, something not hormonal and definitely unpleasant, wafted up her nose. A shiver worked its way down her spine. "What is that? It smells almost rotten."

Fen clapped his hand over his nose and mouth. "I don't know. The smell of fear is still too heavy."

"It's been a week, hasn't it? Why is the fear still so strong?"

He pulled his hand away from his face and sniffed. "The fear was sudden and sharp, condensed into a small frame of space and time and experienced by lots of people. It's going to linger for a while before it truly dissipates. Does that make sense?"

His voice was growly again, his eyes darting this way and that, his body tight and primed to spring. He was reacting to the scent; she'd seen him do this before. She couldn't tell if it had inspired his predatory side or if he was experiencing a type of residual fear.

A police officer picked his way across the parking lot warily, holding his hands up to show he wasn't a threat. "Can I approach?"

The young man tilted his head back slightly, showing his throat in a gesture she knew screamed submission to shifters.

She left the decision up to Fen. He knew his limits.

"Yeah, come on over," Fen answered.

The officer minced over to them, neck still extended. "Are you Inspectors Blair and Classen?"

"Yes," she said, reaching out to shake the young man's hand.

"Nice to meet you. The chief called to tell me you were coming out and asked me to meet you. I was on the scene the night it happened."

She scanned the area. The diner where everything had gone down was only a twenty-minute drive outside of the city, but it felt like they were in the middle of nowhere. Dense woods crowded the road to the left. To the right, the road narrowed, switching from concrete to packed gravel. She was willing to bet it turned to dirt somewhere along the way. There were no other buildings in sight and only one other car sat in the parking lot, which she guessed was the human officer's.

Tension still radiated from Fen, strong pulses of discomfort underscored with a hint of fear. "You okay?"

"Yeah. There's just something really not right here. Whatever happened, it has my wolf anxious."

A fine smattering of goose bumps rose on her arms at the knowledge. What could be worse than the big bad beta wolf that it would cause him so much unease?

She pushed the trickle of nerves aside and faced the officer squarely. "Tell us what happened."

The young man began reciting the events of the week before. Clearly, he'd read his notes enough times to have memorized them. "This diner is owned by a shifter by the name of Carla Defoe. It's mostly frequented by other shifters, although word spread into town about how good the food is. Long story short, when the beast attacked the diner, a couple of humans got caught in the crossfire. I'm guessing that's why I was called out instead of you guys."

A low growl burst from the silence beside her. Fen's eyes had shifted and he looked like he battled his wolf for control. Hopefully, the human remembered his basic training enough to know that running away from an angry shifter was never a good thing. "You need to stay very still," she said in a low voice, keeping a careful eye on her partner.

"Don't worry," he replied in the same, soothing tone. "I know what to do."

Once again, he tilted his head back, fully exposing his throat as he kept his arms loose and limp at his sides, though he did turn his palms so Fen could clearly see they were empty. "I don't mean any harm. I only want to help."

He looked relaxed, peaceful even, and Fen shook his head. "Sorry. It's not you. There's something here. I don't know how to explain it. Your submission is noted and appreciated, thank you."

The officer simply nodded and smiled serenely. "Any time. I've already called the owner to let her know the chief has finally asked you guys for help. She's going to talk to her leo and let me know what we should do. In the meantime, you can look around outside."

Ara covered a snort behind a fake cough. She wouldn't have called the chief reassigning them *asking for help* but there was no need to point it out. It would only serve to irritate her already-jumpy partner.

Fen sucked in a breath and marched toward the diner.

Ara followed, hand on the butt of her gun. She'd never actually used the weapon in the line of duty, though she made sure to visit the shooting range at least once a week. She trusted her partner's instincts and was ready to shoot at the slightest indication from him.

"There's no one in there," Fen said, tapping his nose. She relaxed marginally and stepped closer, inspecting the entrance. Plywood had been installed over the doors.

"The beast tore the doors off," the officer commented. "The owner hasn't gotten around to replacing them yet."

"It wouldn't take that much to get the doors off." She stepped closer and held her hands out to where the handles would have been. "It would have taken a couple of minutes, but I could have done it. And Fen is a lot bigger than me. He'd have them off in under a minute in human form."

"They were reinforced steel doors."

She stared at the plywood. Steel doors changed things. It would have taken a considerable amount of strength to rip the doors off. She eyed Fen, doubting he could do something similar, at least in his human form. Shifters were strong, but they had their limits.

A fully grown male vampire in the throes of blood lust could muster the strength, especially if he was fixed on a target. Not that that observation helped. There hadn't been a single mention of a vampire in everything she read.

Maybe a sole shifter wouldn't have been able to rip a set of steel doors down, but a couple of them could. "Do you think it was more than one shifter?"

The young human shook his head. "Everyone I talked to swears there was only one."

Next to her, Fen crouched and sniffed. She was used to him doing wolfy things. Most humans were slightly weirded out by it, even though human officers went through training provided by human resources to prepare them for working with paranormals. This officer simply watched with mild interest.

"Has the scene been contaminated?" Fen asked.

The officer shook his head. "The owner let me know that there have been shifters guarding this place since the attack. Nothing could have gotten in or out of here without her knowing."

Fen still looked troubled. "Cat shifters don't have the same sense of smell wolf shifters do."

A lightbulb went off in her mind. Of course this place was owned by a cat shifter. If it had been owned by a wolf, Fen would have heard about it.

She supposed the owner could have been one of the local bear shifters, but they tended to keep to themselves. The lone bear shifter she'd met when training for her position on the force hadn't been the most social person in the world. She just couldn't see a bear owning a restaurant.

"So, the owner of the diner is some kind of cat shifter?"

Her partner nodded. "Yeah. I don't know enough cat shifters to determine what species of feline."

She frowned and sniffed the air. There was no hint of shifter blood floating around.

Fen looked up at the young human. "Are they absolutely sure the scene hasn't been infiltrated somehow? Do you have details on the kind of guard they're keeping on the place?"

The disdain in his voice was hard to miss. Canine and feline shifters got along about as well in the shifter world as they did in the animal one.

He didn't need to say anything else for her to catch on to his line of thought. If there had been one small gap in their line of defense, something could have gotten into the diner without them being aware of the intrusion.

"Do you think the scene has been contaminated?" the officer asked.

"A sharp scent is seeping from behind the plywood. Something that feels like it should be familiar, but it's not. It's very distinctive, kind of like ammonia. It's hard to explain. I can't place it, and it's definitely not normal."

She leaned down next to him and sniffed. Sure enough, an odd scent hovered by the wood. It held the distinctive tang of copper. Blood. But not any type of blood she'd ever encountered. She pulled back when the scent burned through her sinuses.

"This must be the weird smell in the reports," she said. She looked over at the human. "Can you smell it?"

"No," the young man answered.

Fen grunted. "I'm not surprised. Human senses are more than a little dull. Honestly, I don't know how humans have survived this long. No offence," he muttered, shooting a look up at the young man.

"None taken."

"Whatever this shifter is, it wanted into the diner really badly," Ara remarked.

"All the witnesses said it seemed like it had some kind of

purpose, like it was looking for something," Fen said.

"Or hunting for something." She straightened. "Did the creature lose interest, or was it scared away? It wasn't clear in the reports we read."

The human shrugged. "No one really knows. All they agree on is that it disappeared as quickly as it appeared."

Her gaze roamed the entire entrance. She'd once spent a summer in Kenya, where she'd helped build a school. They'd installed steel doors instead of the traditional wood ones because they were considered more durable. She distinctly remembered being surprised at how heavy they were. At least one hundred and thirty pounds apiece. And this thing had managed to rip even bigger doors off in seconds, if the witnesses were right. She tried to picture it in her mind. The beast had to be big. Huge even.

She closed her eyes, sinking deeper into the image. It would have been chaos. Complete and utter pandemonium. She could picture the shifter customers attacking the thing. If it was as big and strong as she thought, it would have just swiped the shifters aside.

Humans would have had no chance against it.

Something touched the side of her leg, startling her out of her thoughts. Fen's head brushed against her outer thigh as he bent lower and pushed his nose against the wood. "It really stinks," he said. "It bugs me that I can't place the scent. It feels like something I should know."

Once again, she was struck with how at ease the human officer acted around them. "We're not freaking you out at all, are we?"

The man gave her a startled look. "Why would you?"

She shrugged. "Most humans we work with are a little weirded out when Fen does something so obviously wolfish, even with all the training they receive on working with paranormals. And they always look at me like I'm going to tear their throats out at any second."

"Oh, that." He laughed and rubbed the back of his neck as if he was embarrassed. "My sister is married to a shifter out in California, has been since I was fifteen. I lived with my brother-in-law's pack while I was out there for school. Once I got over my surprise that my sister had a litter of shifter pups, it was actually pretty cool. And I've met a couple of vampires before. They were all decent."

She heard the respect in his voice when he talked about his brother-in-law. Fen still had his nose close to the door, but he'd frozen in the way that only happened when he was paying very close attention to the conversation. More tension eased from him, his shoulders softening.

She relaxed her own rigid posture. Though she'd never admit it, the thought of working with humans and putting up with their anti-paranormal attitudes always knotted her stomach. This kid was the most accepting human she'd met in a long time.

"Should we go in?" the officer asked when Fen stood up.

"Only if we want Fen killed," she said.

The kid looked at her, obviously trying to determine if she was joking. "What?"

Her partner cracked his knuckles. "I have to wait for permission to enter first. This is clearly marked as shifter territory, and I'd be breaching some serious rules if I entered without permission. Didn't the pack you lived with teach you about the permission system?"

The human looked a little bemused. "There weren't any other shifters nearby, so it wasn't an issue. But I thought a criminal investigation would supersede the system."

"Nope," Fen answered.

The officer's cell phone chirped from his front pocket. "I have to take this," he said, raising the phone to his ear to answer. "Yes?" He walked away from them to continue the conversation. She watched him pace along the side of the road. A truck rumbled by, cutting off her ability to hear his side of the conversation.

"What do you think?" she asked her partner when they were alone.

Fen was silent for a full minute. "Honestly, I don't have a clue. We'll have a better idea of what went down when we get inside."

She reached into the kit and snapped on a pair of latex gloves before running her fingers against the plywood. "Something isn't right. I'm beginning to think we don't have the full story here. The lack of forensic reports, even preliminary ones, really bothers me."

"You know how far behind the lab is. It could be weeks before they get to this case. Months even," Fen answered.

She shot him a disbelieving look. "Do you really think the chief would let this rest? He'd normally jump at the chance to push a human death onto a paranormal."

"You think we're being kept in the dark intentionally?"

She rolled her shoulders, trying to loosen her tense muscles. "Yes, but whether we're being blocked by the chief or the leo, I'm not sure."

Fen paced back and forth. "My money's on the leo," he finally said.

"Why? Would Colin keep information from the authorities?"

He pressed his lips into a flat line. "Not from us. But if he didn't know the inspectors, he'd do whatever he deemed necessary to keep his pack safe. If that meant keeping the authorities out of pack business so he could be sure it was dealt with properly, then he would absolutely keep quiet."

The officer walked back to them, slipping his phone into his pocket. "The leo wants to meet you before he lets you into the diner. He said he'll permit you on the pride territory as long as you wait for his second to come down and get you."

She'd been expecting something like this to come up. Shifters were nothing if not territorial. "Listen, we read the shifter witness reports before we came. They were straight forward but lacked any real detail. Can you give us a rundown before we meet him?"

The man grimaced. "You would have read the statements the leo took. He wouldn't allow us to interview his cats. He said either they sent out the paranormal inspectors or he would handle it himself."

The anger was back, turning her stomach into a hot mass of nerves. "Don't tell me. The chief didn't want to call us out until the majority of the human officers were ready to wash their hands of the case?"

The young man nodded. "I told him it was important to get you guys out, but he was determined to handle things himself. Or at least, he was hell-bent that humans would handle it. It didn't matter though. In the end, the leo didn't give him much choice. He cited the law about paranormals having the right to conduct their own investigation."

Fen narrowed his eyes. "You should have told us when we first got here. I wouldn't have wasted my time if I'd known we still had to talk to the shifters."

Ara's nostrils flared when a fresh wave of adrenaline wafted from the young man as he paled. "Sorry. I thought the chief would have told you."

"Don't assume anything about how the chief treats us," Fen growled.

She straightened, breathing deeply to calm her temper. "I suppose the leo demanded he be the one to collect the evidence as well."

"All he allowed us to do was take crime scene photos. He even supervised those. Did you get the pictures?"

Her ire drained. This human didn't deserve her anger. He'd done nothing wrong. "We got them."

The kid glanced at his watch. "We really should go. The leo hates to be kept waiting."

"Right. Off to see the cats." Fen stalked back to their car, clearly unhappy with the situation.

"We'll follow you out," Ara said to the human before taking her seat in the passenger side of Fen's car.

"Did I mention I don't like cats very much?" Fen muttered once they were back on the road.

"The feeling is mutual. Think you can rein it in a little when we get there?"

"I can if you can."

Just as she predicted, the road went from gravel to dirt. Fen swore under his breath when the car ran over a particularly bad rut and something thunked against the undercarriage. "Fucking cats."

Fen's words just about summed up her own feelings.

CHAPTER NINE

The drive to the pride land was silent, which wasn't in itself unusual. They could spend hours at a time in silence and be perfectly comfortable.

No, it wasn't the silence that tipped her off to the fact that he was far angrier than he was letting on. It was the aggression seeping from his pores in waves.

She watched him carefully, noting how his chest rose and fell with his exaggerated breathing, a sure indication of how hard he tried to get himself under control.

"This is why," he said suddenly.

She blinked. What was he talking about? "Why what?"

"Why I'm not alpha. I *am* technically stronger than Colin. I'd win in a physical confrontation. It's not all about strength though. I'm far too aggressive and tend to act before I think things through completely."

"So Colin's strength is the control he has over his wolf?"

"Partly. He also has incredible leadership qualities. Don't get me wrong, he's stronger than the rest of the pack, but they choose to follow him. Non-shifters don't understand, but following a leader simply because they are the strongest doesn't normally make for the most stable pack."

She considered the repercussions of being stronger than an alpha. "Can he force the rest of the pack to obey him if he wants?"

Fen eyes were fixed on the road ahead. He swerved to avoid another pothole before answering. "Almost everyone, anyway."

"Not you?"

He shook his head. Looking back on the years she'd known

him, she should have guessed. He didn't have to submit to his brother, he chose to. He'd never had any trouble looking Colin in the eyes, and there were times she'd sworn he hadn't displayed his throat. "Does your wolf protest him being the alpha?"

Fen shook his head again. "We came to peace about it a long time ago. Maybe if he wasn't my littermate, it would be different."

He seemed happy enough with the situation. She wondered how it had been for him to realize he was physically strong enough to lead a pack, but it would never be a happy one. What had it been like to give that up to someone else?

The officer's car veered right and came to a stop outside a fence. The gate was open. The human drove through. Fen did not.

Fen pulled out his cell phone. "Hang on a second."

She heard the impatience in his voice as he spoke. "Hey, Col. I need to interview some of the local cat shifters. The leo invited us over, but no one met us at the gate. Can you give him a call for me? Great. Thanks."

Ara sighed and stretched her arms over her head. She would never understand shifter politics. As far as she was concerned, they had permission to be on the grounds the moment the leo invited them over.

Five minutes turned into fifteen. When Fen closed his eyes, Ara realized how very close her partner was to losing it. Much longer and she figured he would either throw his hands in the air and drive off or he would storm up the lane and confront the first cat he saw. Eventually, his phone rang again. Fen hit the speaker button without bothering to open his eyes. "You're on speaker. Ara's with me."

"Hey, Ara." Colin's low, soothing voice filled the car. "The leo is sending someone down to meet you now. He's impressed that you've had the patience to wait this long."

Fen snorted. "It's wearing pretty damned thin, Col. Some

strange shit is going down here, and we need to get it sorted out. The delay isn't helping anyone."

"I know. I feel your distress. I'd send one of the pack submissives to help calm you down, but I'm pretty sure your drive to protect anyone weaker than you would outdo any calming affect they'd have."

"Ara's here," he said again.

Was he implying she had a soothing effect on him? Or did he want to stop the conversation before his brother said something else.

"Listen," Colin said, "I've got to go. The pups are here for their weekly training. Just remember, your dominance will be challenged. You need to let the leo win."

"Yeah, yeah. I know." He hung up before Colin could say anything more. Fen cracked his knuckles and slipped his phone back into his pocket.

"You going to be okay?" she asked.

Her partner rolled his shoulders and shook out his hands. "Yeah. I'd rather meet the witnesses on neutral ground. Shifters are damned territorial, and I'm highly dominant. If we weren't here in an official capacity, they would take my presence as an aggressive gesture and would end in a ... scuffle."

She turned his words over in her mind. A scuffle in shifter terms meant lots of paranormal casualties.

"Try to keep your claws sheathed. The last thing we need is more shit for the chief to call us on."

"My claws aren't retractable. Tell that to the damn cats."

Ara had forgotten about the human officer until he knocked on their window. He leaned in when she opened it. "We've been here a while. What do you want to do?"

"I called my alpha, who called the leo. There's someone coming down. Make yourself comfortable. It might be a few minutes."

The minutes ticked by, taking with it any respect she had for the leo and his pride. The leo should have been waiting for them instead of the other way around. She thought about how seriously Colin took his pack's safety. He would have been on the phone insisting for the authorities within hours, not letting a week pass and then making the inspectors wait.

"You guys like crazy eights?" the human asked. He pulled a deck of cards from his car.

"Sure. Let's play," Fen answered with a small smile.

Thirty seconds later, Fen and the human were sitting cross-legged on a patch of grass. "Want to join us?"

She ran through the possibilities in her mind, sorting through the different scenarios. On the one hand, sitting on the ground with Fen would make them seem less threatening. While she and the human didn't really have to pander to shifter sensibilities, it was important that Fen not draw too much attention to his dominance.

And yet, Fen being physically lower than whoever came down would show his absolute submission. Which might not set the tone they wanted.

"I can hear you thinking, Ara. Just come and play. It will help pass the time." Fen pointed to a patch of grass between the two men.

She took careful stock of her partner. His eyes had a wild light, his jaw was tight and his breathing was carefully measured. The wolf was still on edge. If playing a card game while they waited helped him hold onto control, then playing cards was exactly what she would do.

She plopped onto the grass. "Deal me in."

The sun's rays skipped through the leaves and danced in little patches on the ground. It was beautiful, and she could almost convince herself they had simply stopped for a picnic. Minus the food, the blanket and the lemonade.

And the dead humans, of course.

Eventually, Fen's head whipped around, eyes staring down the dirt road. "There's a car coming."

A couple of seconds passed before her own ears could pick up the crunch of tires on compacted ground.

She glanced at her watch. An hour. They'd waited an hour for someone to come and meet them. A fresh wave of anger crashed over her, tightening her muscles and heating her blood. She surged to her feet and propped her hands on her hips.

"Hold up there, killer," Fen drawled. "Let's let the cat live long enough to take us up to the leo."

His words, and the amusement in his voice, would have surprised her if she hadn't caught the glint of danger in his eyes and the dark undertone of his words.

The human tossed the cards inside his open passenger window as Fen pushed to his feet and brushed bits of leaves off his ass.

He ambled to her side and stood completely still, his arms loose and relaxed at his sides.

The young human joined them, peering up the road. "Are you guys sure you heard a car?"

Seconds later, a car appeared around a bend in the road. "Never mind," the young man said.

The car stopped a few feet in front of them, and a tall man exited. She'd grown up around humans. The scent of their blood was so common she didn't notice it unless she was hungry. She'd grown used to the smell of wolf shifter blood.

She'd almost forgotten the difference between cat and wolf shifter blood. The man's blood smelled more feral than Fen's. It was slightly disconcerting.

The man smiled graciously at her, holding out his hand for her to shake. "Hello, you must be Inspector Classen. I'm Tyson, the leo's second."

Tyson had a similar greeting for the human officer, although it was clear they'd met before.

She frowned. Fen was a force to be reckoned with. Normally people greeted him first, or second if Colin was around. People did *not* simply ignore him. It was a deliberate gesture but if it was an insult, a deliberate power play, or some kind of sign of respect, she didn't know. She leaned toward insult.

Tyson's charming smile cooled when he finally turned to Fen.

The two shifters stared each other in the eyes. She didn't have to be a shifter to know they tested each other's dominance. Eventually, Tyson broke the eye contact and fixed his eyes to Fen's chin. "The leo asked me to bring you to the house."

The human officer hopped into Tyson's Jeep without hesitation. The cat looked them both up and down. "Inspector Classen is welcome in my car. I'd be more comfortable if Inspector Blair brought his own."

She forced a smile to her face. "I'll ride with my partner. Thank you though."

Tyson's eyes shimmered. A small smile tugged on his lips and he nodded once. "Good choice, Inspector."

"What was that all about?" she asked when Fen had the car moving.

He shrugged. "Who knows? Cats are weird."

They followed the Jeep deeper into the woods until trees closed around them. The road grew rougher, more pitted, and she worried about the undercarriage.

Suddenly, a house came into view. It wasn't as big as the house she'd grown up in, nor was it anywhere near as large as Colin's house, but as far as most homes went, it was still fairly large. "How big is the local pride?"

Fen drummed his fingers on the steering wheel. "We don't have much contact with them. I suspect they have roughly the same number of members as my pack. From what I know, most cats are solitary shifters. Their hierarchy is more loosely structured than ours. They probably go days between seeing anyone outside of their immediate family socially, maybe even weeks. I can't imagine living in such isolation."

Colin had extra bedrooms so pack members could spend the

night if they needed more contact with their leader. He stocked the closets with extra clothes of all sizes, and she suspected he had more toothbrushes stashed away than a dental office. The pups ran around the lawn freely and even played video games on Colin's entertainment system.

To Fen, a day without spending time with his pack mates, even if most of them were afraid of him, probably was the definition of isolation.

Tyson exited his car and leaned against the door, arms crossed over his chest as he stared at Fen as if he wasted his time. "He's still fixated on your pissing contest, is he?"

Her partner snorted and took his sweet time reaching for his door. "I don't know why he's bothering. I'm stronger than he is, and we both know it."

"Then why is it taking you so long to get moving?" she complained.

He paused, gaze fixed on the front door. "It's not him I'm worried about. It's the leo."

"Why? He wouldn't dare try something shifty. You have permission to be here, both legally and politically. Hell, Colin even phoned for the permission himself."

He sighed and rubbed his temples. "The pissing contest between me and Tyson over there? It was all for show. I'm far more dominant. If we'd had a real match over dominance, there wouldn't have been a contest. If he's the leo's second, I'm a little worried that I'll be more dominant than the actual leo."

Oh. He'd done a very good job of masking the difference between his and Tyson's dominance levels. If Fen turned out to be more dominant than the leo, the situation would become very volatile.

Her partner might find himself in the middle of a cat fight. Literally. Leaders of shifter groups tended to be possessive and would stop at nothing to eliminate a threat to their leadership. "Want me to call Colin?"

Fen pressed his lips together until they were a single flat, white line. "No."

She didn't have time to ask if he was sure, as Tyson marched to Fen's door and knocked on the window. "You coming? Or is the fact cat shifters were attacked not important enough for you to move your ass?"

Fen's nostrils flared slightly.

The words left her mouth before she realized what she was doing. "Apparently it's not enough for you to bother to come and get us in a timely manner. So you can damn well wait for us for a few seconds."

The cat gaped at her and she promptly turned her back to him. "Take all the time you need," she said to her partner.

He cracked a tiny smile. "Thanks."

They spent exactly two more minutes in the car before Fen finally moved. Thankfully, he got out of the car without strangling the other shifter. They followed Tyson up the steps to the front porch and to the front door.

Fen hovered in the entrance, looking more irritated by the second. She barely repressed an irritated sigh of her own. She crossed her arms and glared at the beta cat. "Really?"

The human officer's gaze bounced from Tyson to Fen and back again. "Why aren't we going in?"

"I can't enter unless I'm invited," Fen snarled.

"I thought that was a vampire thing," the human said.

"Hey," she squawked. "Vampire here. I can walk around in the daylight, and I'm not sparkly either. Although sparkly would have been awesome."

She didn't mind the misconceptions though. The kid knew enough about paranormals she figured he was joking. Besides, if the general public wanted to believe vampires couldn't enter their home without being invited first and it made them feel safe, it was fine with her. The safer the humans felt, the easier it was for her to live her life.

The young man cocked his head, his wide eyes making him

look younger than he probably was. "You seriously can't enter?"

"Not without an express invitation from the leo."

Ara gripped the doorframe and squeezed. The wood cracked in her fist, tiny fissures spider webbing above and below her hand. The whole situation was ridiculous.

Ten seconds. She would give the leo ten more seconds before she and Fen would leave and the cats could clean up the mess on their own.

"You really can't go in?" the human asked again.

"No, he's just being polite," a voice said from somewhere in the house.

A gorgeous man glided down a set of stairs to their left. Like Tyson, he was tall, but that's where the similarity ended. Power radiated off him in waves. This had to be the leo.

She momentarily forgot her irritation. The man was breathtaking. He was long and lithe, with muscles in all the right places. His shaggy blond hair should have made him look like an overgrown surfer dude, but it only served to enhance his sharp cheekbones. Bright blue eyes pierced her soul.

She was staring into the eyes of a predator. The leo was more lion than man.

"Beta Fenris Blair, welcome."

Even his voice reminded her of his beast, though she thought it sounded more like a purr than a roar.

Beside her, Fen let out a long, slow breath. She ripped her gaze from the stunning creature and glanced over at her partner to see him tilt his head in submission, an expression of relief on his face. "Yes," the leo purred. "No need to worry about dominance. I am more than capable of leading my pride. And you, of course, Inspector Classen, are also welcome."

His smirk snapped her out of the trance she'd been in. His arrogant, amused expression told her he was well aware of the effect he had on the opposite sex. She was half tempted to snap at him, to rail about stupid power plays and wasting their time simply to save face.

A light touch on her inner wrist warned her otherwise. "Don't," Fen said.

"Officer Jones, it's good to see you again, even if the circumstances aren't the greatest," the leo continued. "I'm glad they assigned you to the case."

"I'm pretty sure no one else will volunteer for a shifter case, Leo. It's good to see you too."

Ara narrowed her eyes. Interesting. The human and the leo were clearly on friendly terms.

"If you will follow me," the leo said, staring at Fen with a smile, "we can begin."

CHAPTER TEN

The leo led them to a large office on the second floor. A massive desk with a huge computer took up half of the room. On one side of the desk, there was a leather chair, the kind CEOs and other boss types always had. A jug of red liquid, cranberry juice if the tart scent was anything to go by, and several small glasses sat on a table in the corner.

A row of bookshelves lined the wall behind the desk. She zeroed in on the various law journals on the shelves. Figured the guy was a lawyer. He seemed like he could talk his way around anything and those people he couldn't convince with words, he would charm. She hated dealing with the lawyers who came through her interview room. They always thought they could get around the rules by spouting some bizarre loophole.

Not that it ever worked.

They weren't interviewing the leo as a suspect though. They were going to interview attack victims and murder witnesses.

She thought back to the photos of the initial scene. They had been grizzly. Shifters might be part animal, the ultimate predator, the top of the food chain, but they were part human too. No one could live through an attack like that and be unaffected. There was a high probability the witnesses would be traumatized.

She glanced around again. She would have preferred to conduct the interviews somewhere more comfortable, like around a kitchen table or even in a cozy living room. Anything to help the witnesses feel more relaxed because comfortable witnesses made for easier interviewing. At least there was a long couch and an easy chair angled in front of the fireplace on the other side of the room

"Before we begin, I need to lay down some ground rules," the leo said. "I will remain present for all of the interviews. Officer Jones will also remain."

She'd been expecting the demand. The leo was so much more than just a leader in situations like this. He provided a calming influence on pride members, a safe haven to those shifters who needed it. And the human officer clearly knew these cats. "I think it's a good idea," she said. "Skittish shifters are never safe for humans, and our presence might make things worse."

"Second," the leo continued. "I will end the interview if I deem it necessary, no questions asked."

She frowned. They were here to gather information, something the leo had not allowed the human officers to do. She didn't like the thought of him arbitrarily ending their interviews.

"Please understand, this incident has shaken my cats, some more than others. I will endeavor to allow the interviews to go on as long as possible, but my pride must come first."

"That's fine," Fen answered. "Alpha Colin would insist on the same conditions."

The leo nodded approvingly. Reaching for the jug, he poured four glasses and handed them around before settling on one side of the couch. "The act of sharing a drink with my cats will put them at ease. It is too early for wine, so I settled on cranberry juice," he explained.

She waited until Fen lifted her glass to his nose and handed it back. "It's fine."

The leo raised his eyebrows.

She shrugged. "It wouldn't be the first time someone tried to poison me. It makes Fen feel better and, quite frankly, I appreciate his concern."

She took a small sip of juice, and the flavor rolled on her tongue. It was good. At least she wouldn't have to force herself to drink it. She pulled out a mini voice recorder as Fen fished a notebook and pen from his pocket.

She relaxed as best she could, trying to push out a soothing vibe. She had no idea if she'd been successful, but Fen nodded at her. These interviews were bound to be far different than the ones they conducted at the station.

Relieved, she faced the leo. "We're ready."

****

The witnesses all said the same thing. They'd never seen any creature like the one that attacked them. The scent terrified them all, though none of them could identify it. No one even agreed on what form the shifter had taken. Some said lion, some said bear, and still others said the thing was a wolf. Hell, one person even swore the creature was a dragon.

Their first new piece of information came from a young woman.

"I was reluctant to allow you to interview the next witness," the leo said, rubbing his chin. "Officer Jones convinced me what she has to say is important. Sarah, darling? Come on in."

Fen's breath caught audibly when she stopped in the doorway. "Submissive," he whispered.

Ah. There were two submissive wolves in his pack, and Ara knew how driven he was to protect them. It probably killed him that a submissive had been in the line of danger.

She lingered on the threshold, her dark eyes peeled wide so they popped against her pale skin. Stress, residual fear, and grief wafted from her. Ara's nose tickled from the strength of the chemicals Sarah's body was producing, but she resisted the urge to rub it.

Next to her, Fen twitched. His fingers clenched and released. The soft groan, almost a keen, told Ara how much he wanted to comfort the young woman.

"It's okay," she said when Fen didn't speak. "I'm Inspector Classen, and my partner is Inspector Blair. We handle any case with paranormal elements."

The girl, who couldn't be far out of her teens, crept into the room and sat closer to the leo than any of the other cats had. Ara wondered if she would end up in the man's lap before the interview finished.

Fen leaned forward, his expression gentle. "Can you tell us what happened?"

The girl's eyes filled with tears. "It killed him. Tore his stomach out with a single swipe. All I could do was talk to him while he died."

She felt Fen twitch beside her, but the leo shook his head slightly. He took the submissive's hand and pulled her flush against his side.

He looked over at them, his own grief reflected on his face. His eyes were glossy with unshed tears, and his nostrils flared as he sucked in a deep breath. "One of the shifters who died was her fiancé."

It wasn't the information they needed, exactly, but it broke Ara's heart. Shifters were often so blasé about the nature of life and death, the intensity of their loss stuck her in the chest. She glanced at Fen from the corner of her eye and tracked his rapid breathing.

Sarah sobbed once and collapsed against her leo. "It's okay, sweetheart," he murmured. His voice broke as he continued. "We won't be long. Just tell them what you told me. About what it looked like."

She took a deep, shuddering breath and wrung her hands. "No one can agree on what it looked like. I watched when it came and swiped at..." She gulped. "It changed forms." Her voice was thick with tears.

"What do you mean, it changed forms?" Ara asked, thoroughly confused. Of course it could change forms. Shifters—at least she assumed the creature was a shifter—could change between their human and animal forms at will. Not quickly, and certainly not without a fair bit of discomfort, but she'd seen both Fen and Colin shift to their wolves in under thirty seconds.

"I saw it. It went from wolf, to cat, to bear. It shifted so quickly, it was hard to see."

Fen growled, low and menacingly. The submissive cat cowered closer to her leader. Her already-pale face turned ashy, and Ara prepared herself to lunge forward and catch her in case she fainted. "I'm sorry," she whispered.

He shook his head. "I'm sorry I scared you. I'm angry with our chief. We weren't informed of any shifter deaths. We were only told of human casualties. We should have been called out a lot sooner."

Something in the leo's expression caused the fine hairs on the back of Ara's neck to rise.

The leo tucked a strand of the submissive's hair behind her ear. "You can leave, sweetheart. Go find Tyson and get him to make you a hot chocolate."

"We're not quite done," Ara said, keeping her voice as gentle as possible. She had to hear the rest of the story. It was possible to glean information from the smallest of details, even if the witness didn't realize the importance of the information.

"We're done." The leo's words brooked no argument. "Rule number two, Inspector Classen."

She clenched her jaw, and only Fen's hand on her shoulder stayed her tongue. "Go ahead," he said to the girl. "If you can think of anything else you want to tell us, the leo has our number."

Sarah sat frozen, her eyes darting around the room as if searching for someone. Or something. After half a minute or so, she reached out to shake their hands, the fingers of her free hand clenched in the front of her leo's shirt. Ara didn't miss the fine tremble in the girl's arm.

She waited until the young woman stumbled out of the room before she turned on Fen. "What the hell? Why wouldn't you insist on continuing the interview? And you," she said to the leo, "don't you want us to solve this attack? It seems like you're doing everything you can to curtail us."

"What did you smell?" the leo asked instead.

"Adrenaline," she answered.

The leo stood and stretched. "Am I correct when I say vampires can only scent the actual hormone the body produces?"

"Yes," she said through clenched teeth. She didn't know how questioning her was helping the investigation, but it was irritating as hell.

"So, in other words, you didn't scent the fact that Sarah was close to a breakdown. You had gotten as much as you were going to get out of her."

Ara closed her eyes and silently counted to ten. God save her from simpering females.

"Not everyone is as strong as you," Fen said softly. "Not everyone has lived through what you have and come out better for it."

The muscles around her eyes tightened. She didn't want the leo to start asking questions about her past. Thankfully, her partner steered the conversation back to the real issue. But his gentle reminder served to drain her anger. She'd once been just like Sarah; scared and helpless. Guilt rushed through her over her irritation but she pushed it aside and focused on what her partner was saying.

"As much of an ass as he is, the chief wouldn't keep paranormal deaths from us," Fen said almost conversationally. His voice remained level, even respectful. "We would have been pulled in immediately if he had known about a paranormal death."

"I haven't heard good things about your chief and how he

treats paranormal citizens. We'd rather track and dispose of this creature without human interference."

He pushed his hair off his forehead and side-eyed them. He was every inch an annoyed lion. "I was surprised to hear the two of you were assigned to the case. I was under the impression he would do anything he could to blame shifters for a human death. There's also a nasty rumor floating around about how he detests humans who interact with shifters even more."

The leo would smell a lie from a mile away. Besides, they had nothing to gain by hiding the truth. "This assignment was supposed to be a punishment," she informed him.

"She broke a blood rapist's nose," Fen explained. "We're not sure why he cares, since you're right, he doesn't care much for paranormals. In any case, we're here now."

"Good for you." He nodded approvingly in Ara's direction. "Scum like that doesn't deserve anything better. You do understand it's our right to exterminate this creature, correct?"

Fen nodded. "I understand. I expect my alpha would feel the same way. We just want to help."

The leather couch creaked as the leo stood. He strode to the window and stared out at the forest. Just when she was sure he was going to reject their offer, he turned around and pinned them with a stare. "We don't have a choice in your involvement, do we?"

"Not really," Ara said.

"Your cooperation would make our job easier. We would certainly appreciate it," Fen answered.

Ara tilted her head and gazed at her partner for a second. He was usually much more direct.

Shifter politics was a sticky subject. She'd known about shifters her entire life, had been close with Fen's pack for years, but she still didn't understand all the subtle nuances to shifter interactions. Fen claimed they didn't formally teach politics, that it was all instinctual.

Luckily, she wasn't bound by the same niceties. Her head ached, she was hungry and tired and it made her snippy. "Can we get a move on? We really need to investigate the scene before it degrades even further."

The leo didn't move, but his muscles bunched. She'd upset him with her tone.

Tough luck. Either they got on with things or they called it a day.

"The owner is one of my cats," the leo responded.

She blew out an exasperated breath. Did he think they were stupid? "Yes, I understand," she responded with exaggerated patience. "And you speak for him. So just grant us permission and we'll get out of your hair until we have something to report."

There was very little they could do until they were allowed into the diner to investigate.

"I have the final say, yes. However, I do take the concerns of my cats into consideration. The owner would prefer to be present during your investigation."

"Fine," she snapped. "No problem."

The leo pivoted and fixed her with a hard stare. "You may start tomorrow morning."

Fen twitched next to her. "It's not that late. We can get started now."

Apparently, her impatience was contagious. His previously calm, soothing voice had a sharp edge to it.

"No, you can't. It's dark. And the owner doesn't like the dark."

Oh, for the love of all that is holy. A shifter who was afraid of the dark?

Her expression gave away her thoughts. "Ever since the attack, several of my cats feel like they are being watched."

Her partner coughed, deep in his throat, like he tried to disguise a growl. "And you waited until the last possible minute to tell us about this feeling? Your cats were attacked by an unknown shifter. It is very possible that one or more of them is being hunted."

"A feeling, Inspector. That's all it is. We have no evidence of any such thing," the leo replied.

"This feeling gets stronger at night?" Ara asked. The attack had happened in broad daylight.

"No, it's constant. At night, it's harder to see, even with our advanced vision. Most feel safer in their homes."

The steel in his voice told her he wasn't going to change his mind on letting them into the diner that night.

"Can we at least see the owner?" she asked, forcing as much respect into her tone as possible.

The leo sighed and rubbed his forehead. "She's the last witness waiting to talk to you. Carla?"

The door flew open and a tiny woman with flowing red hair and curves that couldn't be replicated by any amount of plastic surgery bounded in. "What took you so long?" she barked. "I've been waiting for hours."

The leo's mouth quirked. He was either amused by the woman's outburst, or irritated. Ara couldn't tell which.

"They've been speaking with Sarah," the leo countered, his voice soft.

Carla looked up, contrite. "Right."

The pride leader gestured to the woman. "This is Carla Defoe, owner of the diner."

Ara leaned forward. A comforting scent surrounded this woman. One of fresh-cut flowers and cinnamon. It was completely at odds with her behavior. "If you're anything like my partner, you heard our entire conversation and you already know our names. So why don't we skip the introductions and get started?"

"Great. I was in the kitchen when the thing came in," she began. "I came out when I heard the screaming. I don't know what it was. It had to be at least eight feet tall and built like a house."

Carla took a deep breath and narrowed her eyes, as if trying to recall the episode down to the last detail. This was the kind of witness most inspectors dreamed of.

Ara's heart pounded, the familiar excitement she always associated with getting closer to the truth tugging at her gut. "I understand you didn't see the attack from the beginning. Tell us what you *did* see."

The pulse in the she-cat's neck pounded harder, quicker, as her eyes glazed over. "Like I said, it was huge. Giant claws. No matter how hard I tried, I couldn't make out how many claws it had, which is weird because they were so big. It was moving too fast for me to get a good look at it."

Fen's pen made scratching sounds as he hurried to keep up with Carla's words, but she ignored him.

"Go on."

The leo growled low in his throat, though Carla didn't look particularly intimidated. "I want them to find out what trashed my place, Leo."

"Fine," the leo said. "You can stop at any time."

"I understand," Carla said. "So, anyway, this *thing* is in my restaurant, killing my customers, when it suddenly stops, howls, and bounds back out the door."

Ara frowned. It just stopped? On its own? And *left*? Her mind raced as she tried to picture it. "Nobody chased it out? No one attacked it, causing it to retreat?"

She already knew the answer. Witness after witness had said the same thing. Carla was their most reliable witness yet. She'd been holding out hope that the cat would offer something a little more constructive than *it bounds back out the door.*

The woman shrugged. "I don't know what to tell you. It doesn't seem right, I know. It's like it gave up and decided to go home."

Disappointment frizzled through Ara's veins, causing her

energy to wilt like a leaky balloon. She glanced over at Fen, who quirked an eyebrow in her direction.

They'd long ago established their own method of silent communication. Fen had just told her to roll with it.

They'd played this game before. Usually with suspects, of course, but it would probably work just as well with a witness. Especially if the witness was willing to talk.

Ara folded her hands in her lap and stared expectantly at the shifter, who stared back at her. She was impressed. It wasn't often people tried to stare her down.

Ara didn't move despite the obvious challenge. She'd held the same pose for four hours in the interrogation room before. She doubted Carla would hold out that long.

Eventually, Carla huffed. "Okay. There's something else, but everyone said I was crazy and to just forget it."

"That's all right. We want to hear it." She didn't bother to keep the eagerness out of her tone. Why bother when all the shifters in the room would scent it anyway?

Carla hesitated, glancing quickly at her leo. She huffed and shook her head as if trying to dislodge an unpleasant memory. "It was definitely hunting something specific. It didn't kill or even harm anyone who stayed out of its way. I've been wondering if people had just backed off, it would have sniffed around and left."

Ara frowned. Various people had told them that it seemed like the beast was looking for something specific, but not one of the witnesses had come up with Carla's theory.

The woman rushed to support her statement. "When you see the damage, you'll understand. The thing was clearly cutting a path to the back of the diner."

"You're sure we can't get in until tomorrow?" Ara asked. She held her breath, hoping the leo would change his previous decision.

Carla shivered. "No. There's something in the woods,

watching. Waiting. I don't know what it is. Every time we have a bead on it, it disappears. Sometimes we catch a scent, and it's the same as the beast's. We haven't been able to corner anything."

Anger simmered low in Ara's belly. She hated when people kept information from her. She glared at the leo and opened her mouth to blister his ears.

"Okay. We'll be at the diner by nine tomorrow morning," Fen said, cutting off what she'd been about to say. He tossed her a warning look and got to his feet. "Thanks for meeting with us."

She clamped her mouth shut, squeezing her jaw so tight she wouldn't be surprised if her molars shattered.

Still, Fen knew shifter politics better than she did. And the last thing she wanted to do was undermine him. It was important they present a united front.

She followed his lead and stood, arranging her expression carefully when she turned her gaze to Carla. The woman had been the most helpful thus far, and Ara didn't want Carla to think her anger was for her. "Thank you for your cooperation."

"I'll meet you at the diner tomorrow morning," Carla said in a small voice.

Ara's heart softened. She remembered what it was like to feel so vulnerable when she was supposed to be at the top of the food chain. It must be humiliating to be afraid to go outside at night when the woman had probably been so confident in her own safety prior to the attack.

She inclined her head toward the woman, hoping Carla would understand the silent acknowledgement of her feelings.

The leo saw them to the door. The human officer trailed behind them, as quiet as he'd been during the interviews. Along the way, they found Tyson, softly petting the sobbing submissive's hair. He looked up when they passed and bared his teeth. He evidently blamed them for the girl's distress.

Something about the girl tugged at Ara. Ignoring Tyson's

intimidating growl, she tiptoed toward the miserable female and knelt in front of her, trying to look as unthreatening as possible. Taking a chance, she grasped one of Sarah's hands in both of hers. "We'll find it, Sarah. I promise. I know it won't bring back your fiancé, but you won't have to be afraid anymore."

The girl didn't say anything, but she squeezed Ara's hands.

She reached up and wiped at the tears on Sarah's cheeks. She didn't know what else to say so she backed away and, with one last snarl at the beta cat, she followed Fen out the front door.

"Want me to drop you off at home?" he asked as they watched the human drive away.

Normally, she would thank Fen and decline the offer; she didn't like to be dependent on anyone else. Exhaustion was hitting her hard though, and she got the feeling she would need all the rest she could get. "I would, thanks."

By the time Fen pulled up in front of her apartment complex, she could hardly keep her eyes open.

She trudged up the stairs, stopped in the kitchen to down another bag of blood, and collapsed into bed without bothering to get changed.

The darkness was anything but peaceful. Every time she closed her eyes, an image of something huge lurked on the backs of her eyelids. She felt hunted through the night. Each time it got close enough for her to see what it was, she jolted awake.

She finally gave up, accepting the fact that sleep just wasn't going to happen. She booted up her computer and logged onto a private research website. Technically, she shouldn't have access to the site, but being the granddaughter of one of the vampire elders had its advantages. She pulled up the page on shifters and began sifting through the information.

CHAPTER ELEVEN

When she pulled up to the crime scene the next morning, Fen was already waiting for her. He leaned against his car, camera in hand, looking like he'd stepped out of a magazine photoshoot.

Somehow, he made jeans and a simple black T-shirt look fabulous. His jet-black hair was swept back off his forehead, giving him a boyishly handsome feel. Hell, even his teeth were attractive.

Ara tried not to cringe. She'd tossed her long blonde hair into a messy bun and was pretty sure it was already leaning to one side of her head. She hadn't bothered to put on any makeup and regretted the decision immediately. As a rule, she wasn't a vain person, but she probably looked like she'd been ridden hard and hung up wet.

He sauntered over and opened her door, raising his eyebrows when she glowered up at him.

Reluctantly, she slid out of her car and slammed the door behind her. "Hey," she said when she drew even with him.

"Are you okay? You don't look so hot."

"Way to make a girl feel good about herself," she grumbled.

He sniffed her. "Did you sleep okay? Did you drink enough blood this morning? Seriously, you don't look good."

"Sure, rub it in," she muttered. "Not all of us can look as fantastic as you first thing in the morning."

He didn't smile. "Are you feeling okay?"

She should have known she couldn't hide anything from him. His damn nose told him everything. She popped her trunk and grabbed her kit. "Didn't sleep well."

It was the understatement of the year, possibly the decade. And all her research in the name of insomnia had failed to turn up anything even remotely like the creature that had been described to them.

Luckily, he didn't push for more answers. She really didn't feel like rehashing her night, but he had a way of extracting information from her like no one else did.

The same officer approached them with far more confidence than he had the day before. "Inspector Classen, hi. You guys ready to go in now?"

The tickle of anticipation started in her toes. They typically didn't participate in these kinds of investigations. Usually, the suspects were handed over to them once the investigation was complete. She barely resisted the urge to rub her hands together. She wasn't happy that members of the paranormal community had been hurt and lost, but she and Fen would probably wrap things up before any human ever could.

Needling the chief with their success would simply be a bonus.

Fen smiled at the human. "Sure thing, Josh. Lead the way."

She blinked. Her partner never called any of the officers they worked with by their first name.

Once upon a time, she'd had plenty of human friends. Her mother had warned her of the pitfalls of befriending mortals. She hadn't listened. Until her friends grew up and started to question why she wasn't aging with them. It had been difficult to separate herself from the friends she'd truly cared for.

By the time the paranormal community had come forward and revealed their existence to the humans, she'd already sat at the back of countless funeral homes as her former friends died one by one. Any ties with humans didn't seem worth the heartache, so she'd simply stopped trying. Her emotional state was no reason to forget her manners though, and she imagined the lecture she'd receive from her mother if she ever discovered the situation.

She stuck her hand out toward the human. "Sorry. I haven't properly introduced myself. Arabella Classen. Please call me Ara. 'Inspector Classen' reminds me of the chief."

"Joshua Jones. You can call me Josh." He grasped her hand firmly.

It was refreshing to see him not cower from her. They may have been out in the open for a number of decades, but most humans still feared vampires.

"Are we allowed to go in?" she asked.

"Yeah. The leo called down a few minutes ago, giving us permission to do whatever we need. Carla will be here in a few minutes."

"Let's get started," Fen said.

Plywood had been nailed to the door frame. Josh produced a hammer from his trunk. "Sorry. The chief reminded me, for the hundredth time, that I was supposed to take the lead on this. I'm not supposed to let you touch anything if I can help it."

A squad car drove by, slowing down to a crawl as it passed. She narrowed her eyes. People often underestimated a vampire's abilities because they'd been told said abilities were significantly muted when a vampire lived on bagged blood.

It was true, of course. Heightened senses were a sure signs of live blood addiction.

But the absence of live blood didn't dull her vision, or anything else for that matter, to the level of a human. She could see inside the squad car perfectly, even from the diner entrance. "Chief," she muttered.

"Of course," Fen growled. He blew out a breath, the frustration practically vibrating off him in waves.

She was tempted to wave at the man, maybe flip him the bird, but kept her hands at her sides. There was no point in getting him all riled up. He'd probably find some way to suspend her if she pissed him off enough.

"Sorry," Josh said again. He flipped the hammer and pried

at the nails from the door.

They waited exactly one minute after the chief finally drove away before attacking the wood. She hooked the tips of her fingers in the tiny crack between the wood and the door jamb and pulled. Several nails popped out, clattering to the ground. She continued working away at the plywood until one side was completely free of nails.

"For the love of God," Fen growled. "I know you can tear that thing down in a matter of seconds. Why are you taking so long?"

"What if Carla wants to put it back up?"

Fen rolled his eye. "We'll never get in at this rate."

He stepped forward and kicked the plywood, sending broken shards of wood flying in every direction. The flimsy plywood was no match for an impatient wolf shifter. One kick and a few punches later, there was a gaping hole wide enough for a truck to fit through, though she suspected a few of the punches were more to relieve Fen's frustration than anything else. The scent of fear assaulted her. It was thick and oppressive, yet so sharp it hurt to breathe. She gasped, sucking in oxygen, desperate to relieve the sudden heaviness pressing down on her chest. Was this what it was like to drown?

Inhale. Exhale. Inhale. Exhale.

It was no good. Her brain buzzed, goose bumps covered her skin, and her muscles twitched. Her respiration sped up. Logically, she knew she was on the edge of hyperventilating.

Inhale. Exhale. Inhale. Exhale.

She'd studied meditation for a few years in Tibet, long before it had become all the rage in North America. She searched her mind for peace, forcing herself into a trance until breathing became bearable again.

Opening her eyes, she shot a quick glance at Fen. If *she* could smell the terror so sharply, he had to be close to losing control of his wolf.

Fen stood ramrod straight, though his arms hung loose at his sides. Then again, he would have smelled everything from outside, and had time to prepare himself. His golden wolf eyes were the only indication the scent had affected him at all.

"Better?" he asked.

"You could have warned me," she said. "But yes, better. I've never felt anything like that before. Can you scent anything or anyone in there?"

He shook his head, but she drew her gun, just in case. She stepped over the shards of wood, ignoring the way the residual feelings pressed on her chest, and swept her gun in a wide arc.

Josh followed her. Out of the corner of her eye, she saw him repeat her action.

Fen pushed his way in, his own weapon still holstered to his side. "I told you there was no one here."

A row of gouges caught her attention. Like the ones outside, they were deep, six inches into the steel frame at least.

It was the difference in them, not their similarity, that had her bending down immediately. "Fen? Look at this."

Her partner crouched next to her and reached out to touch the indentations. "They look like a wolf made them."

She frowned. "Really? I didn't think you guys made claw marks like this."

Josh hovered behind them, a pen flying across a notebook page. "What do you mean?"

She straightened and extended a hand toward her partner. He stared at the marks for a few seconds longer before accepting her hand and pushing up to his feet. He gestured to the marks, inviting Josh to look closer. "Wolves have four claws. Well, five, but one wouldn't leave a mark. They are spaced the way I would expect if I searched for a wolf suspect."

"But?" Josh prompted.

Fen stared at the marks, a troubled look crossing his face. She'd only seen wolves fight once, but she knew what was bugging him. She asked the human a question instead. "When you were living with your sister's pack, did you ever witness a fight?"

The officer narrowed his eyes as if digging through his brain for a specific memory. "The alpha tried to keep me away from anything like that. I only saw a fight once, right at the very beginning."

"You would have seen them snapping at each other, posturing and attempting to pin each other, right?" she asked.

"Yes."

"You wouldn't have seen them swipe at anything. It's not how wolves attack. If they're fighting for survival, they're more likely to bite at the throat, not claw at their enemy. Besides, their claws are pretty dull, definitely not sharp enough or strong enough to gouge so deeply into a steel doorframe."

Understanding dawned in Josh's expression. He turned to Fen. "Can you think of *any* wolf who might be able to do damage like this.

The shifter shook his head. "No. Even the most powerful alpha I know isn't big enough to leave these kinds of marks. A normal wolf's claws wouldn't be spaced this far apart either. Whatever did this had to be massive."

Ara inspected the rest of the diner. She picked her way over a broken table and into a corner, digging around in her kit until she found her flashlight. Flicking it on, she crawled the perimeter of the room, searching for additional evidence. There had to be something, *anything*, that would point to what the creature actually was.

She only looked up once when she heard someone else shuffling. Fen crept on all fours with his own flashlight, peering under tables and chairs.

She found nothing. Absolutely nothing.

She straightened and perched on her knees. "You find anything?"

"No."

How was it that something that did so much damage left so little evidence? All she saw were claw marks and broken furniture. There had been casualties. There should be blood, lots of it. If the cat shifters fought as hard as the witnesses said, there would be fur of some sort scattered around.

And yet, neither she nor her partner had managed to find anything of the sort.

She thought back to the slim case file they'd reviewed. Forensic reports took time and probably wouldn't be available for a couple of weeks yet, and they would be lucky if the chief even let them have immediate access to them anyway.

There had been photos though. And they had shown a lot more carnage than this. There should be bloodstains everywhere. Hell, the smell of blood alone should be enough to trigger her hunger and instinct to hunt, but there was nothing that had her gums tingling or her heart pounding in anticipation.

She closed her eyes and took a deep breath, sorting through the different scents that floated to her. They were faint, almost like the scene was months old instead of just days. She caught human blood, coppery and tangy, lingering lightly. Under that, she could smell shifter blood. It wasn't anything like Fen's blood. It was lighter, with less power behind it. It carried the same wildness she'd smelled at the leo's house. Definitely some kind of cat shifter.

Below the scent of shifter blood, so faint she could hardly smell it, was a scent that caused a shiver to work its way up her spine. It was the same scent they'd detected leaking from behind the plywood the day before, only greatly diluted. The fine hairs on her arms rose, her stomach clenched, and her muscles bunched.

"Do you smell it?" she asked.

Fen drew in a deep breath and released it slowly, like he was trying to control his respiration. "You mean the sour smell?"

"Yeah." She propped her fists on her hips and inhaled again. "Sour and acidic all at the same time."

"It makes my wolf crazy," Fen said. His voice was gritty and his words were slightly slurred, like he was talking through a mouthful of marbles.

She ignored his obvious distress, having learned from experience that he would inform her if he had trouble controlling his beast. "It's pretty distinctive. I can't believe it isn't more potent than this."

She took another sniff, concentrating on the smell with all her might. There was something else in the air, a scent that shimmered and sparkled and made her nose twitch. "Magic," she said.

"The leo probably had a witch come in and clean it. He is determined to deal with this himself, remember. He made it clear, at least to me, that he wasn't willing to play by human rules. Besides, the last thing we need is an out-of-control monster loose in public. A spell would explain why the scent is fading quickly. Some magic needs time to work."

She wrinkled her nose and glanced around. The scene certainly had been cleaned since the crime scene photos were taken, which made their job harder. She'd dealt with her fair share of witches in her lifetime. It wasn't something she was eager to repeat.

All magic had a distinct feeling to it. The last time she'd encountered a spell, she had nearly thrown up, much to the witch's delight. This magic smelled clean, almost like rosemary and thyme. "Do you recognize the magic?"

"No. Colin has a witch on standby in case he needs to clean up any pack fights or anything he needs to hide from the human government, if you know what I mean, but this magic smells entirely different."

"What are the chances the leo is trying to hide something from us?" she asked.

Fen squinted and shook his head like he was trying to get rid of an irritating bug. She almost smiled at the action. It was a very wolfy type thing to do. "I can smell when someone's lying. He was telling us the truth."

Or the leo had *convinced* himself he was telling the truth.

"You said wolf shifters only have four claws? Or they only use four of them?" Josh asked from across the room.

She turned on the spot and saw him standing in a far corner, near the back booth. He was staring at something on the wall. She frowned and wove her way through the wreckage of broken furniture to stand next to him. So far, she and Fen had only had time to inspect the floor. They usually started from the ground up. Neither of them had inspected the are Josh was staring at yet.

The booth had taken the most damage. The upholstery had been torn to shreds, foam pushing through the splits in the fabric and scattered on the floor as if the animal had been digging in the seat for something. The table had been damaged, cracked down the middle, reminding her of the Grand Canyon. Only the half attached to the wall still stood, the rest reduced to splinters. The wall was clawed as bad as the door frame. Even the ceiling sported a set of claw marks.

"Yes." Fen's joined them. "Why?"

"What shifter has five claws then?" Josh asked, pointing to the wall.

She leaned forward and ran her gloved fingers over the gouges. Five. Just like Josh said.

"There were four at the door," she mused, more to herself than the men. "And there are five here."

Her mind raced. Everything indicated the presence of multiple shifters, though every single witness had sworn there had been only one.

"A bear has five claws," Fen said.

"Do bear shifters live this far south?" Josh asked, dropping to his knees to inspect the underside of the table.

"They are rare," Fen said. "I've never actually met one, but I know they're around. Apparently, there's a family of bear shifters not far from here. Colin knows about them. He's even met them once or twice. I expect the leo knows as well."

Ara smelled the woman a full ten seconds before she spoke, just enough time to have her gun ready in case the leo had changed his mind about allowing them to investigate and had decided to have them forcefully removed.

"I never thought to count the claw marks," Carla said from the door.

Ara stifled an irritated sigh and holstered her weapon. Most of the time, she would have spun around and snapped at the woman to get out of her crime scene, regardless of how much she liked her. She was very particular about how she liked things done, and civilians tended to mess things up.

However, the laws were very clear on the subject. Once the leader of a paranormal sect took over a police investigation, they called the shots, not the police. And if the leo allowed Carla to crash their scene, Ara had to suck it up and play nice.

Josh pushed away from the booth and crossed to the woman. "Carla. Thanks for coming over. We just got started."

"No problem, Josh. Inspectors Blair, Classen. If there's anything I can help you with, please just let me know."

"You can start by telling us exactly what evidence was saved before the witch came in and did her bippity-boppity-boo thing," Ara snarled.

Maybe playing nice wasn't as easy as it sounded.

The she-cat peeled her lips away from her teeth and hissed.

Ara rolled her eyes. She hadn't managed to live over ninety years without tangling with a shifter before, much to her grandfather's dislike. "Please. I may not be as strong as I was when I drank live blood, but I can still wipe the floor with you. However, I do apologize for my comments. It's not your fault your leo…" She trailed off. It was never a good thing to insult a wolf's alpha, and she assumed it was the same with the leo.

Carla backed down, apparently mollified by the apology.

The energy in the room calmed somewhat, though there was still a thread of tension sparking in the air. "I tried to convince him to leave it until you guys showed up. He said he wasn't sure you would even hear about it. He wanted the place cleansed because of the smell. It was creeping everyone out. The witch went a little overboard on the cleaning. He was angry, but she'd collected some fur and even a vial of blood before she did her thing. He sent it with me."

"Tell me about the fur," Fen said suddenly. His voice was gritty again, eyes completely shifted to his wolf's. She wondered briefly if she would have to break up a fight between the two shifters. There was no doubt Fen would win a physical confrontation. Her respect for the female cat shifter increased exponentially when she didn't balk or hesitate. "The witch we hired was less than clear about what we dealt with. She couldn't determine the species of shifter from the fur. The blood sample also confused her."

Behind her, Josh made a noise in his throat. "Why didn't he give us the evidence yesterday?"

She didn't blame him for his irritation, especially since it appeared he knew most of the cat shifters well. She also knew how this part of shifter politics worked at least.

Fen answered before she had a chance. "He wants to make sure we know who is in charge. It's not us, in case you hadn't noticed."

God save her from macho shifters. If the leo wasn't careful, she would start suspecting he was the real culprit. Ara held out her hand. "Let me see the blood."

She might not technically have as good a sense of smell as wolf shifters, but when it came to blood, she could smell things that even shifters couldn't.

A small vial was pressed into her palm, and the smell assaulted her even before she uncapped it. She took off the stopper and nearly dropped the tube.

Both shifters in the room flinched, Carla even taking a large step back. Ara didn't blame her. Something was definitely not right with this sample. It smelled acidic and alkaline all at once.

A shiver ran down her spine, the fine hairs on the back of her neck stood on end, and her gums tingled where her fangs tried to drop. The vial inspired a fight or flight instinct in her she hadn't experienced since the last time her father beat her.

She searched her mind, trying to understand why she was suddenly so afraid, but she couldn't put her finger on it. It was almost like some old instinct evolution carved into her rather than an actual familiarity, the same as how some humans were irrationally afraid of spiders.

"Do you know what it is?" Josh asked.

She shook her head. "No. And that scares me more than anything."

"Why?"

"It's not common knowledge, but vampires can tell so much more than just species by the scent of blood. Normally, I can tell you whether the blood belonged to a male or a female by the amount of hormones I detect. I can tell if the person is sick, and I can sometimes even pinpoint exactly what illness that individual is suffering from."

Fen cleared his throat and inched closer to her, still clearly put off by the scent of the blood she held. "And you can't get anything from that?"

She almost smirked at the disgust in his voice, would have if she weren't so creeped out herself. "Nothing. It's frustrating."

Carla shivered. "Can you cork that thing again, please? It's giving me the willies."

"My pleasure." She capped it again and dropped it in the resealable baggy the woman produced from her pocket. "You know, magic tends to contaminate things, blood especially. I doubt you need to seal it for evidence."

Carla dropped the whole thing into her purse and zipped it

up. "I know. I want to try and mute the scent as much as possible. I still can't believe I'm carrying it around with me."

Ara frowned. She hadn't been able to scent it when Carla had walked in. Fen hadn't given any indication of being able to smell it. Either the plastic was doing a *very* good job at masking the blood's scent, or the magic was much stronger than she'd realized.

Carla placed her purse gently on the counter like she was afraid something might jump out of it if she jostled it too much. "Have you ever come across blood you couldn't identify before?"

She shook her head again. "No. And that's what's so frustrating."

"Is there any way someone from your pride could have made these marks?" Fen asked from across the room. "There's another set of five gouges, but it's spaced differently from the bear-claw ones. This one looks like a cat."

Carla was silent for a moment. "I guess it could be from one of us," she said finally. "We put up a pretty good fight. Though I'm sure that's where the humans were sitting."

"Tell me about the humans," Ara said. She stripped off her gloves and grabbed a small digital recorder from her kit. It was easier to record Carla's responses than write them down. She wanted to be sure she got every single detail and didn't want to risk missing something in her rush to copy the woman's words onto paper. "Hold on a sec."

The recorder made a little beeping noise as it turned on. "This is Inspector Arabella Classen, Paranormal Investigation Unit, interviewing Carla Defoe. Ms. Defoe, please tell me about the human victims. Did they frequent your diner often?"

"Yes." Carla's response was firm and clear. Just what all inspectors wanted when questioning a witness. Or a suspect.

"They were regulars here," the cat shifter continued. "They came in at least once a week. Said they had a fondness for my roast beef special."

"How long had they been coming?"

The woman paused to think. "At least five years. At first, I think they were intrigued by the idea of shifters. They didn't talk much, but they were respectful."

"How were they acting just before the attack? Were they nervous at all? Did it seem like they had any idea of what was about to happen?"

Carla shook her head before she'd even finished the question. "No. They were perfectly normal. It was a typical Tuesday night, except that Josh wasn't here."

Josh wasn't here? She cocked an eyebrow at the human. "Officer Jones comes in as well?"

"Yes. A few times a week. He likes the shepherd's pie."

Josh nodded. "I come here to eat, yes. And I've gotten to know a few of the local pride members, the leo included. I wasn't here during the attack, I didn't know either the human victims or the shifter victims, and I was assigned to the case by the chief. It really doesn't make a difference if I'm familiar with the diner or not."

No help there.

She turned back to Carla. "So, the humans acted perfectly normal as far as you could tell. Did you see their deaths?"

"Yes. I came out of the kitchen just after the screaming started, so I saw most of what happened. Like I said yesterday, it looked like it was searching for something. It went straight to the humans and sort of sized them up before turning away. Honestly, it probably would have left them alone, but they freaked out and bolted. They got in its way and it swiped at them. They hit the wall." She pointed to the wall with the unknown claw marks and swallowed. "I didn't see what happened next, the thing moved too fast. Maybe it made those marks in the process. I don't know."

Josh summarized the scene in a few neat sentences. "So, all in all, we've seen evidence that a wolf, a bear, and possibly a cat attacked this place. All the witnesses say there was only one creature. It didn't seem to care who got in its way, which resulted in deaths all around."

"Well, remember what the submissive said yesterday? That the shifter was actually all three? Is it possible that there's a species of shifter we haven't discovered?" Ara ventured.

Fen heaved a sigh. She'd never seen him so tired. Concern for her partner wove through her mind. He hardly ever let her see his exhaustion, let alone two strangers.

"I'm starting to think that's what we're dealing with. Even if this thing is some undiscovered species of shifter, we can't just let it roam all over. Is there anything else you can tell us?" he asked.

Carla pursed her lips. "I will say that it seemed like it was especially interested in the booth." She shot a look at Josh, who seemed a little green.

Some kind of awareness tingled in Ara's toes. She'd learned long ago to trust her instincts. "What's the matter?"

Josh licked his lips. She could hear his heart pounding, going a mile a minute. The blood rushing through his veins buzzed faintly, and it caused her mouth to water. She swallowed and focused on his eyes instead of his throbbing pulse. "What?"

"That's where I sit."

"Every time?" Ara asked.

"Yes. Every time."

Something clicked in the back of her mind. "Could it have been hunting you?"

The human officer shifted uncomfortably. "I guess. But I wasn't here. I hadn't been here for more than two weeks. The chief had me pulling overtime, and it was all I could do to get home and crash."

Fen tilted his head and considered the young man. "Ms. Defoe," he said, without tearing his gaze from Josh. "The magic has pretty much wiped the diner clean of any scents other than the lingering fear and grief. On the day of the attack, did the diner carry Josh's scent at all?"

"No." The answer was quick and firm. "I have a crew that comes in and cleans every night. In the morning, the only thing I can smell is disinfectant. And the food pretty much drowns out every other smell by midmorning. There's no way his scent could have been around for that long."

Except cats didn't have the same sense of smell as a wolf did. Ara pinched the bridge of her nose and turned to Fen. "Do you scent him in the booth at all?"

Her partner shook his head. "No. Like I said…magic. Whatever that witch did, she totally wiped the place clean of all human scent."

She made a note to have a talk with the leo about calling them before he brought a witch in if something ever happened again.

She glanced out the gaping hole where they'd torn down the plywood. "So it gave up searching and took off. Into the woods."

"Yes," Carla said. Her voice quavered. She wasn't as unaffected as she seemed.

"I guess the only thing we can do now is track it," Fen said.

Ara picked her way across the rubble and stood in the door, staring at the woods. They looked dark and foreboding despite how sunny it was outside. A memory of the monster from her nightmares surfaced again, and she rubbed her arms against the sudden chill.

Unfortunately, tracking angry, out-of-control paranormal monsters was definitely part of her job description.

CHAPTER TWELVE

It had taken a call to the leo in order to make Carla stay at the diner instead of following them into the woods. She'd growled and hissed but had eventually stayed behind, hovering in the doorway.

Ara, Fen and Josh stood at the edge of the forest, peering into its dense darkness. It was like she was waiting for a monster to pop out at them any second. Everything in her was on high alert and her own heart rate, normally much slower than most shifters, was sky-high.

Actually, it wasn't far from the truth. "Are we sure this is a good idea without backup?"

Fen snorted. "It's the worst idea we've ever had. I could call Colin to send a few wolves with us, but that would mean calling the leo and waiting for permission, and who knows how long that will take us. At least if we get eaten, the chief will be happy."

She forced a laugh at Fen's attempt at humor. "Someone may as well get something out of this."

Her partner turned to Josh. "You don't have to come with us. In fact, it's probably a good idea if you stay back with Carla and protect her if something happens."

It was Josh's turn to snort. "Carla doesn't need my protection. I hate to tell you but if that thing decides to kill someone, I'm the least protected."

It wasn't often a human admitted their physical weakness in front of paranormals. As a rule, they liked to pretend they were superior in every sense.

The young man was quickly becoming her favorite human.

She might even break her own rule about becoming friends with them.

Still, tromping through the woods looking for killer maybe-shifters probably wasn't the best thing for Josh.

He must have caught the look on her face, because he interrupted her before she could even start. "Don't even try. This is my job. And I have my gun."

She had a feeling their duty pistols would do little to slow down the creature. This thing certainly didn't sound like a normal shifter. It would probably take a very accurate shot to the head or heart to have a chance of stopping it, and hitting a moving target was a lot harder than people thought. She decided not to mention it. He was right. It was his job, even if he'd somehow drawn the short straw and been assigned to this case.

A warm hand settled on her shoulder and she looked up at Fen. He stood at least a head taller than her, and she sometimes forgot how small it made her feel when he towered over her. He handed her his weapon and holster. "Take this."

As soon as she'd accepted the gun and holster and strapped it to her side, he stripped off his shirt. She averted her gaze and caught Josh's smirk out of the corner of her eye. Evidently, he knew exactly what was going on. Fen was making sure he had on as little clothing as possible so there wasn't a chance he'd get too tangled in it if he had to shift quickly.

She had been raised in a time where showing off an ankle was considered taboo. Times changed and she had changed with them. The sight of a woman in a bikini didn't strike her as scandalous anymore, and a man's bare chest was almost commonplace. Still, she didn't need to see her partner's naked ass.

Even if it was a really nice ass.

"You can look, Ara. And for God's sakes, get your mind out of the gutter. I'm not that shameless."

She wasn't sure how him strutting around in his underwear was much better than being completely naked. At least he'd kept those on though, so she didn't have reason to complain.

Embarrassed, Ara fixed her gaze at the tree line. There were several likely paths the creature might have taken.

A soft tickle of scent teased her nose.

Ammonia.

The same scent the blood from Carla had carried.

She activated the navigation app on her phone and followed the smell fifty meters down the road, doubling back when the scent started to fade, finally stopping at a patch of trees about twenty-five meters from the restaurant.

Fen was already there, staring into the trees. "This is where it went into the woods."

"Probably. The scent is the strongest here." She crouched and stared at the ground. The brush was destroyed in some places, tree trunks cracked and smaller trees toppled over.

The ground was muddy and deep footprints led into the forest. "Wolf," Fen said.

Ara had been around Fen in his wolf form before. She'd seen any number of his pack members sauntering around in their wolf forms whenever she'd been over to visit Mandy. She'd never seen a wolf big enough to make paw prints the size of what they looked at. She grabbed a ruler from her kit and laid it beside the indentation. Regular wolves had front paws that topped out at around five inches long. Some wolf shifters had paws as long as nine inches. These tracks were an astonishing twelve inches long. She dictated the measurements into her recorder, keeping the surprise out of her voice as much as possible.

"Check out the toe spread," Fen suggested.

"That's next. I want to get a measurement of depth and see if we can determine how much it might weigh."

"I don't think depth would matter in this case. The ground would have been so soft from the rain it probably sank deeper than it normally would. The toe spread would give a much more accurate picture of its size. More weight means a larger distance between each toe."

She ignored him, measured the depth of the print, waited for Josh to snap a photo and moved on to the toe spread.

"Wow," Josh said when she laid the ruler down. "That is one big wolf."

"Have you ever met a wolf shifter that big?"

"No," Fen said.

"I have," Josh said from behind them.

She straightened. "Where?"

"My sister's husband is almost that size. Not quite as big. Close though. I measured his paw size once, just for kicks. It was ten inches long. But his toe spread was quite a bit smaller. It seems our monster might have a hell of a lot more muscle than the average shifter."

She pushed the implication to the back of her mind and went back to staring at the paw prints. There were four, all close together, indicating the creature had entered the forest at a dead run.

She peered through the trees, searching for the next set of tracks. She found them, in the same formation, some ways into the woods. Her twelve-inch ruler was not going to cut it this time. She pulled her measuring tape from her bag on her way back to the men.

"Here," she said, handing Fen the end.

Her partner crouched next to the tracks and held the end of the tape firm while she walked slowly to the next set of tracks, mentally counting her paces as she went.

Twenty-five feet.

Her stomach did a funny little dance. A wolf shifter could bound at a distance of twenty feet, give or take a foot. She waited until Josh took pictures of the tracks and measuring tape, narrating her findings into her digital recorder, before letting go of the end of the tape.

"Wow," she whispered. It wasn't professional, nor was it

enlightening, but she couldn't think of any other way to describe what she saw.

"We should get going," Fen said as he approached them. "We're losing daylight, and something tells me we don't want to be in those woods after dark."

Normally, she would have scoffed. Her night vision was excellent, although not as good as a shifter's. Between the two of them, she and Fen could have searched through the night without so much as tripping over a tree root.

But there was a monster on the loose, one that a room full of predator shifters couldn't take down, and neither of them was stupid. She might be hard to kill, but not impossible. And the human at their side was far more fragile than either of them. "Lead the way."

Josh stared into the trees pensively. "I guess you guys didn't get everything in the reports the chief gave you."

"It wouldn't surprise me," Fen said. "Why do you think that?"

"It's just that a couple of officers followed this trail a couple of days ago."

Ara wasn't surprised. It was standard procedure. And she'd read the report. Something in Josh's voice had alarm bells ringing in the back of her mind. She remembered the report he was referring to. It had been sketchy. Then again, paranormal investigations were, at worst, often brushed off by the human police or, at best, handled poorly. "They got lost, right? What happened?"

"They reported seeing something weird and then their walkies went silent. We couldn't get in touch with them for over an hour. I was sent in with a couple of other guys as a search party. We eventually found them wandering back toward the diner. They said they were fine, but people who are fine don't look so damn traumatized. They insisted they just got lost. I don't believe them. Now nobody else will come into the woods."

"That would have been good information to have earlier," Fen said. "Why didn't you say anything?"

Josh shrugged. "I thought you knew. I guess the chief really didn't see the need to add the fact that the officers were clearly creeped out. I mean, they did say they were fine."

Ara huffed. "Don't ever assume the chief fills us in. From now on, tell us every little detail. We'll decide if it's important or not."

They followed the broken brush through the woods. The creature had left a clear physical trail. Footprints changed from wolf, to bear, to cat and back again. Sometimes the order changed. There was no pattern, no rhyme or reason she could see behind the changes. Each time the paw prints changed, they would pause to take measurements and for Josh to take a photo. The scent of the beast thinned until it faded completely, leaving only the path of destruction to follow.

The trail seemed to go on forever. Her watch showed they'd been at it for more than four hours. While they hadn't travelled more than a few kilometers, stopping every few minutes to document and collect some kind of evidence ate up a big chunk of time.

"How far could it go before being spotted?" she mused. "The diner is half an hour outside of the city. The woods aren't that big, and we're heading right into Toronto. The forest is going to start thinning out soon. There's no way it's going to stay dense enough to hide something so huge for much longer."

Fen shrugged. "A wolf shifter can hide pretty effectively. I'm guessing most cat shifters could as well. And the bears, well, I know they hide incredibly well seeing as almost no one has ever seen them."

Josh bent down to take a photo of another set of tracks, bear ones. "There's got to be something we're missing."

The human was right. Something was off. She didn't smell any magic, didn't see any evidence that anything had been around to contaminate the trail in any way. Which was odd. It had been a full three days since the incident happened. The woods around the city were a haven for coyote. The ground was still wet enough for a rabbit to leave faint tracks. Why hadn't they seen any evidence of other wildlife along their way?

They walked for another hour. She counted the animal's form shift fifteen times. The stride length between prints shortened where the creature had slowed down. The prints even circled around a few times, as if it had been searching for something. The sky peeking through the tree tops had darkened as night started to fall.

Over to their left, a patch of mist hung low to the ground. Something about the way it lingered, the way it moved, triggered a long-forgotten memory of her great-grandmother. *"Stay away from the mists, child,"* she used to say. *"Nothing good ever crawled out of the mists."*

She wrinkled her nose. The stories Gran used to tell could curdle a kid's blood. But they were just stories.

Josh took a few more photos of broken branches and trampled brush. "It's getting dark. Do you think we should call it a day?"

"Did you bring your flashlight?" Fen asked.

"Yes."

"I can see fine without it. Ara can too. And you have your light. I think we should keep going, at least for a little while. We're not actually that far from the diner."

"I thought you said you didn't want to be out here in the dark?" Josh countered.

Ara interrupted them before they could start flexing their muscles. "Look, guys, as long as there's a trail, we should follow it. It's the only thing we have going for us right now. We can head back in another half hour and start again at first light."

She stared down the trail of wrecked branches and ruined brush. She thought about the human officers who had become lost along the way. What had they seen that left them so traumatized? "Fine," Josh said, pulling a flashlight out of one of his vest pockets. "If we run into this thing, I'm blaming you."

She smiled at the human. "Fair enough. Shall we?"

"Yep," Fen said.

She tromped ahead, eyes peeled for anything that seemed out of place. She held her gun steady in her right hand. Fen's weapon pressed reassuringly against her hip.

She didn't have to lead for long.

Abruptly, the trail ended.

It didn't fade into an ending. There wasn't evidence of a larger struggle.

It just ended.

They'd been following a trail of destruction, clawed trees, cracked branches and broken brush when they suddenly stepped into a patch of pristine forest.

She studied the trees, looking for evidence that it had scaled one.

Nothing.

"What the hell?" Fen muttered when he drew even with her.

"How could it just disappear?" Josh asked.

"I don't think it did," she replied. "We know it can shift into three forms. What's to say it can't shift to a bird and fly away? Or a snake? Or hell, a cute, fluffy bunny?"

"I thought about that. Why wait until here to do that?" Josh asked. "Why wouldn't it have flown away from the diner? It's not like the cats could have grabbed it once it was in mid-flight."

Fen disappeared into the trees ahead as she and Josh talked.

"Maybe it's not intelligent enough," she said. "Maybe it's more comfortable in those three forms and only shifted to a less predatory form once it felt safe enough to do so."

She doubled back until the trail became visible again. The tracks showed the creature had been in its cat form.

She took out her own flashlight and shone the light on the leaves where the trail disappeared. A large snake would have left some kind of disturbance as it slithered off.

Nothing.

There were no birds in the tree branches overhead, not that most would stick around while they were tramping through the woods.

Fen appeared again, a frown gracing his handsome face.

"Nothing?" she asked.

He shook his head. "I was hoping the trail would pick up again. I could have gone farther, but it's getting dark and Josh can't see as well as we can."

"We don't need to stop on my account." Josh crossed his arms over his chest and stared around. "What are the possibilities that the witch the pride hired followed the creature with a cleansing spell?"

"I don't smell any magic. Fen, do you?"

He paused and shivered. The movement was so small she doubted Josh's human eyes could track it. "Every witch's magic has a distinct scent. The one who cleansed the diner smelled of grass and wind. Definitely a white witch. That's not what I smell here."

"You do smell magic then?"

His nose twitched. "I smell something that's not right. It's not something I've ever encountered before. Something faint."

She contemplated his words as she stared around. A strange shimmering caught her attention. The fog she'd noticed earlier drifted a few feet away from them. She frowned. It was larger than before.

Significantly larger.

She ignored the sudden increase in her unease. It couldn't be the same fog. Fog didn't *follow* people. Night was falling and the air was cooler than the ground. Patches of fog would be forming over any area of lower ground and probably over any puddles. It was just that time of year.

Her great-grandmother's voice echoed in the back of her mind again. *Beware the mist.*

Her heart picked up speed when it drifted slowly closer. Fog didn't move like that.

"Guys?" she said, trying to keep her voice even. "We should go."

"Is it me, or is that fog acting really strange?" Josh asked, straightening to his full height.

"Yeah." Ara couldn't make herself explain that a patch of mist made her nervous. She was supposed to be a police officer, damn it. She regularly interviewed the worst of the worst. She didn't want to ruin her reputation.

The smell hit as she was searching for the right words to explain her unease.

It was the same scent they'd encountered at the scene, only far more concentrated. Complete and utter terror chased away her unease.

The fog rolled closer, expanding and pulsing with a life of its own. She stumbled back, grabbing the men's arms and pulling them with her. "*Run.*"

CHAPTER THIRTEEN

A low growl rumbled through the air, and Fen's muscles rippled under her hand.

She dropped his arm and jerked Josh out of the way. Suddenly, the fog wasn't their only problem. When a wolf chose to shift, they retained a part of their human self. He would recognize them in wolf form. If Fen lost control and shifted against his will, however, it meant the wolf part of him was in charge. And if that happened, there was no guarantee the animal would recognize them as friends.

"Fen," she called out.

She watched the fog out of the corner of her eye and took a deep, calming breath. "Fen."

He growled again, hunching over as he began to shift. His jaw lengthened into a snout and he stared up at her, his lips peeled back over deadly teeth.

When he didn't answer, she decided to pull out the big guns. Literally. She pointed her weapon at his face and hollered, "Fenris Blair, you listen to me. If you make one move on us, I will shoot you. It will kill me to do it, but I will do whatever I have to do to keep Josh safe."

He blinked and stared at her. He still looked at her with his wolf eyes, but he seemed far more in control. Or at least she hoped so.

The mist creeped slowly toward them, shimmering and sparking arcs of lightning.

She grabbed Josh's arm. "Let's go."

She didn't wait for him to answer, just took off with Josh in tow, hoping the fog didn't overtake them and that they hadn't inspired Fen's hunting instincts. Either option would probably end in their deaths.

She ran as fast as she could. It wasn't her top speed by any means, but she was dragging a human behind her. If she went much faster, she risked dislocating his shoulder.

A glance back showed the mist gaining on them. Colors flashed in its depths and sparks shattered the growing darkness.

She put on a burst of speed.

Josh stumbled, falling to his knees. She scooped him up and threw him over her shoulder. "Keep your head tucked in," she called.

A wall of white appeared in front of her. A shadow loomed in its depths. She wasn't about to wait around for whatever it was to leave the fog and try to kill her.

She veered left, narrowly missing colliding with a tree. Her running shoes slipped on the wet leaves. She didn't let it slow her down.

Pounding footsteps behind her told her Fen had copied her move. She didn't look over her shoulder to make sure. She was moving too fast and needed all her concentration to navigate through the trees.

The mist kept forming in front of her. By the third direction change, she was well and truly lost.

But still alive.

Suddenly, Fen froze. "Stop."

Her heels skidded as she stilled. Fen had never steered her wrong. If he told her to stop, she was damn well going to stop. "What?"

"It's gone."

"It was just behind us," she insisted.

"I know. And it's still here. I can smell it."

She sucked in a long breath. Sure enough, the faint stink of ammonia hung in the humid air.

"Put me down." Josh squirmed, nearly upending himself.

She'd forgotten she still had a human slung over her shoulder. Lowering him to his feet, she passed Fen his gun. She gripped her own weapon in both hands, aiming it in the direction they'd last seen the mist. "We still need to get back to the diner."

"I agree," Fen said. "We have to do this carefully. It's stalking us."

"Great. Intelligent fog."

Something cracked to their left and all three of them swung their pistols in the direction of the sound.

A branch crashed to the ground behind them.

"Here's what we're going to do," Fen whispered. "Ara, you and Josh take the front. I'll take the rear, protect your flank. We shoot at anything that so much as fucking moves; I don't care if it's a goddamn bunny or what."

"No, I'll take the rear. I'm lost, and I can't smell anything over the fog other than you and Josh. You'll need to use your nose to get us out."

"Deal. Slow and steady."

Josh's eyes were wide, his mouth set flat. His blood thundered through his body, and Ara could smell the adrenaline and testosterone pouring from him. He was in full fight-or-flight, mode but his hands were steady.

"Move out," Josh said.

She scanned the forest, sweeping her gun from side to side in a never ending arc. If it had just been her and Fen, she would have pressed her back against his as they moved and trusted him not to lead her into an obstacle. Since there were three of them, she kept one ear open for the sound of his careful footsteps and followed them as best she could.

The stink of ammonia rose from the ground. White mist curled around her ankles and tugged at her. She yanked her foot away and aimed her gun at the dirt. She shot it once and paused. If it didn't work, she didn't want to waste ammunition. There was no telling when she'd need it.

The mist cringed, curling in on itself. It pulled away from her slightly and hovered less than an inch from her legs.

Before she could say anything, Fen shouted wordlessly. The terror and rage in his voice was plain to hear.

She spun on her heel. "Shoot it," she screamed.

"I can't," he yelled. "I don't want to risk hitting him."

Horror crawled over her. Josh had stopped dead in his tracks and was staring at the mist around his ankles, apparently fascinated. It crept up his legs, swirling around his knees.

Fen yelled at him again. The human didn't turn around.

She aimed her weapon at the edge of the fog and shot again. It shuddered and rolled closer to the human, winding around his thighs instead of backing off.

Sucking in a breath, she stepped into the fog. Every cell in her body, every fiber of her being, protested but she was out of options. She waded into the mist toward Josh anyway. It was like moving through quicksand, slow and laborious, until the fog reached her waist and it was nearly too hard to move.

Fen grabbed her arm, growling, and tried to force her back. She charged on, tearing her arm out of her partner's grasp and latching on to the young man. She wrapped her arms around his chest and yanked, using all her strength, but something was fighting her, trying to drag him down. He didn't move, didn't even look at her.

The ground turned mushy. Her feet sank into... nothing. The dirt closed around her ankles, sliding up her calves until it was just under her knees.

This was it. Getting swallowed by fog was a really crappy way to die. At least, she hoped she died. She had a bad feeling she wouldn't want to live to see where the fog was dragging them.

Suddenly Fen was there, gripping her hips and pulling.

She kicked out as hard as she could. One leg came free. With a scream, she wrenched her other foot from the sludge. "Help me get him out."

The irises in Fen's eyes bled out so there was no hint of white at all. His chin bulged a little. "Get out of here."

"No. We can't leave him behind. Now help me."

She had to constantly move her legs to keep from being sucked down again, which made getting a solid base difficult, but she wrapped her arms around Josh again.

A feral growl ripped from Fen's throat as he wound his arms around Josh's waist. "Wasn't going to leave him behind. I can get him free myself. You should go. The tree line is just over there."

He jerked his head to the side. Sure enough, there was a break in the woods. A cool breeze filtered through the trees. She hadn't realized how humid the forest had become until that very moment.

"You'll never get him out on your own," she countered. "Now, pull."

The strain on her shoulders was unlike anything she ever remembered. Slowly, they pulled the human free from the mist. She gave one last tug and all three of them tumbled backward.

Josh blinked and looked at her. "Ara? What's going on? Where are we?"

His memory loss chilled her to the bone. The fog was advancing, shimmering with blues and greens and some other colors changing so fast, she couldn't even identify them.

She rolled off Fen and scrambled to her feet, pointing her weapon at the mist. She squeezed the trigger, shooting right into the middle of the mass. As it had before, it drew back slightly.

Her earlier concern about running out of ammunition became null and void. The hell with saving ammo. She would do what she had to do to get the three of them out alive.

"Run," she said. "Don't look back. Just get out of the woods."

She had no evidence the mist would stop at the tree line, but having a goal gave her something to focus on. Getting them all out of the forest seemed like a good one.

Josh struggled to his feet. Instead of running, he fidgeted. "Fen doesn't look too good. He looks like he's about to shift."

If she had to choose between running from a crazed wolf shifter or getting engulfed by the weird mist, she figured she had a better chance of surviving the wolf attack.

She emptied her weapon into the fog as fast as she could, savagely pleased to see it pull away a couple of feet. Acting on pure instinct, she released the magazine and jammed in her backup.

Next to her, Fen and Josh began shooting. They backed away, keeping the mist in check, until they all ran out of ammunition.

It was all the time she could buy them.

"Run!" she screamed.

Thankfully, Fen kept control. He rushed forward and grabbed Josh around the waist. He hauled the man over his shoulder in a fireman's carry and stared at her. "Keep up."

She matched his pace, glancing over her shoulder only to see the mist gaining on them.

It was almost on them again when they broke through the trees. A number of people she recognized were milling around, including Fen's brother and alpha, Colin.

She was about to scream for them to run when Josh gave a surprised yelp. Wheeling around, she gaped when the mist suddenly dissipated.

"What in the *hell* is going on?" Colin shouted.

CHAPTER FOURTEEN

Fen struggled to draw in enough oxygen to stay on his feet. He dumped the human on the ground and stumbled over to his brother.

His wolf was close to the surface, too close for safety. More than once in those woods, he'd nearly lost control. Shifting that way would have been disastrous.

He only managed to stagger halfway to Colin, desperately needing his alpha's presence to center himself. He might not have to obey the other wolf, but he'd long ago chosen, to and that was all his wolf needed.

Colin, for his part, didn't say a word. He closed the distance between them with a few long strides and gripped Fen's shoulders, pulling him close enough so their foreheads touched.

Fen waited, soaking in his alpha's calm, soothing vibes, until he was reasonably sure he wouldn't shift and tear the human's throat out.

He pushed his beast down, though the wolf growled at him and paced restlessly in the back of his mind, still ready to take control and defend those he considered his.

"Is that Fen's alpha?"

Fen tensed as Josh's whisper floated to his ears. His temper returned with a vengeance but his wolf simply flopped, content in their safety and the presence of his alpha for the moment.

He turned around, though he kept a firm hold on Colin's wrist just to center himself. "What were you thinking?"

His sister had once told him it was his voice that scared people. How quiet it could get even when it carried the edge of violence.

The human's eyes, still wide and glazed with a hint of confused panic, got even wider. He rubbed his hands on his thighs and refused to meet Fen's eyes.

"You put all of us in danger," Fen continued. "You should thank Ara for the fact that you're still alive. I would have left you behind, but she insisted."

It was a lie, of course. He'd been honest when he'd told Ara he'd stay behind and get Josh out of the mist. Josh didn't need to know that.

"Well?" he asked when the human didn't respond.

"Fen, he doesn't remember all of it," Ara said softly. "When we got him out, he didn't know what was going on."

Great. Freaky fog and amnesia. This day just kept getting better and better. "What do you remember?"

"The fog was… following us," Josh answered, squinting as if trying to remember. "And then Ara screamed at us to run. You almost shifted. That's it."

"So, the mist was following us, a shifter is losing control of his human side and a vampire is screaming at you to run, and you thought it was a good idea to stop and stare at some freaky-ass fog? Especially when we're trying to track down some kind of unknown shifter?" Fen asked.

It was an unfair accusation, given that Josh had no memory of doing it, but he couldn't help it. Not when he'd come so close to losing his partner.

"Back off," Ara said, though without any heat. "It's no use harping on it now."

The sound of tires rolling along the pavement caught his attention and he looked up at his brother, finally realizing Colin had crossed into the leo's territory. "Do you have permission to be here?"

"Nope." Colin used Fen's grip on his wrist to pull him a little closer. "Don't worry, brother mine. Everything will be fine."

Maybe. Maybe not. An alpha crossing into another shifter's territory for more than just a few minutes was a serious breach of shifter etiquette. Things could get ugly very fast. And having a vulnerable human around was not a good idea, even if the local pride seemed to like the man quite a lot. "Josh, get in the car."

"What?"

Fen didn't bother to disguise his irritation. "Get in the car. If Colin and the leo start getting aggressive, leave immediately."

The human held his ground, his chin set at a defiant tilt. "What about you and Ara?"

He frowned. He didn't like the idea of Ara hanging around in the open with a couple of angry shifters, but there was no way she would let him send her away. "She can take care of herself."

Ara pushed the young man toward his squad car. "Don't worry about me. I'm hard to kill. A little scuffle between a couple of shifters won't hurt me. Get in."

She all but shoved him in the car, slamming the door so hard the windows shook.

Fen glared at Josh until he heard the locks click and the key slide into the ignition.

He turned back to his brother. As quietly as he could, he whispered, "Thanks for coming. I needed you."

Colin cupped his jaw and smoothed a thumb over his cheekbone, just like he did when one of the pups was scared. "I felt your terror and your near loss of control. You did good keeping it together."

Praise from the alpha was what a shifter lived for, even him. Warm, reassuring feelings vibrated through their pack tie, and he wanted nothing more than to curl up at Colin's feet and sleep.

He was positive that whatever hunted them in the woods wasn't gone though. It was just waiting for another opportunity. He felt it watching them. Was this how rabbits felt just before he pounced when he was hunting?

A black sports car rolled into the parking lot. The door opened and the leo eased out, unfolding his long legs and standing to his full height. He stalked forward, every inch of him a prowling cat, and bared his teeth at Colin.

Fen stiffened and moved a few inches to the side, putting his body between his alpha and the leo. He didn't want a fight, didn't think he'd be able to come back from his wolf if forced to shift, but he was a beta. And betas protected their alphas.

The leo didn't even blink. He stopped a few feet from them and snarled. "Did you really think I would overlook such a slight? Did you think I wouldn't find out? How *dare* you come into *my* territory?"

Colin nodded once. Fen knew his brother wasn't apologizing for his behavior. That would be akin to accepting defeat. He was simply acknowledging the breech of acceptable behavior. "I'm here because I sensed my beta's distress. It was quite pronounced, and Fen is a very hard man to ruffle. There wasn't time for me to call for permission."

"No time to call for permission?"

It was clear the leo didn't believe a word he said.

"I'm not quite sure how you knew I was here," Colin remarked instead of answering. "I've only been here a couple of minutes. Just in time to see my beta and the other inspectors come through the trees. Your cat didn't have time to call you."

Fen wouldn't have been surprised if the leo hissed. "I felt Carla's extreme fear and came as fast as I could."

"So you didn't know I was here?"

The discussion was pointless. Colin had indeed knowingly trespassed on the pride territory, and the leo had cause to be upset. Fen knew it was all a distraction designed to get the leo talking and away from any violent acts. He was looking for common ground so they could work things out instead of killing each other.

It was a perfect example of why Colin was the alpha and he wasn't.

"Leo, may I speak?"

Carla stepped forward and the leo softened. "Of course, Carla. You don't need my permission to speak."

"You should know that the wolf alpha arrived just as I heard something start to crash in the forest. It sounded like the beast..." She swallowed and squared her shoulders. "The first thing he did when he got here was ask for his beta. When he found out he was in the woods, I thought he would go in after him, especially since we could hear them screaming. Instead, he put himself between me and the treeline and told me to run, that he would keep whatever was coming away from me long enough for me to get away."

The corner of the man's mouth lifted a little, but he seemed slightly mollified. "If the creature didn't come out of the woods, what did?"

She waved her hand at Fen. "Those three. It looked like they were being chased."

Having worked with Ara for so long, Fen was highly attuned to her scent and body language. He didn't miss the shiver that wracked her frame, nor did he miss the slightly acrid scent of her fear.

He strained against his brother's hold, trying to get to her. Colin held strong. "Ara," Colin snapped. "You need to get a hold of yourself. Your unease is upsetting Fen."

It took all the remaining control he had not to growl at his brother. Ara never liked having her vulnerabilities pointed out.

Instead of snapping back at the alpha, Ara shook her hands and took a deep breath. "Sorry. It's a little hard not be freaked out after just about getting eaten by a patch of sparking mist."

At the mention of the mist, his wolf growled and it took another squeeze on his shoulder from Colin to make it behave.

His brother turned to Ara. "Look, why don't you and Fen go over there and talk? Your presence will probably do him a lot of good."

This time, it was Fen's human side that growled. The alpha cocked his eyebrow at him, clearly daring him to deny the suggestion.

He smirked a mere second later and turned his gaze to his partner. Colin's words had been more of an order and less of a suggestion. She didn't take kindly to being ordered around and, unlike their boss, she didn't need to listen to a word Colin said. She might like his brother, might consider him a friend, but she didn't answer to him.

Sure enough, Ara stiffened. "Actually, I think Fen might need a few minutes by himself."

Fen hoped that would be the end of that. He should have known Colin wouldn't let it go. "I think you greatly underestimate the influence you have on my brother."

Ara rolled her eyes and gestured to Fen. "Come on. Let's let the two macho men work things out. I don't want to get caught in a pissing contest."

He followed her to the car and, just as Colin had suggested, his wolf immediately relaxed a little. He closed his eyes and drew in a few breaths, needing to reassure himself that she truly was unharmed.

She stank.

She reeked of ammonia and sulphur and rotting leaves.

He leaned closer, practically jamming his face into the crook of her neck, and inhaled again.

"Are you sniffing me?" Ara asked.

"Stay still. I'm making sure you're not injured. You did sink to your waist in… whatever that was."

It wasn't until his nose was brushing against her skin that he caught her natural scent. He concentrated, sifting through all the sensory information his nose was feeding him, until he was satisfied she wasn't hurt.

Behind them, he caught the last bit of Colin and the leo's

conversation.

"I would have called for permission, but I was genuinely worried for the safety of my beta. If I'd waited for your response, I wouldn't have made it on time and I don't know if he would have been able to control himself."

"I understand," the leo said. "And my thanks for thinking of Carla. We've recently lost a pride member and have yet to recover."

"My condolences."

Fen pushed away from Ara. "Great. You're not going to start a shifter war. Now can we talk about the fog that wants to eat everybody?"

CHAPTER FIFTEEN

Well, that was one way to get everyone's attention. Ara might have put it a little differently, but Fen had cut to the heart of the matter in seconds.

"Before we begin, are we all good?" she asked. She waved her hand to where Josh still sat in his squad car. "Nobody's going to kill anybody? We're not going to scare the natives?"

"Yes, yes. It's safe for him to come out."

The leo knocked on Josh's window and crooked a finger at him.

"What can you tell us about the woods? And what had you all so spooked?" the leo asked as he and Josh approached.

They told him about the scent, the mist, the weird feelings, everything. She rubbed her arms when describing how it felt to get sucked into nothing.

"You didn't see any sign of the creature?"

"Yes," Ara replied. She tried her best to sound patient. "We followed its trail until it ended. I think I saw the outline of something huge in the mist. It all happened so fast, I can't be sure."

"How do you know the trail was caused by this creature?" Colin asked.

Josh spoke to the two men for the first time. "What else could it have been? I can't think of anything else that would have created such destruction."

The two leaders looked him over then apparently decided to dismiss him. She felt slightly sorry for the young man. Shifters were forever dismissing humans for being, well, human.

Josh pressed on. "Besides, both Fen and Ara said the scent was the same. I don't know too many vampires, but I've never known a shifter to be wrong about a smell."

"Know many shifters?" Colin asked.

"Actually, yes. I lived with a pack in California for four years."

Colin raised an eyebrow again, only this time he seemed intrigued. "Which pack? Who is the alpha?"

"I think you met him a couple of times. Mike Donovan?"

"I do know him. He's a good wolf."

Josh nodded. "Anyway, we were wondering how something so big could just disappear right before that patch of fog started chasing us."

"Fog? Chasing you? You do know that fog isn't alive, right?"

If the statement had been addressed to her, she would have snorted and said something snarky, possibly punch someone in the face. The human merely let it roll off his back. "Yes, sir. This wasn't normal fog. I don't remember much about it …."

There was silence for a few moments. Finally, the leo spoke. "We'll have to worry about the fog later. My first priority is locating and destroying the creature that killed my cat."

"I agree," Colin said.

Ara glanced at Fen from the corner of her eye. Her partner looked like he wanted to protest, but he kept his mouth shut.

She, however, was under no obligation to keep quiet. "They have to be connected."

"How do you know?" the leo asked. "There're all kinds of magic in this world, you of all people should know that. For all we know, the mist was a by-product of a spell witch spell gone bad."

"You have to be kidding me." She looked at the cat shifter incredulously. "You think the appearance of an unknown, very destructive shifter *and* killer mist is coincidental?"

"Do you have proof?" The leo's tone was snide.

Heat coiled in her stomach. Stupid man.

"Josh already told you," Fen said quietly. "The scent was

the same."

She smiled at her partner. It had to be hard to go up against someone more dominant than him, especially when he had to walk the fine line of shifter etiquette. She appreciated his backup.

The leo narrowed his eyes. "Are you suggesting I should just sit back and wait for this creature to attack again?"

"Are you suggesting we send people to tromp around in the woods so they can get sucked into some kind of abyss?" she shot back.

Colin continued talking as if the whole exchange hadn't happened. "I'd like to offer my pack's help with tracking the creature. Wolves generally have a much better sense of smell and we hunt as a pack, so that should help negate any danger the mist might be."

Fen fidgeted. She could tell he was reluctant to have anyone go back into the woods. There wasn't much he could say about it once Colin had made the offer though, and clearly, the two leaders didn't see the fog as much of a problem.

"Thank you. I would very much appreciate the help," the leo said.

Leave it to the only human in the area to point out the obvious. "With all due respect, I don't think it's wise to send anyone else into the woods. At least not until we know what that mist is, regardless if it is connected to the creature or not."

"Fen?" Colin asked.

Her partner cleared his throat. "I agree."

"Why?"

Fen cleared his throat again and gestured toward the treeline. He was still holding his gun. Then again, she hadn't holstered her weapon either, even though she was ninety-five percent certain it was empty.

"You just said it could be dark magic floating around. I'm not sure how adding more wolves to the search neutralizes its danger. There were three of us. Ara emptied her pistol into the mist and it barely slowed down. I don't know why you aren't taking this seriously."

"I understand," Colin said after a full minute. "My beta isn't easily rattled, and I believe there is concern with this mist. Regardless, our offer to help still stands. I suggest we go back to the Pack Hall. I'll call a pack meeting and we can sort things out from there. Leo, Carla, you are, of course, welcome to join."

"What am I supposed to do?" Josh asked.

Colin looked him up and down. "You lived in Mike Donovan's territory for four years?"

"Actually, I lived with the pack itself, not just on their territory."

Colin raised an eyebrow. "Your sister must have married someone high in the pack. You would have been privy to just about everything."

"Mike is my brother-in-law."

"Ah. Well, there is little you don't know about shifters then. Perhaps you should join us. Your insight might be helpful, especially since you don't feel the need to submit."

Josh accepted and Colin turned to her. She fully expected him to thank her and send her on her way. They might be close friends, but she wasn't a shifter.

"Ara? Perhaps you should join us as well, if you don't mind. Fen still seems a little off, and your experience with paranormal creatures may come in handy. Besides, it's not as if you're completely unfamiliar with shifter customs. You spend enough time with Mandy, and you do work daily with my brother."

Ara separated herself from the little crowd and caught Josh's arm, pulling him aside as the four shifters continued the discussion. She needed to make sure he understood what had just happened. "You understand this is no longer a police issue, right? Since Colin and the leo have decided to take care of it, it's strictly a paranormal issue, specifically a shifter one. The only reason I'm being included at all is because my partner is the pack beta. And make no mistake, just because Colin and I are friends, doesn't mean he won't tear my throat out if it comes down to protecting his pack."

"Yeah, I know. I can at least offer some help."

She smiled at him. "You're remarkable."

"For a human, right?" Josh smiled, cushioning the joke.

Something in the woods cracked and they both jumped, swinging their firearms around. Out of the corner of her eye, she saw Fen do the same.

My gun has to be out of bullets. We should drive away. That would be the best option. Terror froze her to the spot. Her muscles tensed so tightly, she thought they might snap. Josh's heart thundered beside her. Fen's low, menacing growl ripped through the air.

A raccoon came tearing out of the trees, skidding to a stop at the side of the road, its nose twitching. It spun wildly and took off down the street.

She didn't relax. The mist was somewhere in the woods. Who knew if it was confined to the forest.

"It's a raccoon, guys," Colin eventually said. "You can stop with the guns now."

"Can't you feel it?" Josh asked. "Even I can feel it. It's like a tingle of low-level electricity."

The leo moved forward, coming to a stop between them. "I do feel something," he admitted. "And it doesn't feel good, that's for sure. I am inclined to think we have a rogue witch on our hands."

Fen materialized at her side. "Josh, you can ride with Colin. Ara will ride with me."

The leo started toward his car. "I'll follow the alpha. Carla, do you want to drive separately or with me?"

Ara forced her feet to move, heading toward Fen's car. He held her back with a hand on her forearm, waiting until Colin's and the leo's cars drove out of sight before letting her go. She wasn't sure what was going on, but she was sure it wasn't a good idea to hang around alone.

"Ready to go?" she asked when they drew level with Fen's car.

"Do you mind driving?"

She blinked. Fen always complained she drove too slowly. His question told her just how out of control he'd actually been. She was touched he would show such a vulnerability to her.

"Sure." She kept her voice even, unwilling to voice her thoughts in case Fen changed his mind. "Do me a favor though? Keep your gun at the ready until we're far, far away from this place. I can still feel it."

"So," she said when she finally eased the car onto the road, steering it as far away from the woods as possible. "What do you think we're dealing with?"

He sighed and kept his weapon trained out the window. "I have no idea. I'm leaning toward magic, but that scent isn't like any magic I've ever smelled before."

"Me too. I can't imagine any white witches being able to pull something like that off. And dark magic smells like tainted blood, not ammonia."

"Also, if it *is* magic, then did whoever cast the spell create the creature? Or did they just free it from… somewhere?"

She glanced at him out of the corner of her eye. She hated, absolutely *hated* dragging her family into her work. Even having Bo around sometimes felt like she was being smothered. Unfortunately, she didn't have a choice in this. "Hey, Fen?"

"Yeah?"

"What if this mist isn't new? What if it's been around before?"

"It's possible, I guess. What makes you wonder about it?"

She took a deep breath. Vampires and shifters didn't work together often, at least not on big things. "We've never seen this magic before, if that's what it is. That doesn't mean no one has ever seen it."

"Okay, continue."

She took a deep breath. "My great-grandmother used to tell me and Bo this story all the time. It was about a girl who disappeared into the mist and found herself in another dimension. With the Fae. It wasn't a happy ending either. It was like those old Grimm fairy tales. Really gruesome. My mom got upset with her once because the story gave Bo nightmares."

She paused and glanced up at her partner. If there was one thing vampires and shifters had in common, it was their shared dislike of the mention of their creators.

"It was a story, Ara. Your great-grandmother was born in Ireland, right? It was probably one told to keep little kids from wandering around in the forests and getting lost."

"What if it wasn't? What if it started off as a real warning? Mist that transports you somewhere else? Think about it, Fen."

"Okay, so I can agree that the coincidence is rather strong. I'm assuming you want to talk to your great-grandmother about it?"

"Not her. She's dead. Vampires do age, just slowly, you know that. Perhaps someone on the Vampire Elder Council can help us."

"You want to ask your grandfather for help? Is that what you're saying?"

She almost laughed at his tone. "Not really, but I don't see any other choice. Not if we want to explore every lead."

"When was the last time you saw him?"

She made a face. She loved her grandparents, she really did. They only wanted the best for her and Bo. It was just that they were both so old, so stuck in their ways they couldn't understand why she wanted to work when she could have her pick of nice vampire husbands. "Two weeks ago, for Sunday dinner. They'd invited someone for me to meet. It didn't end well."

"Do you think the council would help us? They're not exactly forthcoming with information."

"If we ask, they would help. It comes down to whether Colin and the leo would let us ask."

Fen didn't say anything else. The rest of the drive passed in silence.

Fen still hadn't relaxed his hold on his gun by the time she drove through the pack gate. "I think you can put the gun away," she said. "At least for now. Should I park at the Meeting Hall?"

While most shifters lived on pack territory, it wasn't possible for every shifter. Some worked in the downtown core, and travelling through the rush hour traffic every day to get home wasn't something that interested most wolves. For those shifters, Colin made a special allowance, letting them stay in the city during the week and come back on the weekends. The arrangement had eventually resulted in the Alpha House running out of space in the driveway, so Colin had built a parking lot in front of the Meeting Hall.

Her partner didn't answer. One look at Fen and she pulled up to the Alpha House instead. Most of the pack would be at the hall already, so few people would be around to see her driving. The last thing she wanted was for everyone to connect his previous fear, which would have been broadcast to the entire pack, with her driving. While the pack was pretty stable, it was never a good idea for a dominant wolf to display a weakness to other wolves.

"Thanks," Fen said quietly.

She nodded brusquely. "Shall we?"

She waited until he got out of the car. There was no hint of ammonia, and the ominous feeling had eased back. Not completely, but enough for her to relax a bit.

The air was cool and crisp, and the sky was a deep navy speckled with stars. A perfect early fall night. She allowed the breeze to wash over her face, soothing her nerves and calming her racing thoughts. Still, she kept her hand on the butt of her gun, though it wouldn't do her much good if it was indeed empty. She'd lost count of how many rounds she'd discharged into the fog. "Just a second."

She slid the magazine out and made sure the gun wasn't loaded.

Definitely empty.

Great.

Now she had to go back to the station and explain how she'd emptied two magazines into a patch of fog.

"We've got more," Fen said, watching her. "One of our wolves has a strange hobby. He likes to make his own ammunition. He's always sure to make enough to fit my weapon."

"Thanks. I'll pick some up on the way back."

"You sure you don't want to get some now?"

"They're waiting for us, Fen. The leo doesn't strike me as the patient type. I don't need to tell you that shifter wars have been started over punctuality and the perceived insult of lateness."

It wasn't like him to stall for time. She tilted her head and stared at him. His pupils shimmered, like he was fighting to keep them human. The fine hairs on his arms stood on end. He took a deep breath and released it slowly. She'd only ever seen him do something similar when he was trying to keep his patience with rowdy teenage shifters. "You okay?"

"I'll be fine."

He wasn't fine. Not by a long shot. His gaze darted from side to side. He licked his lips and took one deep breath.

"I know that fog was scary as all get out, but why are you having such a hard time settling? We've seen crazy things before."

"It's not about the fog," he muttered.

"Well, what is it then?"

She didn't want to seem so short with him, but he needed to snap out of his funk. Mandy had once told her there were at least four wolves who were just waiting to see one small weakness before they would pounce on the chance to challenge him.

He narrowed his eyes at her. "I wasn't thrilled with the way you put yourself in danger back there."

Oh. She wasn't quite sure how to respond. "I can't promise it won't happen again. I can promise to be more careful," she said finally.

Fen cracked a small smile. "Good. It took me long enough to get you on track. I don't want to break in another partner."

The small joke broke some of the tension and she snorted. "Same here, buddy."

The smile he shot her way was much more genuine than before. "Thanks, Arabella."

"No problem, Fenris. Better?" she asked.

"Yeah. You ready? This promises to be one of the more entertaining meetings we've ever had."

"Lead the way." She followed him to the door.

The hall was packed. She acknowledged the wolves she knew as Fen wound his way through the crowd. He paused every few steps to shake someone's hand or to greet someone he obviously hadn't seen in a while.

Mandy sauntered over, one hand on her hip, a big grin stretching across her face. "Fog, huh?"

"Shut up," Ara replied. "You would have freaked out too. It was scary as hell."

Her friend shrugged, the smile still firmly fixed in place. Irritation swept through her and she struggled to keep her words nice. "All I can say is that I hope you never have to see it."

When Mandy's expression didn't change, she growled. "Why are you acting like I'm a scared little girl? I've been around a lot longer than you. And I'm far from helpless. I can snap your neck before you even see me coming."

"Whoa," Mandy exclaimed, raising her hands, palms forward. "Settle down."

"Quit it, Mandy," Fen muttered when he drew close.

Mandy gawked at them. It wasn't often Fen used his beta influence over her.

She was silent for a few seconds before speaking again. "I see you brought a human with you."

Fen rotated his head, the vertebrae popping and snapping. "Colin brought him, not me. He's a good guy."

He walked off without a word, wading through the shifters until he stood next to Colin.

Mandy frowned after him and looked back at Ara after a few seconds. "Any human who can live with a wolf pack for more than a month is aces in my book."

"You already talked to him?"

"Sure. He's a cutie. All that dark skin and those big brown eyes. It makes me wonder what he looks like—" She cut off her statement, suddenly looking up at the front. "Gotta go. See you later."

Mandy didn't wait for her to answer, making her way to Colin and standing slightly behind him, next to Fen.

Ara scanned the crowd and finally found Josh standing against one wall. She gestured for him to join her as Colin started talking.

CHAPTER SIXTEEN

She was mildly surprised when Josh shook his head and waved her over. Confused, she picked her way through the milling wolves, smiling at a few of the pack members as she went.

Ara genuinely enjoyed spending time with wolf shifters. They treated their female members as equals. The strong females, like Mandy, were expected to train as pack soldiers, same as their male counterparts.

It was quite different from how vampires treated their females. To say that she'd caused a few raised eyebrows when she'd joined the police force was an understatement.

She put that to the back of her mind as she finally reached the human.

She latched onto the young man's arm and towed him toward the door.

Josh went easily enough, stopping just short of the exit. "Alpha Colin told me to stay here. And an unescorted human wandering around pack territory is just asking for trouble."

She glanced up at the front to find Colin staring at her. He shifted his gaze between Josh and the door before shaking his head. She nodded her understanding.

Fen frowned, looking out over the wolves with something akin to disapproval. She knew he prided his pack on their discretion, but having both a human and unfamiliar shifters on their territory would make any wolf antsy.

She blinked when Colin stared intently at her again. This time, the alpha looked from her to Josh and back again. Once again, she nodded. He wanted her to protect the human if anything went wrong.

At least he had faith in her abilities.

"Josh," she whispered, even though she knew every single shifter within a foot of them would be able to hear her, "it is very important that you stay calm and unobtrusive."

"I know." His whisper was hardly louder than a sigh.

She knew Colin would do whatever he had to do to keep Josh safe. Most of the shifters wouldn't care about a human among them. Plenty of them worked with humans on a daily basis. It was the presence of the two cats that threw everything off balance.

She listened as Colin ran through introductions, ignoring the hostility the wolves were emitting. Both the cat shifters looked around defiantly, as if daring the wolves to try anything. It was hard not to compare them to hissing kittens, but she was pretty sure the leo was a full-grown lion in his animal form. He probably wouldn't hesitate to claw the throats out of any poor soul who suggested he was cute.

"Despite our differences, when something attacks a shifter, it attacks all of us. As such, I have offered the leo our help."

The note of finality in Colin's voice was enough to stop anyone from complaining. About the presence of the cat shifters, anyway.

"Alpha, why is there a human here?" a wolf Ara only vaguely recognized questioned. She felt the sudden need to bare her own fangs at the wolf in question, an unexpected wave of protectiveness for the young man washing over her.

Next to her, Josh stiffened slightly, though he did a remarkable job of remaining calm. He didn't acknowledge the speaker, waiting instead for one of the ruling wolves to answer the question.

Colin sent an approving glance Josh's way. "Officer Jones is here to satisfy the human authorities that they have been involved in the investigation. He has agreed to stay out of our way."

She let her attention drift from Colin's speech, turning the events of the day over in her head, looking for any detail she may have missed.

The trail had been clear. And then it had disappeared.

Had the creature shifted into a different form and escaped without leaving a trace behind? The three forms they knew of were huge. She tried to picture it shrinking in size to a bird. It was entirely possible, of course. It just didn't seem to jive with its behavior.

And the fog. It couldn't be a coincidence that it began to actively pursue them at the end of the trail. Was the fog some kind of gateway? And if it was, what was on the other side? Who'd created it?

The questions piled up until her mind spun.

She blinked when a few of the wolves around her snickered. She looked around to see what was so funny and one of them jerked his chin in Fen's direction. The beta wolf was wearing an irritated expression and staring right at her, clearly put out. She could practically hear the thoughts running through his head. *Pay attention to the alpha.*

She rolled her eyes and gave him a middle finger salute. A few gasps sounded around her, but Fen merely rolled his own eyes and cracked a smile.

He wasn't wrong though. She turned her attention back to Colin in time to hear him invite the leo to speak.

She listened with half an ear as he described the creature they were attempting to track. Her thoughts wandered back to the woods. She pushed the memory of the strange fog to the back of her mind and focused on the memory of the trail. Her great-grandmother's story floated back to her. *Beware the mists.*

Most legends had some kernel of truth to them, no matter how small. The story had intrigued her when she was little. She remembered wishing a gateway would materialize in her room any time her father started screaming at her mother. She would ask her great-grandmother to tell the story over and over, and fantasized about tumbling into an alternate dimension, one where her father wasn't an abusive jerk and where she, her mother, and Bo could live without fear. The girl in the story hadn't met a happy ending, but Ara always hoped her own ending would be better.

She'd cried more than once when the woman stopped telling the story because of Bo's nightmares. It was the only time she'd ever resented her brother.

She only tuned back into the conversation when Colin took over again, inviting Josh and the two cats to stay for a meal.

Murmurs of surprise rippled through the wolves at the invitation. Even she was taken a little aback. The wolves ate together in the hall at least once a week. She and her brother had been to several of these meals, and she knew that being invited to eat with the pack was a tangible sign of the alpha's respect.

Josh clearly understood the honor and even bowed respectfully as he accepted.

Mandy was already on the phone, ordering so many pizzas they would probably clean the pizzeria out.

"Bo will also be joining us," Colin said as he and Fen drew closer. "Do you need any blood? I can have Mandy run to the house to get some."

She really should have a bag or two, just in case. But she'd made sure to drink enough at breakfast and the last thing she wanted to do was send Mandy out into the night on her own, even if she was still a little irritated with the woman. "I have to go back to the house with Fen later to get some more ammunition. I'll grab some then."

Her partner frowned at her. She brushed it off and looked around for a place to sit.

****

At a normal pack meal, people sat wherever they wanted. Fen usually sat at a small corner table with Mandy. Colin sometimes ate with the pups, other times with the elders. Ara usually found herself with Mandy and Fen, and, when he was around, Bo. The presence of other shifters, especially someone whose dominance was equivalent with the alpha's, called for something a little more formal.

It was a little weird, being at a head table surrounded by two alpha males, one beta, a human and her brother, especially when the meal was a slice of pepperoni pizza.

The conversation made it even more awkward.

"So, what was it about the fog that freaked you guys out so much?" Colin asked.

She shot him what she hoped was a death glare when she saw the corners of his lips pull up.

In the bright, warm hall, surrounded by fifty-plus vicious wolf shifters, running from mist seemed rather silly.

Thankfully, Josh didn't seem to think the fog was silly at all. "It was weird," he said. "I first saw it when we came to the end of the trail. I know Inspector Classen saw it, and it looked like it kind of creeped her out. It seemed to just float along. At first, I didn't think anything of it but when we got to the end of the trail, it sort of surged."

Josh went on, capturing the attention of everyone within hearing distance. "It was more like it was stalking us, just drifting slowly around, getting closer and closer. I was going to mention it when Inspector Classen said we should run. I remember her picking me up and running like a bat out of hell. And then I remember coming out of some kind of trance with her emptying her gun into the mist."

"Wow. That's not something I've ever heard of before. The whole pack felt your fear, Fen. It was more than a little unsettling," Colin said. He scratched his chin, looking thoughtful. "What do you think it was?"

Fen shrugged, looking a little lost. "Is. It didn't disappear. It just chose to wait for a better time. Even before it started trying to get to us, it made me uneasy. It was like I was pre-programed to fear it."

"Me too. There was this feeling deep in the pit of my stomach. I felt sick, like I was dying," Ara said. She shivered, remembering the lost, hopeless feeling.

She paused, trying to collect herself. She hadn't even been aware of the feeling until she started describing it. "Honestly, I thought that if the fog touched me, it would kill me."

"It whispered," Josh said softly.

The room was dead silent. Everyone's eyes were fixed on the human, who had turned pale and looked more than a little scared.

"Whispered?" Fen finally said. "It *whispered* to you?"

"I was afraid I was losing it, like those other officers. To tell you the truth, I'm still not entirely sure I'm not going crazy."

She could understand the feeling. "You're not crazy," she said firmly. "If you are, then we are too."

"Can I ask you guys something?"

Her brother's voice almost startled her. She'd forgotten for a moment that Colin had invited him. It wasn't like him to stay so quiet or ask for permission to speak. She leaned across Fen to see him clearly.

"This fog… Did it smell funny? Bad?"

"Yes," she and Fen answered at the same time. Fen gestured for her to continue. "It was weird. Sharp, like ammonia."

"It smelled exactly like the blood sample the leo sent with Carla," Fen added, wrinkling his nose. "Only concentrated."

He frowned. "Do you remember that story Nana always told us?"

"I thought about it," she admitted. "I'm going to call Grandfather in the morning, ask him if he's ever heard of such a thing."

"What story?" Colin asked, leaning forward.

Before she could tell them about the story, Bo chimed in. "Our great-grandmother used to tell us this story about the mists being a gateway to Under."

"Under what?" the leo asked.

"Where," Bo corrected. "Under is what they called the Fae Realm in the old days."

The leo scoffed. "The Fae? Are you seriously suggesting what I think you're suggesting?"

"Why not?" Bo shot back, unconcerned by the leo's attitude. "Both vampires and shifters were created by the Fae. It's in our history books, and I would bet it's in yours too."

"Fairies are real?" Josh said. "We were always told they were just in stories."

She nodded. "Yes, they're real, though fairies are actually a sub-species of the Fae. Vampires were created by the Fae as slaves. Of all kinds, if you get my drift. The earliest vampires were treated very poorly by the Fae. Their previous race of slaves, which died out as far as I know, had rather short lifespans. They didn't want to go through the trouble of re-training their servants every few years, which is why we were created with such long lifespans."

"Wow," the human breathed. "Why did they create you with a flaw then? I mean, wouldn't it be better to create creatures that didn't need to rely on the blood of humans to live?"

"I don't know." The Old Books spoke of the reasoning, but it had been so long since she'd studied them she couldn't remember.

Bo took over. "To control us. It wasn't like there was an abundance of humans wandering around in the Fae dimension. Those stories our great-grandmother told us about the girl disappearing into the mist were probably true. They probably harvested humans by watching the gates. It's probably also why we were created to need food too. They needed some way for us to gain nutrients to live long enough between humans.

"The vampires they created eventually escaped into this world through the mist gates. Fae don't like this world. It has too much iron, which is essentially poison to them."

Bo sat back and took a bite of his pizza.

Ara smiled. Her baby brother was as smart as they came. Once he read something, he never forgot it. He didn't always display his talent. Far too many people thought him a mindless killing machine, and it made his job easier if people believed that's all there was to him.

"What about shifters?" Josh asked, his eyes so wide Ara wondered if they would pop out of his head. She didn't blame him in the least. It was one thing to believe in creatures you could see and interact with. It was something else entirely to believe in creatures who hadn't made an appearance in eons.

Colin answered easily enough. "Our books say the Fae are quite a brutal race. They make war at every turn but don't want to fight it themselves. They created us to fight those wars for them. Later, they used us as entertainment. It's said our ancestors fought their wars for generations until they also escaped through the gates."

"When you say created, what do you mean?" Josh asked. "How did they create you?"

Colin shrugged. "Magic."

"Magic," Josh echoed. He chewed his pizza for a few seconds. "And here I thought faeries were supposed to be nice and cute. Like Tinkerbell."

Bo snorted. "Yeah, right. They're bastards, all of them. One of our history books tells of the Fae saving the human children. They didn't give them to the vampires for lunch."

"Do I want to know why?" Josh asked.

Ara dropped her pizza to her plate, her appetite suddenly gone as the memory of reading that chapter returned to her. She shuddered. No, Josh didn't want to know why. He needed to know though, especially if the Fae were finally making an appearance again.

"The Fae considered them delicacies. They were saved for special feasts, then eaten," she said.

Josh's eye widened. "Tinkerbell ate people?"

Something inside Ara snapped. She was so sick of everything tonight. "Tinkerbell isn't exactly a great role model," she said. "She tried to have Wendy killed multiple times, even in the cartoon. First, she abandons Wendy to find her own way to Neverland, and then she convinces the Lost Boys to shoot Wendy down. She is vain, selfish, and murderous. A pretty accurate representative of the Fae, actually. Humans just can't look past her pretty face."

"Do you actually believe all that crap?" the leo asked. "Gates to Under, being created as soldiers, the Fae eating children?"

"Don't you?" Colin shot back.

The two dominant males stared each other down until Josh cleared his throat. "Okay. So the fog was actually a gate to this Under?"

"It would explain why the scent would throw off both vampire and shifters," Bo explained. "Evolution. Why are humans so afraid of spiders? Because at one point, they posed a real threat to human safety. The fear of spiders was bred into humans along the way. So think about it this way. Evolution couldn't breed the fear of the scent out of us. Avoiding falling into Under would have been essential for our survival, thus the fear remains."

Bo leaned forward, reaching for another slice of pizza. "The only problem with that theory is, according to everything I've ever read, these gates haven't been seen in over five hundred years."

CHAPTER SEVENTEEN

After Bo's statement, no one said anything else about the mists. Everything in her told her the mist was essential to their investigation, but she had absolutely no proof, other than a legend and some history. And a feeling, of course.

She listened half-heartedly to Colin and the leo discuss tactics to capture the beast while managing the risk of sending anyone into the woods. Every once in a while, the leo tossed her a look of dismay, like he couldn't believe she would actually think a shifter would be in danger in their own environment.

She wanted to tell him to go tromping around in the forest, tell *him* to follow the trail until the mist found him. She clamped her mouth shut, swallowing the comment. It wasn't her place. If he wanted to send his cats out into danger, then it was his right.

Then she looked at Carla and realized it would be a shame to lose someone like her. She was exactly the kind of shifter the humans needed to see. Strong, independent, self-reliant, but concerned for others.

"You're zoning out again. You need some blood." Fen stood over her, peering down at her. His brow was wrinkled, his eyes narrowed, and his lips set in a flat line.

"Just thinking," she said. "But yes, I do need some blood."

Her partner scowled. "Stubborn."

She snorted. "To the end. Colin offered to send Mandy to the house to get me some but…."

"You didn't want to send her out alone," Fen finished. "You're a good friend."

"I try," she replied.

"Come back to my place," he said, holding out his hand to help her up. "The leo and Carla are coming as well. Bo can drive you home if you don't feel up to it."

She opened her mouth to tell her partner she was fine and yawned instead. "Sorry. I just realized how tired I really am."

"The adrenaline crash takes a toll on your system," Mandy said from beside her. "You'll sleep well tonight."

Ara suppressed a snort. Any sleep would be better than the night before. Hopefully it would be a dreamless sleep. She had a feeling visions of strange mists would fill her mind for a while.

She allowed herself to be pulled to her feet and ushered along as the crowd dispersed, some going home and others trailing behind them.

The way the wolves made themselves at home in Colin's house was one of the things she loved most about spending time with Fen and his family. The pack treated the Alpha House like a community center. Colin had set up a giant games room for the pups, complete with arcade games, an air hockey table, and a big-screen television that seemed permanently tuned to a children's station.

She always got a kick out of seeing the children interact with Fen. While many of the adults avoided her partner like the plague, a side effect of being his brother's enforcer, the kids didn't have the same inclination. All he had to do was sprawl out on the plush carpet and the children swarmed him.

"You have a nice stretch of woods here," the leo commented. "How big is it?"

She heard the smile in Colin's voice when he answered. "Two hundred acres. The pack hunts on more than a hundred of them a couple of times a month."

The leo nodded. "We don't have quite as much. Actually, I've considered expanding the property. I want to build some shelters in case of emergency."

"It's a smart idea," Colin said. "We've got the panic room

in the Alpha House, of course. We also have a safe house. We call it the bunker. It's impossible to get into once the door's been shut. The only way to get in is if someone inside lets you in."

"That's exactly what I'm looking at. Humans have been getting closer and closer to my pride lately. I'd rather have a safe place for my cats instead of them being forced to defend themselves."

The two leaders walked ahead, still chatting. Fen tossed a toddler into the air, making the little girl squeal with delight, before handing her off to her parents.

Mandy sidled up next to her. "Your partner is really cute," she whispered.

"Fen? Gross, he's your brother," Ara whispered back, grinning at Mandy's disgusted expression.

"Not him. Josh Jones."

"I'm just teasing. You really like him, don't you? It's the second time you've told me he's cute."

Mandy shrugged. "I don't suppose he'd want anything to do with me though. Most human males look at the fact that I'm in an alpha's inner circle and decide I'm too masculine for their tastes."

Ara eyed her best friend. Masculine was the last thing she thought of when she looked at Mandy. The woman was tall and curvy in all the right places. She had long dark hair that fell to her hips and expressive green eyes. She was one of the most beautiful women Ara had ever seen, and she'd seen a lot. "Want me to put in a good word for you?"

"God, no." Mandy's voice was scandalized. "That's so middle school?"

Ara forced a smile. "How do you know? Shifters don't go to regular school."

"Hey," Mandy said. She nudged her until Ara looked up. "This evening really rattled you, didn't it?"

"Yeah. There's something going on, Mands. And I don't think it's a good thing."

She glanced over her shoulder to look at Josh, who lagged behind, staring at the woods. "You go ahead," she said to Mandy. "I need to talk to Josh a little."

"Don't say anything to him about me," Mandy whispered frantically. She grabbed Ara's arm and shook it. "I mean it, Arabella."

Ara shook Mandy off. "God, are you twelve or something? I need to talk to him about what happened this afternoon. He looks a little traumatized, don't you think? And why does everyone feel the need to call me Arabella today?"

She backtracked before Mandy could say anything else. Irritation made her crabby, and she didn't want to say anything she might regret. She ignored her friend as she fell into step next to Josh. "What's up?"

He jerked, clearly startled to find her next to him, and then shrugged. "Just thinking."

She nodded, sympathetic. "You learned a lot today. Probably a lot more than they taught you about paranormals in school. I'm sorry I went off on you about the whole Tinkerbell thing."

He sighed. "You know, I never questioned how vampires or shifters came into existence. I sort of always thought they were just... there. The idea that something created you is a little scary."

It wasn't the answer she'd been expecting. "Why? Most humans believe in a creator, whatever they call him. You might not call that power *magic*, but it's essentially the same thing."

"I guess it never occurred to me that we were created by two different beings. Humans and paranormals, I mean. Humans weren't created by Fae, right?"

She could hear the uncertainty in his voice and her heart went out to him. His faith was shaken, and he didn't know what to do to get it back.

"No," she said as gently as she could. "We have no records

of humans ever being in Under in large populations. The only time humans are mentioned at all is when they accidentally fell through the gates. Chances are, humans were already here and we stumbled into your world."

"Thanks." He lowered his eyes. "It seems like a stupid thing to be worried about when there's so much going on. I just can't help it."

She patted his arm. "Don't worry about it. You okay otherwise?"

He snorted. "As good as can be, given I almost got eaten alive by a magical mist. I don't think I'll ever look at the woods the same way again."

"If it makes you feel any better, I think the same thing. And fog is forever ruined for me."

He smiled at her. "It does make me feel better, thanks."

They walked another few feet in silence. She didn't know the man well enough to know if he needed some time to gather his thoughts or if he needed some kind of distraction.

"Is it true that those mist things are gates to this Under?" he eventually asked. "It's a little unnerving, to be honest."

She contemplated telling him a little white lie. She had no doubt in her mind that Josh was only there because he supported paranormal citizens and cared about their well-being. The chief wouldn't have forced him to be on this assignment otherwise. As such, he deserved the truth. "The thought should scare you."

He was pale and she could hear his heart pounding. She wondered if she should have changed the subject but forged ahead. It wasn't like she could stop now. "Our books tell us of what happened when a human accidentally stumbled through one of the gates. Apparently, the Fae enjoyed hunting the adults for sport. And their human victim never had it easy. They never walked away alive. It would have been a mercy to be handed over to a hoard of hungry vampires. At least their deaths would have been quick."

"And the children?" Josh asked. "They really ate them?"

She had been hoping he wouldn't mention children.

He must have seen the reluctance on her face because he grabbed her hand. "Please. I need to know."

She swallowed and stared into the woods so she wouldn't have to look at him. "Yes. And sometimes, much worse." Josh's breath caught and she prayed he wouldn't ask her to relay what their ancient books had said. "Don't ask. Some things you can't unhear. It will haunt you."

And that was as far she went. The look on Josh's face told her he didn't need to hear anymore either.

She cleared her throat and followed his gaze back to the woods. "Don't worry about it too much. The gates to Under haven't been seen for hundreds of years."

"What if that really is a gate?"

"If you really knew about everything that walks this Earth, you would never sleep again."

"There's more than just vampires and shifters?"

She thought of the little vindictive creatures that were a part of human lore, creatures that were real and ready to feast on human flesh should they ever get the chance. They lived at the bottom of ponds, in seas, lakes, in swamps, deserts, and anywhere a human might accidentally fall to their deaths.

"Yes," she said finally. "You don't need to concern yourself with them, as long as you're careful. They don't kill." They just waited quietly in the wings for a human to die so they could have an easy meal. She didn't think he needed to know that last part.

He didn't seem comforted by her words at all. He looked back at the woods, his face still troubled. "Why are you staring so hard at the forest?" she asked.

The young man rubbed his chest. "I still feel the tugging."

The blood rushed from her head so fast she swayed. Taking a deep breath, she steadied herself. "You've felt it the whole time?"

He continued to rub tight circles over his heart. "No. It eased after we left the forest before. It's back now."

"What's back?" Fen asked.

The wolf shifter had doubled back to see what held them up. Josh looked troubled. "I feel like I need to go somewhere."

"Like when we saw that mist in the woods?" Fen asked.

Josh nodded and actually took a step toward the forest.

"Don't," Fen said, grabbing the young man's wrist and pulling him back. He took a deep breath and blanched. "Colin, it's here."

Less than a second later, a roar echoed through the woods.

A huge creature barrelled out of the trees.

Sparks flew from its fur. It shifted so fast she had trouble tracking its change. One second it was a hulking wolf, much bigger than Fen was in his animal form, the next it was a giant lion. A bear's head appeared only to be replaced by the wolf again.

It lurched in their direction and the child behind her let out a high, thin scream.

She acted on instinct, grabbing the little girl and clutching her shoulders. "Run to the bunker. Don't stop. Go as fast as you can."

Colin shouted the same order. Two men grabbed up the youngest children and took off while three more shifters hustled the older ones along.

Her gun was in her hand in seconds, pointing at the rampaging monster, determined to give the pups the time to get to safety.

She pulled the trigger.

Nothing. Empty.

Shit.

Shit, shit, *shit*.

She should have gotten those extra magazines from Fen when she had the chance.

Fen grabbed her arm and spun her around. He pushed his face into her line of vision and she blinked. She'd never seen him more ferocious. "Take Josh and run. Go to the house. Get him into the panic room."

"Take Carla with you," the leo growled. "She's not strong enough for this."

"Where's Bo?" she screamed over a persistent shrieking somewhere off to her left. She scanned the crowd, searching for her brother.

"Here." He stopped by her side, his executioner's blade in hand. "Take them and go. Keep them safe. I'll be fine."

Her training kicked in and she seized Josh's arm. The screaming was coming from Carla, who, thankfully, was only a few feet behind her. She snagged the enraged cat shifter and yanked. Carla struggled in her grasp. "Let me go. I want to kill it. It murdered my pride mate."

Ara managed to get a grip on the woman and dragged the two forward, through the throng of shifters already changing into their animal forms. "Run," she ordered.

She half carried them toward the Alpha House, dodging random wolves as she went. Recognizing Mandy's wolf as she ran past, Ara sent a silent prayer to anyone who was listening to protect her loved ones.

She risked a glance over her shoulder and gasped. The creature was less than ten feet behind them and gaining.

Its fangs dripped and it stared at them with crazed eyes, ignoring the shifters attacking it. It swiped at Colin's wolf and the alpha went sprawling. She turned away before Colin's body stopped skidding.

CHAPTER EIGHTEEN

Ara ran, ignoring everything going on around her and focused directly on her goal. The Alpha House was only a few feet in front of them. She heard a sickening snap, like a breaking bone, as she mounted the porch steps. Josh hollered but she didn't stop, running headlong into the door with a desperate hope that it would open under her weight.

She turned slightly at the last minute, hitting the door hard with the front of her shoulder. It cracked but didn't open.

She let go of Josh and grasped the doorknob. It refused to budge.

Locked.

"Get ready to shoot the creature," she screamed at Josh.

She kept her grip on Carla's upper arm steady as she stepped back. There was no way she was letting go of the woman, not when she was determined to exact revenge herself. Except she needed to get them into the house and she couldn't get the right angle to break through the door if she kept a hold of the cat shifter.

"Don't do anything stupid," Ara growled, then let go of her and aimed a side kick at the door, right where the lock was located.

She put all the power she had behind the movement and the framing imploded with a shower of splintered wood. The lock snapped with a satisfying crunch.

She grabbed Josh and Carla and shoved them in front of her. Josh stumbled under the force of her push and she struggled to keep him upright.

"Basement door to the left," she ground out. She herded

them along, glancing over her shoulder.

When the creature didn't crash in behind her, she figured something, or someone, had succeeded in slowing the creature down. *Oh, God, Bo.* God, please don't let her brother be whatever had distracted the monster. Or Mandy.

Or Fen.

An ache, sharp and sudden, pierced her heart at the thought of her partner. She pushed it out of her mind and steered her charges through the basement. She'd only been down here once, but the panic room was easy enough to find.

At the end of the hall, a large metal door waited.

Carla balked, digging in her heels and refusing to move. "I'm not going in there."

Josh eyed the room. He didn't look much more enthusiastic about entering it either. "My brother-in-law's pack had one of these. This is where they put blood-mad shifters until they can be put down."

"It's not the holding cell. It's a panic room. You can get out if you need to. And it's the safest place for both of you right now," she insisted.

"That thing tore the steel doors right off the frame at my diner," Carla protested.

Ara made an impatient noise in the back of her throat. If they didn't get in the room on their own in the next thirty seconds, she would throw them in herself. "This is reinforced and you know it."

The sounds of fighting drifted in and Ara glanced toward the stairs. "Get in now," she said. "Don't make me force you."

Nothing was stronger than a vampire in full fight mode, not even a shifter. It was clear they both knew she outclassed them in that category and, though Carla sent her a dark look, they entered the room.

"Don't come out unless you are 100 percent sure it's safe. And I'm trusting you to protect Josh." She spoke directly to the cat shifter, who still looked as if she were on the edge of a mental breakdown.

She didn't swing the door shut; Carla still had a wild, almost feral look in her eyes, and the last thing she needed was to lock a human in a panic room with an out-of-control cat shifter. Ara hovered by the door, listening hard for a sign of what went on outside. It wasn't hard to hear the commotion, even without the heightened hearing of a shifter.

Her mind flashed to Bo. Technically, this wasn't his fight, but she knew he wouldn't leave while his friends were in danger. He would fight to the death for people he cared about.

Mandy too. She swallowed thickly around the lump in her throat. Her friend was one of the warrior commanders. She would be the first person to throw herself in front of danger.

And Fen.

She couldn't even think about her partner.

"Ara."

She wheeled around at Josh's voice and found him holding out his service weapon. "Take it. I changed out the magazine earlier so it's fully loaded. They need all the help they can get. You should go."

She swallowed again, torn. "I need to stay here and keep you safe."

The young man shook his head. "No, you need to be out there trying to stop this thing. Go. I'll keep us safe. I'm a good shot. And I have another weapon." He lifted the hem of his shirt, showing off another hip holster.

She looked at the butt of the gun. It was smaller than the standard-issued police weapon. "There's no way your pistol will kill that thing. Not if a bunch of fully grown shifters can't."

"I don't need to kill it. I just need to hurt it enough for us to get out."

"How are you supposed to do that?"

"My brother-in-law taught me to aim for the most vulnerable parts of a shifter. Their eyes."

She stared at him. "And you can hit a target that small when it's moving?"

He stared straight at her, a steely look entering his eyes. "I can. Besides, it won't be moving around all that much once it's in the room. It's too big."

A shout, loud enough to wake the dead, ricocheted off the walls. Her gut clenched at her brother's voice.

Then silence.

"For God's sake, go," Carla shouted. "I'm not going to do anything to the human."

Oh God, how would she be able to look at her mother and tell her she'd done nothing to help her baby brother? How would she be able to look at herself in the mirror? It didn't matter that Bo was a fully grown vampire and he was more than qualified to take out the creature. She'd sworn long ago that she would protect him with everything she had, and there was no way she would back out of that oath. Not when she was standing around doing nothing.

"Fine," she said and grabbed the gun. "Fine."

She slammed the panic room door shut and raced up the stairs.

Somewhere along the way, the front door had swung shut again. She flung it open and stepped out into a bloodbath.

CHAPTER NINETEEN

She took a breath, bracing herself for what she might see. When shifters died, they reverted to their human form. Wolves and large cats littered the lawn, injured but not dead.

Her gaze raked the surroundings, searching frantically for her brother. She spotted him a few feet away, locked in a furious battle with the creature.

He jumped back, spinning in midair as he avoided a vicious swipe. His gaze locked with hers. "Get back down in the basement. Get into the panic room."

"I can't," she shouted back. "Not when you're up here."

"Please, Ara, for once in your life, stop being my older sister and just listen to me. I need you safe."

"Forget it," she yelled. "Where is everyone?"

He swung his executioner's blade at the creature. He missed but succeeded in driving it back a few feet. "Fen's rallying the troops. They should be here any second. Colin's out for the count. So is the leo."

Taking a page from Josh's book, she drew her weapon and advanced slowly.

A low growl came from her left. She took her eyes off the beast to see who was chastising her. It could only be one of two people.

Mandy or Fen.

Sure enough, Fen stood next to her, the fur on his neck standing straight up. "I can't go back," she whispered. "Not when Bo's out here, or Mandy. Or you. Do what you have to do and I'll do what *I* have to do."

His reluctance was reflected in his eyes, but he fell back. She followed him with her gaze and found a line of shifters between them and the house.

It looked too much like a last line of defense to sit well with her.

She glanced back at her brother. He was still going strong, slicing at the beast with every chance he got. He made contact a few times. It didn't even slow the thing down.

The line of wolves at her back growled as one.

She closed her eyes and centered herself, ignoring the smell floating off the creature and saturating the air. Closing out the situation was probably the stupidest thing she'd ever done in her life and she knew she would hear about it from multiple people if she survived, but she needed a way to focus.

She sorted through the situation as fast as she could. She didn't have a sword, like her brother, or claws like the wolves.

Her fangs might to do some damage, especially if she could get to its throat. Unfortunately, if the monster could throw off a pack of wolf shifters without a problem, she doubted she could get close enough to sink her fangs into its flesh.

The only thing she had was Josh's gun. It had at least slowed down the fog earlier. Maybe it would have the same effect on the beast.

She scanned the area, looking for the best location to angle her shot. Her gaze fell to a spot on the front porch, right in front of the front door. It was high enough to shoot over the wolves' heads if they didn't rear up.

"Stay down," she cried as she clambered up the steps. "Fen, tell them to stay down."

A low growl was the only answer she got.

Just as she got into position, the beast knocked her brother aside and charged the line of wolves. It broke through the shifters, who stayed down as she'd requested, and lunged at her.

Time seemed to slow as Josh's words floated in her mind.

She didn't need to kill it. She just needed to give Fen's

wolves a chance to regroup and attack a second time.

Pulling her weapon from her hip holster, she took aim. There was no way she would be able to hit it in the eye, as Josh had suggested. It was moving and it changed sizes every time it shifted into a different form.

But a direct hit to the face would probably hurt like a bugger.

She pulled the trigger and caught it mid-shift.

The bullet missed the beast's head and lodged into its shoulder.

The creature howled and reared back. Thick smoke poured from its wound, nearly obscuring it from view. It reared on its hind legs and spun around, racing back toward the woods.

"Ara? What did you do?" Bo yelled.

"Shot it."

Bo's eyes widened a split second before he pulled out his own pistol, the one he'd never drawn in the line of duty.

She was at his side before he even had it in position. "You'll never hit it from here."

"I know. I can't convince you to stay here, can I?"

"Not on your life."

Together they ran after the creature. It had a decent head start on them, and moved far faster than either of them could manage. The smoke trail dissipated but they plunged on.

Bo froze in mid-stride and she nearly stumbled over him.

"What?" she asked, sweeping her gun in a wide arc.

"Does it always smell this strong?" Bo asked.

The scent had become so familiar she hadn't noticed it intensifying. "No. We're getting closer."

"Okay. Let's go a little slower." Bo didn't sound especially anxious to continue. She could sympathize.

They crept forward silently, still following the smoke until it trailed to nothing at a patch of shimmering mist.

"What the hell?" Bo whispered.

"Oh, hell, not again," Ara moaned.

Sure enough, the fog drifted toward them. It sparked, and smoked, dark shapes moved inside as the foul smell intensified. Something howled from within it, sending a wave of goose-bumps across her skin.

The mist roiled, flashed and heaved, like it was trying to spit something out.

Or maybe make room for a couple of vampires.

She grabbed Bo's arm and yanked him back. He came easily, looking as spooked as she felt. "That's some seriously messed up fog."

Branches snapped behind them, accompanied by the sound of something big running through the woods in their direction.

She swung around, horrified. Crazy fog that might eat them to one side, and a psycho shifter on the other side. They had nowhere left to run.

Heat, heavy and somehow reassuring, pressed against her back. She didn't need Bo to tell her what to do. She pushed against his back and aimed her gun at the oncoming sound, confident that Bo aimed at the fog.

She figured they had very little chance at surviving. At least they would go down fighting. Her mind flashed to her mother and her heart broke. They were all she had, and she would have to live with the loss of both of her children on the same day.

A huge gray wolf broke through the trees, growling and frothing at the mouth. The only thing that stopped her from shooting it was the fact that, while it was much larger than a regular wolf, it wasn't nearly as big as the creature she and Bo chased.

She wasn't stupid though, and kept her gun trained on the wolf even when it started to shift.

The air emptied out of her lungs when she recognized her partner, standing tall and very naked. How she hadn't realized it was him before, she didn't know. Her knees buckled in relief.

"What in the hell were the two of you thinking?" Fen

shouted.

A litany of comebacks raced through her mind. Her brother yelped before she could say anything. "It's gone."

"What's gone?" she asked.

"The mist," Fen said, his eyes now trained on a point over her shoulder. "I don't like it. Something is seriously fucked up. We should get back."

She didn't protest, even when her arm was clamped in a brutal grip and she was marched back the way they'd come.

It wasn't until she stumbled over a stray tree root and bumped her forehead into Fen's shoulder that she noticed the large bruise on his ribs. Forgetting his nudity, she bent closer and examined the wound. She prodded around the edges a little, watching for any signs of pain.

He winced and pulled away from her. "Quit it."

"Anything broken?" she asked.

"I'll be fine once I shift again. So straighten up and start walking."

She bit her tongue on the reply. He was snippy because he was hurt and worried, which made him feel vulnerable.

Bo stuck close to them, brushing against her arm every once in a while. "That thing was smoking," he said.

"Well, no shit, Sherlock. And the fact that it was smoking instead of bleeding made you want to chase it?" Fen snapped.

Irritation bubbled in her gut. They had only done their jobs. "We couldn't just let it go."

"And how were you going to capture it? Or kill it?" Fen shot back. "Do the two of you have death wishes?"

The scent of blood, thick and sweet, hit her. Her stomach clenched with need and her fangs dropped. She stopped, inhaling through her mouth, trying to control her reaction. Her body clamoured for blood.

It had been so long since she'd hunted something, since she'd tracked something. And she'd just hunted for the second time in twenty-four hours. It didn't matter that she hadn't been hunting for sustenance. Her predatory instincts had been triggered, and it was all she could do to keep from sweeping in and latching onto the nearest blood source.

She closed her eyes and counted to ten.

"Is everyone okay?" she asked when she finally had control of herself again.

They broke through the tree line and Fen swept a hand in front of him. "See for yourself."

CHAPTER TWENTY

She couldn't remember ever seeing such a sight, and she'd seen some pretty horrific things in her line of work. Maybe it seemed worse than it really was because she had a connection with these people.

A number of shifters, both in wolf and human form, were lying scattered on the ground.

"Don't eat anybody." Fen stalked away, converging on the few submissive wolves milling around. It took her a second to realize they submissives were triaging the injured shifters. She spotted Mandy a short distance away, cradling her arm against her stomach.

"Mands?" she said when she reached her. Her vision shimmered at the amount of blood running from a hole in her friend's abdomen. She pushed away her hunger and bent over the woman. "Stay still. I'll find someone to help."

"Whoa, Ara. Slow down. I'm okay. I just need to shift a couple of times and then eat a boatload of protein. Bo?" she called. "Come look after your sister. She looks like she's about to pass out."

A large hand cupped her elbow and pulled her back a few steps. "You all good, sweetheart?" Bo asked.

Ara kept quiet. She knew he was talking to Mandy and not to her. Bo would never call her *sweetheart*.

Her friend nodded. "It's just a surface wound. Ara doesn't look so good though. I've never met a vampire afraid of blood before."

The joke was meant to ease her, but it did the opposite.

Mandy only joked like that when she was trying to hide something. "Mandy," she breathed. "Let me see."

"Are you sure that's a good idea?" Bo whispered. "I saw you back there. You need to eat."

"I'm not that hungry," she pushed out through gritted teeth. "My more … basic … instincts were triggered. I'll be fine."

She shook her brother's hand off and bent over, gently pulling her friend's arm from around her middle.

The cut didn't seem too bad, just as Mandy had stated. "See?" Mandy said. "I told you. I'll be fine. Now, go get some blood to tide you over. I've lost enough already."

The joking was back. "Mandy? What's wrong?"

Her friend cast a quick look at Bo, one that neither Ara nor her brother missed. "Where's Colin?" Bo immediately asked.

"He's around," Mandy murmured. "He took quite a hit in the last assault. Try and see if you can get him to rest soon. He won't listen to me or Fen, but he might listen to you."

"I doubt it," Bo said darkly. "Look, leave everything to us. You just shift and get better, okay?"

Her brother loped away, looking for his friend.

Mandy must have been waiting to get her concerns off her chest before she shifted because barely an instant later, a black wolf panted at Ara's feet.

Shifter healing abilities never failed to amaze her, and she watched, with a great deal of awe, as Mandy's wound sealed itself.

Ara gripped Josh's gun in her hand, still ready to attack anything that came out of the woods, as she collapsed next to her friend. Mandy put her head in her lap and looked up at her with wide eyes.

The absolute trust her friend showed effectively shut off her hunting instinct.

Colin hobbled into the middle of the throng, with Fen and Bo close to his sides, and glanced at them, his eyes bouncing between her eyes and Mandy's form. She nodded, hoping he understood that she wouldn't leave his sister alone while she was vulnerable.

He cracked a small smile at her, and she knew her message had been received.

She didn't know how he smiled so readily. The area around his knee was swollen to twice its normal size. It had to be painful, but the last thing he would do in this situation would be to show any type of weakness. His pack needed him to be strong, so he would be strong.

"Okay," he called, as if trying to quiet everyone down. It was unnecessary, really. The clearing was silent and watchful.

"We've just encountered the same beast that attacked the leo's pride. So this is no longer us simply helping them. This is the pack and pride working together to destroy a common threat."

Mandy stirred, causing Ara to tear her gaze off Colin's face and look down at her. "You shouldn't shift back so quickly," she commented when she saw the telltale ripple work its way across her friend's skin.

The woman ignored her, or maybe she was too far into her shift to actually stop it. Whatever the case, Mandy was back in her human form before Colin finished his next sentence.

She shook her head at her friend's stubbornness and focused on the alpha again. "Luckily, while there have been a few injuries, some more serious than others, we didn't lose anyone. None of the pups are hurt and Josh and Carla are safe."

Guilt swept through her. She'd totally forgotten about the two she'd left locked in the panic room in her concern over Mandy. She leaned to the side in an attempt to see behind Fen, breathing a sigh of relief when she caught sight of Josh and Carla standing on the porch with the leo. They looked angry but otherwise fine.

Beside her, Mandy struggled into a sitting position. "Feel like I'm going to throw up," she muttered.

"Better than bleeding to death," Ara commented.

Both women stopped talking when Fen cleared his throat and shot them a dark look.

Colin continued speaking as if they hadn't interrupted. "No one is to stay alone for the time being. Families with pups will be housed at the bunker and my place. The rest of the pack will temporarily move into the houses close by. Keep in mind that you will be living in someone else's home, so no marking your territory."

Ara would have laughed out loud if she hadn't known Colin was dead serious.

Colin spent a few more minutes arranging temporary living quarters. His hands shook a few times, and she marveled at how he kept going.

Mandy finally pushed to her feet, where she swayed. Ara jumped up and steadied her. "What are you doing?"

"I have to get everyone relocated."

"Are you sure you're well enough to do that?" Ara asked. She tried to keep the concern out of her voice, but even she could hear it plainly in her tone. "You lost a lot of blood."

Mandy shrugged and stepped away. "I'm fine, Ara. I'll shift again once everyone is settled and then grab something to eat. We're tough. It's how we were bred."

Goose bumps skittered over her skin at her friend's statement. The reminder of their shared roots brought the image of the beast's trail ending in a patch of fog into sharp reality.

She picked her way across the field, careful not to step on anyone, until she drew even with Colin, Fen and Bo. "We need to talk."

Fen glared at her but said nothing as Colin spoke. "I agree. Do me a favor and get the leo, Josh, and Carla into my office. We'll join you in a few minutes.

****

A few minutes turned into twenty. Luckily, the leo had other things to distract him from the wait. He made use of Colin's phone and quickly put in call after call, assuring himself that his pride was okay.

"They're fine," he said when Carla asked. "No sign of the creature."

"Are you going to have the pride stay together too?" Ara asked.

It seemed like the smartest thing to do, at least to her. The leo shook his head. "Cats are solitary creatures. Wolf shifters might fight over territory occasionally, but they tend to be happier living close together."

Carla pushed her hair out of her eyes. "We'd probably do more damage to each other than that beast would."

Ara snorted. Clearly, the two cats hadn't yet grasped what the creature was truly capable of.

Eventually, Colin, Fen and Bo trooped in, Bo with a small mountain of blood bags piled in his arms.

He collapsed on the couch next to her and tipped half the bags into her lap. "You good?"

"Yes," she answered. "You?"

"Yup. I think we can agree never to tell Mom what we did."

She shuddered at the thought. Now that they weren't in imminent danger of dying at the claws of some mysterious beast, the idea of the lecture her mother would deliver if she ever found out was enough to make her want to curl up in a ball. Their mother might have finally come to the conclusion that both of her children were in law enforcement and accepted there was some risk attached to their profession, but that didn't mean she wouldn't tear a strip off them if she thought they'd acted stupidly.

Colin walked stiffly to his desk, nodded at the leo, and eased himself into his chair. Fen took up position behind him, still glaring at her.

"Where's Mandy?" she asked.

"I've ordered her to rest. She needs to recover, and you know how she is."

She did indeed know her friend. The woman would work until she collapsed.

"I don't mean to rush things," the leo said, "but can we get started? I want to get back to my pride and make sure we have our bases covered in case we're attacked again."

Ara didn't waste any time explaining how the creature started smoking when she hit it with a bullet.

Bo took over, describing their chase and how the trail ended in a patch of mist. While her brother talked, she turned and bit through a bag of blood as discreetly as she could. She emptied the first bag quickly and was about to grab another when Fen interrupted.

"Yes," he said. "Ara and I will be having a conversation about chasing monsters in the woods without backup."

Rage bounced around inside her skull. She wasn't eight. "I'm a fully grown vampire," she said softly. "And a trained police officer. I don't need your permission to do my job. Nor your concern about my safety. I don't need a father. I already had one. It didn't work out so well."

Fen's head reared back and he paled slightly. He looked like he'd just been slapped. She felt bad for the words almost as soon as she said them. It was a low blow. They'd worked together long enough to form a strong friendship. She would be just as concerned, and probably just as angry, if he'd went into the woods without backup.

The difference was she wouldn't berate him in front of a room full of people. She wasn't the helpless little girl he seemed to think she was.

Not anymore.

Before she could say anything else, Bo spoke. "We were together, so she had backup."

His voice was light, but the menace behind his words

peeked through. The look he gave her partner would have had any normal person shuddering with fear. Carla pressed her entire body against the leo's in an attempt to get away from him. Fen simply raised an eyebrow and stared back. Eventually, Bo nodded, as if understanding something, and continued. "What's really important is the connection between this beast and the mist. There are shapes moving in the mist. Sounds coming from it. It flashes and sparks. It carries the same scent as the monster. It is some kind of magic, and it's not something I've ever seen before. It's certainly not witch magic, either dark or light."

No one spoke. Ara was content to break into another bag of blood while she let everyone else in the room digest the meaning behind her brother's words.

"As much as I hate to admit it, it seems as if the fog is connected to what's happening. I think we really do need to investigate the possibility that we are dealing with a new gate to Under," the leo finally said.

"Well, that's not good," Carla said.

"Why?" Josh asked.

"It could mean that the thing is either some kind of Fae or it has been created by the Fae the same way we were," Fen answered.

"And the gates haven't been spotted in centuries," Colin added. "Their presence is definitely something we should be concerned about."

Josh frowned. "How can we be so sure? What if it's just some kind of shifter we don't know about?"

The leo shook his head. "No. Our books are quite clear. Wolves, cats, and bears were the only animals the Fae had merged with mortal bodies, at least it was at the time our ancestors escaped."

"We still don't know if it's a Fae. Couldn't it be something of this world?" Josh asked.

"We can't rule it out. My gut says the creature we're searching for is Fae though. It would explain why my sword didn't so much as slow it down when Ara's bullet sent it running. Our duty ammunition may contain small amounts of iron," Bo answered. "But my sword is silver and steel."

"They might," Fen agreed. "Iron is poisonous to Fae. Our bullets are most likely some kind of metal alloy, although trace amounts of iron would definitely explain why the wound smoked, especially if the creature really is Fae."

"I think we can stop with the ifs," Colin finally said. "As much as no one wants to think about it, it seems the gates to Under have reopened. Although, what we should do about it, I'm not sure."

"Have you ever seen the gates before?" Carla asked, staring at her.

Ara puffed out her cheeks. "I'm not *that* old. I can try to arrange a meeting with one of our elders. Her name is Catriona MacDougal. She might be able to give us information on the Fae."

"Our history books should be enough," the leo said. "By all accounts, the gates closed and the mists disappeared six hundred years ago."

Ara rolled her eyes. Sometimes looking far younger than her age meant everyone felt the need to *enlighten* her. "I know. Dame MacDougal is well over eight hundred years old."

She tossed the bags into the trashcan next to Colin's desk. "I've already spoken with Fen about contacting my grandfather. He should be able to arrange a meeting with her. If it's okay with both of you," she said, looking at the two leaders. "I understand the case is technically now managed by shifters, but if it does turn out to be the Fae, the repercussions for the entire paranormal world will be unthinkable."

"It's fine by me," Colin said. The leo hesitated only a few seconds before nodding.

Fen sighed and handed her another bag of blood. Her earlier

blood lust had been assuaged, but she accepted it anyway.

"The other thing we need to discuss," he said as she drank, "is what exactly the creature's hunting. Both Carla and Josh are possible targets. The beast originally attacked Carla's diner where Josh eats frequently. She has also been present during one of the mist's appearances. Josh has been present for both."

"I need to get going," the leo broke in. "Carla will be staying at the Pride House with me. Josh, I suggest you find somewhere safe to crash for the next little while."

"You can stay here," Colin offered.

Josh accepted. Bo and Fen accompanied the leo and Carla outside, their duty pistols drawn and ready.

Colin stayed where he was until Fen came back. "You should shift so your leg heals properly," Fen whispered to his brother.

"I will," he said. "As soon as I get upstairs. Can you do me a favor and bring me some scissors when you come up? I'll have to cut the leg of my pants open to get them over my knee."

Fen nodded. "I'll stand guard outside your room tonight."

The alpha shook his head. "I'm fairly sure I only tore a ligament. It should heal almost instantly. Ara, you should stay as well."

It was a nice offer and probably a smart idea, but there were some things she needed to do alone. And arranging a meeting with her grandfather was one of them. She shook her head. "I don't think I'm the target. Besides, I have to speak with my grandfather."

"Ara," Fen said. "I really don't think it's a good idea for you to be on your own."

Colin stared at her before nodding. "As she pointed out before, she is a fully grown vampire. I can't force her to stay. Besides, pack life isn't for everyone."

Meaning he understood she wanted to speak with her grandfather without the chance of being overheard, which was impossible in a house full of wolf shifters. "Fen, take her back to the diner so she can drive home, please."

Fen looked reluctant to leave. He wouldn't want to leave his brother unguarded while he healed. She knew, however, he wouldn't disobey a direct command from his alpha, even if it was phrased as a request.

Instead, her partner turned to her. "Are you ready to leave?"

CHAPTER TWENTY-ONE

She didn't bother to ask if he wanted her to drive, digging into her pocket and handing him the keys.

She waited until he'd eased out of the driveway and was on the road before she asked how he was feeling.

"Fine. Why?"

She shrugged. "You had quite the bruise on your ribs."

"I'm fine," he snapped.

She waited a few minutes before trying again. "What do you think that thing really is?"

"Don't know."

Talking in single syllables was never a good sign. She really should keep at him, bully him until they were back on even ground and could have a productive conversation. But exhaustion hit her hard, and she was too tired to deal with his moods. If he wanted to give her the cold shoulder, she wasn't going to go out of her way to try and talk to him.

Instead of trying to coax him from his sulk, she busied herself by loading a new magazine into her weapon.

She blinked when the car pulled to a stop. Without a word, she pulled out her weapon and reached for the handle to let herself out.

"Ara?"

Oh, now you're going to talk to me. She swallowed the sarcastic comment. There was no point in making things worse. "Yeah?"

"Can I ask you something?"

"Sure."

She expected him to berate her for denying Colin's offer,

maybe another lecture about being reckless.

He surprised her instead. "Is the only reason you don't date because of what your father did?"

She sat back, a little torn as to what she wanted to say. "It's only part of the reason," she finally said.

He was silent for a few seconds. When he spoke again, his voice was soft and gentle. "Only part?"

She chose her words carefully. "I don't think shifters or humans can really comprehend what it means to live such a long life."

"What do you mean?"

"The short answer is that I learned early on not to get attached to people I know I will have to watch die."

Fen stared at her and she looked away. How was she supposed to meet his eyes when she was talking about his eventual death?

"You're still young for a vampire though. Surely you couldn't have run into that too often," he whispered.

For the first time in years she thought of another group of people she'd once known. The memories made her eyes fill with tears, and she impatiently brushed them away. "When I was a teenager, I didn't understand why my mother kept trying to convince me to stay away from the neighborhood. Then the second world war broke out. A lot of my friends marched away and never came back. It was the first time I realized I would outlive any humans I became friends with."

Of course, it hadn't stopped her from becoming emotionally invested in humans and shifters as she got older. Try as she might, she just couldn't help herself. A little over a decade ago, she'd gone to the funeral of her last remaining teenage friend. They hadn't seen each other in years, even after vampires had come out to the humans. It didn't matter. She still felt the loss. She'd sat in the back and cried quietly as the girl's family spoke of a long life well lived.

What was a long life for a human, even for a shifter, was

nothing more than a blink of the eye to a vampire.

She was already far too attached to Fen and his pack than she should be. Losing him would create a hole in her soul. And yet she couldn't pull back now. She was stuck. And sometimes, the knowledge that time would creep up on him faster than it would her made her ache.

She blinked back tears and popped open the door. The quiet safety of her car called to her. "Thanks for the ride. I'll see you tomorrow."

"I'll follow you home," Fen said.

On the brink of an emotional breakdown, the last thing she wanted was for Fen to witness her crying. She cleared her throat. "I'll be fine. I'm not the target, and I have my weapon. We know shooting it will make it run away."

Fen didn't say anything, just continued to stare at her.

"Really, Fen. Thanks for your concern. It's not necessary."

His face tightened and his mouth pulled down into a frown. "We're more than co-workers, Ara. We're friends. I don't know about you, but I don't let my friends charge off into the night blindly without backup."

She took a deep, calming breath. "I understand you're still upset about what Bo and I did. I'm sorry I worried you, I really am, but I can get home fine. Besides, Colin is injured and your pack probably needs their beta more than I do."

It was a low blow and she knew it, especially given the fact that she'd heard Colin insist he'd be all right and probably didn't want Fen standing guard outside his room anyway.

It worked though. "Fine. Promise to call me when you get home."

The demand chafed at her pride a little, but she would do whatever she had to do to get out of there. "Yes, I'll call."

Fen waited until she got into her car. She drove off, watching as he got smaller and smaller in the rear-view mirror.

****

As much as she wanted to crawl into bed and let sleep take her away from the memories of both the past and that day, Ara pulled out her cell phone and dialed her partner's number as she trudged up the stairs.

"Hey, Fen," she said when he answered. "I'm home. I'll see you in the morning."

She hung up before he could say anything else. She was so strung out, so emotional, she didn't think she could have another conversation with him like the one they'd had in his car without bursting into tears.

She needed to set up a meeting with the old vampire, and the only way she could do that was to go through her grandfather.

He was of the old school of thought, that females should get married and let their males support them so they could stay home and have little vampire babies.

She couldn't blame him for his attitude, really. The man was about five hundred years old.

But she really didn't feel like arguing with him. The best thing would be to have her mother call him for her. He never was able to refuse her mother anything.

It was late. Late enough that her mother might actually be in bed. She contemplated leaving the conversation until the morning, but she just couldn't resign herself to doing absolutely nothing while people were in danger.

She dialled her mother's number, collapsing on her couch as she waited for her to pick up.

"Hello, darling," her mother answered.

Something in Ara softened. Bo and her mother were really the only constants in her life, and she couldn't stay irritated with the woman for long. "Hi, Mom. Did I wake you?"

"Oh, no, darling. I'm watching a lovely documentary about

the fall of the Berlin Wall. It's amazing how many humans believe the fall was really because of them. You didn't call just to chat, did you?"

What was really amazing was how her mother always knew when something was up. "Actually, I was wondering if you could get Grandfather to arrange for Fen and me to meet Catriona MacDougal? We need information about Fae."

"Hmm. I can't arrange the meeting myself, but your grandfather certainly can. I'll call him and get things started. You know you're going to have to meet with him at some point, right? I know you've been going out of your way to avoid him, but he loves you, Ara. He only wants what he thinks is best for you."

Ara sighed and tiredly rubbed her eyes. "That's fine. Can you tell him to text me with the details? I'm exhausted, and I'm going straight to bed as soon as I get off the phone."

"Of course. I should let you go then, darling. Could you do me a favor?"

"Sure."

"The next time you see Boris, tell him to call me. I have met a wonderful young woman I think would be just perfect for him."

She chuckled. "Sure, Mom. I'll tell him."

Her phone rang as soon as she disconnected with her mother. "It's me," Bo said when she answered. "I'm downstairs. Let me up?"

He helped himself to one of the bags of blood in her fridge as soon as he walked in. She cringed when he popped his fangs straight through the plastic. "At least put it in a glass."

He threw the empty bag into the trash and reached for another. "You know, most people would find a vampire drinking blood out of a wine glass just as disturbing. And this way, I'm not leaving any dishes for you to wash. Besides, you didn't use a glass at Colin's. Did you phone Grandfather yet?"

She winced as he slapped another bag to his teeth and a little fleck of blood landed on her floor. "I called Mom instead. She's going to set it up for me. And before you say anything, yes, I know I'll have to see him."

"If you don't want to see Grandfather, I can go for you."

She sighed and reached for her own bag, considered getting a glass, but in the end mimicked her brother. She just didn't have the energy to take her own advice. They sat quietly her living room sofa. She sipped at the blood, not really hungry but not wanting to waste it. She'd had enough at the Alpha House.

"Thanks," she said when she finished. "I need to learn to stand up to him. It's not like he'll hurt me or anything. He's the one who arrested Father after he beat me and Mom so badly that one time. And he also made sure Father was never getting out of prison."

Her brother didn't answer. Instead, he wandered over to her kitchen and rooted around in her cupboards until he extracted her favorite pair of wine glasses. He filled them both with more blood and carried them over.

She smiled at him when he turned around, remembering all the times she used to take care of him. She never considered there would be a time when he'd try to take care of her.

Bo, however, didn't smile back. He looked at her as if trying to see through her. "Ara, I need to tell you something."

That didn't sound good. Especially when he looked at her as if she were about to run away. "Okay," she said.

He rubbed at the side of his nose, a habit he'd had since he was about five years old and learning to lie.

"I've wanted to tell you for years now. I really didn't know how to bring it up."

"What is it?" she whispered.

"I don't know how you'll react. I don't want you to worry."

His hesitation was scaring her. "What's wrong?"

He blew out a breath. "Father wasn't arrested."

"He wasn't?"

Panic threatened to overwhelm her, and she immediately cursed herself for caring. She wasn't a little girl anymore. He couldn't hurt her. She'd shoot him before she let him near her or her mother, and Fen would look the other way.

"Don't worry," Bo rushed to say. "He can't hurt you or Mom."

She drummed a finger on her thigh. "If he's not in prison, and he's not around anymore, where is he?"

"Don't be angry. Granddad had him executed right after the last incident. He didn't want either of you to know because you were already so traumatized."

Her panic drained away, leaving her shaky and weak. "He thought I would be upset over that man's death? I guess he doesn't know me very well. When did you find out?"

"See, that's what we didn't want to tell you."

She stared at him. "He told you right away, didn't he?"

He looked even more uncomfortable than before. "Well, he didn't exactly tell me."

It wasn't like her brother to beat around the bush. "Bo? What aren't you telling me? Oh, God. He didn't take you to witness the execution, did he?"

He shook his head. "I didn't witness it."

She had a sick feeling she already knew what her brother would say. Her mind flashed back to the last time she'd seen her father. The man had beaten her and their mother until they couldn't move. It had been Bo who'd finally had enough and called their grandfather.

He had been eight.

"Granddad allowed me to perform the execution."

Bile pushed up her throat and she gagged a few times. How could he do something like that to a mere child?

"It's okay," Bo insisted. "I wasn't traumatized or anything. I hated him, even then. Once Granddad explained that execution was the only way to make sure he wouldn't hurt you or Mom again, I was okay with it. Better than okay, actually."

"Oh, Bo …" She didn't know what else to say.

"I still feel the same way. It's part of the reason I became an executioner. I like knowing the criminals I kill can't hurt anyone again. Sometimes I wonder if there's something wrong with me."

She swallowed, grabbing Bo's glass and chugging back a few mouthfuls to get rid of the awful taste in her mouth. She tried to smile reassuringly at him but had a feeling it looked more like a grimace. "I don't think there's anything wrong with you."

The relief on his face broke her heart. She could only imagine how it had felt to carry that secret around for so long.

"My offer still stands," he said. "I know he's always getting on your case about quitting."

"Thanks. I'm hoping he'll set up the meeting without having to talk to me first. If he doesn't, don't worry. I won't let him bully me into quitting."

Bo fiddled with the stem of his wine glass, still looking troubled. She knew what it was like to finally put your fears into words. He was worried there was something seriously wrong with him, and there was nothing she could do about it but offer him company. "You want to spend the night? I'm sure Fen would feel better knowing I'm not staying alone."

"Thanks. I don't want to be alone either."

"Same."

She gathered their glasses and carried them to the sink, trying to stop the moisture in her eyes from welling over. Bo didn't need her tears. He needed her strength.

"Ara?"

"Yeah?"

"Thanks for not hating me."

She nearly choked on a sob. Tears ran down her cheeks and she rinsed out the cups as an excuse not to turn around. "I could never hate you," she whispered when she had some sort of control again. "Never."

CHAPTER TWENTY-TWO

Thankfully, her grandfather hadn't seen the need to question why she and her partner needed to meet with Catriona. He'd simply arranged for the meeting and texted her the details.

When she pulled up to the station she found Fen already waiting outside, his arms crossed over his chest as he leaned on the hood of his car.

He didn't bother to wait for her to get out. Instead, he slipped into her passenger seat and smirked. "What took you so long?"

Apparently, she was forgiven for charging into the woods after the creature. "I was talking to my grandfather."

Texting counted as talking, right?

"Did you get us the appointment we wanted?"

"Yes, and it's in a few minutes. Don't we need to go in and update the chief? You know, fill out some paperwork?" Not that she actually wanted to speak to the chief. The thought of talking to the man made her blood pressure skyrocket.

He shook his head as he buckled his seatbelt. "Already done. I called the chief last night and gave an oral report. He said since the shifters have taken over the case, as is their right, he didn't give a damn what happened as long as there weren't any humans involved."

She snorted. "I should have known. So I guess Josh is off the case then?"

"Actually, he assigned Josh to us permanently."

"Permanently? As in, until this case is solved?"

"As in, we've got ourselves a new partner."

Something seemed wrong. "Josh is a human. Doesn't that

go against what the chief said about involving humans?"

Fen shrugged. "I get the feeling Josh isn't too popular around the station. He's too friendly with the local paranormal population."

Anger tightened her gut. "Josh is a good guy. He doesn't deserve to be stuck doing the less-than-desirable things we do."

"Don't worry too much," Fen answered, patting her hand. "The man charmed the entire pack last night. They're already referring to him as an honorary shifter. He called his brother-in-law and explained what we're dealing with. He's offered Colin any help he can provide, because he's so grateful we've taken Josh under our wing."

"Where is he now?"

"Moving into our office. Think we have enough room for another computer? Where are we going, anyway?"

She pulled out of the parking lot before she answered. "We'll make it work. And we're meeting our contact at her home. It's not far, but she's older than dirt and I don't think traveling to the station would be easy for her."

They didn't say anything else until she found the address she was looking for. It was in one of the city's oldest, most prestigious neighborhoods. Even Fen, who lived in his brother's mansion, whistled when they pulled up.

A massive black car idled outside and the door opened to reveal her grandfather. She took a deep breath and steeled herself for the inevitable confrontation.

"What's up?" Fen asked.

"That's my grandfather. I love him, but he's not happy with my decision to work. I've been avoiding him for the past couple of years, because all he does is harp on at me about being a good daughter, quitting my job, and letting him take care of me."

Fen frowned. "Don't worry. I've got your back."

She wanted to remind him that she didn't need to outright fear her grandfather, but she appreciated his support too much to say anything. Instead, she pushed open the door and got out. "Hi, Granddad."

He greeted her with a wide smile and a hug. She tried to hide her surprise as she was folded into his arms. He'd never been a demonstrative man, at least not in public. She kissed his cheek when he presented it to her. "How have you been?"

He squeezed her again. "Better now that I've seen you. It's been too long, love."

She soaked up the affection, kissing his cheek again. "I know. I've been busy with work."

"Hmm," her grandfather hummed. He turned and surveyed her partner, looking him up and down critically. "Are you going to introduce me to the man who's been taking up so much of your time?"

"Grandfather, this is Fenris Blair, otherwise known as Fen."

Fen stepped forward, his hand outstretched. "Nice to meet you, sir. I'm sorry I've taken up so much of your granddaughter's time."

"Nice to meet you as well. You're also the beta of the Toronto wolf shifter pack, correct?"

"Yes, sir."

"Hmm." Her grandfather turned back to her. "I've heard your mother is trying to set you up on those blind dates again."

She prepared herself for the lecture she was sure she was about to hear. About how she would be a better daughter if she'd just settle down.

So she was taken by surprise with his next words. "I'll be sure to tell your mother to cool it when I see her next. You should do what makes you happy."

"Um, thanks?" she said. As discreetly as she could, she pinched her arm, just to make sure she was actually awake.

"I've never told you before," he said. "Your grandmother and I are so proud that you're doing exactly what you want. It's what your grandmother fought so long for. And we're always so happy to tell our friends that you're the first female paranormal inspector ever."

She wondered at the sudden change in his attitude but didn't say anything about it. She didn't want to ruin the moment.

Her grandfather seemed to understand her confusion. "It has been pointed out to me, by your grandmother, that if I stop hassling you about your job, you may come and visit more often." He frowned. "I just want you happy. That's all I've ever wanted for you, ever since you were born and I held you, all tiny and indignant, for the first time. Your grandmother has told me that times are changing. And I need to change with them."

Ara smiled. "Thank you. I *am* happy."

Granddad smiled. "Your mother mentioned you needed information about Under. Is it true, Arabella? Have the mists really come back?" he finally said.

It was Fen who answered. "It's possible. We need to find out more about them before we confirm anything."

Her grandfather looked over at Fen again, as if assessing him, before he nodded. "Catriona is waiting for you in the house. Please, go right in."

She mounted the steps, noticing the yellow mums in a container on the porch. The bright flowers seemed out of place when they had such grim suspicions.

"You ready?" Fen asked, his hand on the doorknob.

"No," she said. "Let's go in anyway."

CHAPTER TWENTY-THREE

"Come in here," a thin, reedy voice commanded.

Catriona MacDougal sat in a large wingback chair. She was tiny, so old she looked shriveled, and yet she managed to look nothing short of regal.

So regal, in fact, that Ara fell back on her years of etiquette training and curtsied. She couldn't help but stare up at the woman from under her lashes. They were standing in the presence of the oldest vampire in existence, probably the oldest living being in the world. It was a little disconcerting, to say the least.

"Tut. Get up, girl."

Ara obeyed immediately. Though the old lady's voice was thin and reedy, it carried an unmistakable kind of authority. This was a woman who was used to getting what she wanted.

"Madam MacDougal," she said. "Thank you for agreeing to meet with us."

"Yes, yes. I've actually been asking your grandfather to meet you for some time. First female in the police force. That's quite an accomplishment."

"Well, the first female vampire, anyway," she said.

"Don't be so humble. You should hear the way your grandfather talks about you. Now, you and your young man should sit down there, where I can see you." The dame pointed to a small couch on the other side of the dainty table. "I'll ring for refreshments. Tea, Arabella? Mr. Blair, I can have some meat brought in. I understand you are a wolf shifter."

Ara hid a smile behind her hand as Fen assured the old woman he was fine with the tea.

They made polite conversation until a young woman hurried in, carrying a tray laden with a teapot, three cups, cream, sugar, assorted pastries, sausages and two wine glasses filled with blood.

She accepted the blood with a small smirk, remembering Bo's assertion that drinking the liquid out of a wine glass would be disturbing for most people. At least she wasn't the only one who liked to have some manners. And Fen didn't seem to think there was anything off-putting about it. He was far too interested in the sausages.

She sat back and sipped at the blood, letting Fen explain the situation. Although she didn't think Catriona was one of them, most older vampires didn't respect her position or authority. It rankled her more than she liked to admit. Most of the time, though, it was easier to get the cooperation of older vampires when Fen explained.

The enzymes in the blood she drank trickled through her, reminding her she hadn't stopped to drink before driving to work. She hadn't realized how awful she'd felt. Bo was right, she didn't drink often enough.

"Well, Arabella? What is your opinion?"

She blinked, startled from her thoughts. She wasn't used to being asked her opinion on cases. "Pardon me?"

"Tell me what you think happened in the forest."

For the first time since they'd been assigned to the case, she dared to put her greatest fear into words. "The smell, like ammonia and sulphur mixed together. It was so distinct, like something I should remember and fear. Somehow, I just knew that mist was dangerous but I can't explain why."

The woman pointed at her. Her hand trembled just a little. "Always listen to your instincts, girl. Fearing that mist is a good thing. You stumble into one of them, you're not coming back out."

Fen cleared his throat. "What exactly do you mean?"

Catriona gazed at him, her eyes sharp and intelligent despite the haze of age. "You should have had the same reaction. All Fae creations would and *should* fear it. The mists reek of the scent of Fae. Somewhere along the line, an enhanced sensitivity to the stink of Fae became ingrained in us, along with the physical reaction."

"Have you ever seen a gate?" Ara whispered. Her fist was clenched so tightly, she felt her nails digging into her palm.

The old woman stared at a spot over Ara's shoulder, lost in her memories. "I have," she said finally. "And I've lost plenty of loved ones to Under. The gates closed and disappeared centuries ago though. We were never sure why. Personally, I always thought the Fae closed the gates to stop their creations from escaping like the vampires and later the shifters did."

Ara's heart dropped. She'd been hoping against hope that they'd been wrong about the Fae. Instead, their fears had been all but confirmed.

Catriona stayed silent, seemingly lost in memories. Eventually, she looked up and pinned them with a gaze so sharp Ara shivered. "The question is why the gates have opened again after all these years."

"Do you have any thoughts about that?" Fen asked.

The woman shook her head. "I will tell you this: I hope I'm dead long before the Fae invade."

****

"Well, that wasn't helpful," Ara muttered out of the corner of her mouth as she and Fen left the house. "All we learned was that we should be afraid of fog and Fae invasions."

"It's okay," her partner said. "At least we know what we're dealing with now."

Ara sighed. Sarcasm wasn't a good look on her. "I don't know how it will help though. She didn't give us much to go on."

Her grandfather stood beside his car, as if standing guard. "Did you find what you need?' he asked.

"Not enough," she answered.

The older man looked her over and nodded, apparently satisfied. "The old woman gave you some blood, did she? She must have liked you. She comes from a time when a regular supply of blood was scarce, and she's a little possessive over her stash."

"Yes, I had some blood. She had sausages for Fen. I'm surprised they were cooked." Ara stifled a giggle.

"You really should think about increasing the amount of blood you consume," her grandfather continued as if she hadn't just spoken. "You look peaky and have lost weight since the last time I saw you. Would it be so bad to move back in with your mother? She would make sure you drank enough."

Ara covered her eye roll by pretending to scratch her ankle. Strange mist and rampaging monsters aside, she generally made sure to ingest enough blood.

At least he wasn't suggesting she quit.

Fen's voice suddenly joined the conversation. "You're right, sir. If it makes you feel better, I'll make sure to remind her."

She straightened, not bothering to hide her eye roll that time. Fen looked her straight in the face with a shit-eating grin.

"It would make me feel better knowing someone was looking out for Ara at work. I think I can trust you with my girl, even if you *are* a shifter."

Her partner's grin widened, his eyes sparkling.

She blew out a puff of air, sending her bangs flying, and propped her hands on her hips. "Are we done with figuring out who's going to babysit Ara? Can we get back to the case?"

The older man's expression sobered and she immediately regretted her words. It had been a long time since she'd seen him in such a good mood. "What did Madam MacDougal have to say about your case?"

"She came to the same conclusion we did. The gates to Under have re-opened and we have a killer Fae running around, using the gates to get in and out of our world. Or dimension. Whatever."

Ara stopped. The last thing she wanted to do was scare her grandfather. It didn't matter that he'd apparently had some kind of breakthrough when it came to her job. If he thought she was in danger, he might insist she quit and move to the mountains, or some strange place. If he pulled his council card, he could force her to quit.

Or get her fired.

It didn't matter. His smile faded completely. "What can we do?"

"Who is we?" Ara asked, relieved he hadn't insisted she abandon her job.

"The Vampire Elder Council. A Fae invasion would be very bad for everyone involved."

She considered his question. They really needed more information on the gates before they charged off in an attempt to guard them. How could you guard something when you had no idea when or where it might appear next?

"Well, let's not start a mass panic. It would end very badly, especially for the humans."

She paused and eyed her grandfather, wondering how much help he was really willing to provide. "Access to the Old Books would be helpful. I want Fen there too. He's got a good eye for detail."

Only vampires had ever laid eyes on those books. Asking that her shifter partner be allowed to handle them, let alone be in the same room as them, might be pushing the limit of her grandfather's generosity.

"What old books?" Fen asked.

"The Old Books," she corrected him. "With capitals. What do you think, Granddad?"

"I will authorize the both of you for unlimited access to the library and its contents. By the time you get there, the rest of the council will be informed."

The speed with which he agreed surprised her. "Thanks, Granddad. We're going to head right over."

"Give your old grandfather a kiss before you leave," he insisted.

She complied, kissing the man's cheek. "I'll come visit you and Gran soon."

He kissed her cheek. "Be sure you do."

"Don't worry. You and I are going to have a long talk concerning Bo and a certain execution."

Her grandfather grimaced. "Finally found out about that? It needed to be done, Ara. And it was a long time ago. Besides, he was a sorry excuse for a male. Why are you upset?"

"Oh, I agree he deserved what he got. But Bo... was eight. How could you?"

"I assume since you aren't tearing a strip off me, you and Bo have worked everything out. He's not traumatized, and he grew up well."

"He did grow up well. I don't know about him not being traumatized. We'll talk about it later."

Her grandfather gripped her hands. She was surprised to feel the tremor running through him. "You have no idea how much I regret what happened. If it makes you feel better, I had him see a therapist as soon as therapy became an option."

She closed her eyes. Sometimes it was hard to look at her grandfather and remember how old he actually was. He'd grown up in a time when similar situations were not only encouraged but the norm.

"Let's go, Fen," she said, leading the confused shifter to her car.

He didn't ask her about the last bit of her conversation with her grandfather, for which she was grateful. He didn't say anything at all until they were moving. "Where are we going, and what the hell are the Old Books?"

"It's easier to show you than tell you."

CHAPTER TWENTY-FOUR

True to her grandfather's word, they were granted access to the library immediately upon arriving. She and Fen passed the vampire guarding the door without incident, and she led her partner straight to the archive.

"Whoa," Fen said.

She smiled at his awe. He looked suitably impressed. She didn't blame him in the least. The first time she'd entered this room, she'd stood in the same spot, staring for hours.

She'd thought the faces of their ancient kin carved into the façade of the building would have impressed him. It did, to an extent.

The inside impressed her partner even more.

The archive housed thousands upon thousands of books. It should have smelled musty but somehow, it smelled like eucalyptus and mint. "Cool, right?"

"You really have all your history books housed here?"

"Yes." She slipped behind the main desk and gazed at the rows of metal filing cabinets. "Don't shifters have something like this?"

"Sort of. It's nowhere near as extensive as this." He approached one of the shelves and stared at the tomes. "These are ancient."

"They are," she agreed. "We have to wear gloves to read them."

"Are they really called the Old Books?"

"Yes. What else should we call them?"

He smirked and slipped a pair of white gloves over his hands. "I mean, you could be a little more creative when naming them. It's like naming a puppy *Dog*."

She pulled the drawer open on an old metal filing cabinet, fishing out the file that contained the index. "Don't you guys call your monthly hunts The Full Moon Hunts?" she shot back. "Maybe you should call them The Most Awesome Hunts of the Month instead."

"Touché. So, what exactly are we looking for?"

Spreading the papers out across one of the tables, she jabbed at it with her index finger. "Lots of these books have stories that have been passed down through the generations in addition to the official records of our history. I remember reading quite a few about the Fae."

He crowded close, staring over her shoulder at the table. "There isn't a digital index we could access? Something that would help us pinpoint which books we should look in?"

The laugh bubbled up her throat before she could stop it. "There are far too many books for something that detailed. I think they're trying to index things as they come in. I can pretty much guarantee that what we're looking for hasn't been added to the database yet."

She ran her finger down the column until she came across a likely looking entry.

"Here, go find this," she said, jotting down the volume on a scrap piece of paper. "It should be on those shelves over there."

The next entry also listed something about Fae. She found the giant ledger on a shelf close to Fen. "We'll start with these. Only take one book at a time," she warned. "The librarian gets crabby if they get out of order."

Hours passed, the scent of musty pages filling the air. "Any luck?" she asked.

Fen shook his head. "The only thing I've learned is that the real Vlad was as ruthless as his fictional counterpart."

"Yeah, I've heard he was a jerk. He's the one who gave vampires such a bad reputation. We've always needed blood to survive but we've never, ever sanctioned killing a human. His distaste of sunlight was because he was quite ugly, hideous even, and the humans around him interpreted it to be an allergy to the sun."

He was quiet for a few minutes. "I've never heard of this library before. I kind of thought I knew everything in the paranormal world."

She nodded absently, still carefully flipping the pages. The last thing she wanted was the sour-faced librarian breathing down her neck because he was worried she would damage the books. "It's a pretty well-kept secret."

"Then how do you know about it?"

She closed the book and carried it back to the shelf, making sure to place it in exactly the same spot she'd found it. "It's not a secret to vampires. We have to spend a year studying the Old Books when we turn twenty-five."

"Every vampire?" he asked, the doubt plain in his tone.

She led him to a coffee maker and poured him a cup. "Well, not a whole year. The term is about forty weeks long. But yes, every vampire. They come from all over the world to study the texts. There's a dorm nearby. I'm actually surprised there aren't any students here today. They must have closed it because of our investigation."

The librarian scuttled over, scowling. "Make sure you don't drink that near the books. I've been known to commit murder for lesser things."

Fen raised his eyebrows as the little man hurried away again. "I don't think he's kidding."

"Probably not."

He drained his cup in one long swallow. "So, you spent almost an entire year of your life in this room?" he asked when he was done.

She watched the liquid pour into the mug as he served himself another cup. "There are other rooms," she answered. "This one only holds the oldest books. There are far too many to fit into one room."

"How do they enforce it?"

"It's part of our schooling."

He shook his head and, once again, drank the cup in one go. "I can't imagine still being in regular school at twenty-five. I mean, most people have graduated university by that time."

She wandered back over to the table where the index was still spread out. She didn't know how to respond to his statement. To most people, still studying at twenty-five seemed like a long time. For a vampire, twenty-five was still young enough to be considered a child.

The realization that Fen was already more than a quarter into his short life reminded her that she shouldn't allow herself to get too attached to him.

"Everything okay?" he asked a few minutes later. He joined her at the table and bent over the papers.

"Yes," she replied, then jabbed her finger at a listing. "Here, you grab this one. I'll take this one."

He gave her a funny look but obeyed.

Another hour passed before she finally found something. "Here."

Fen looked up at her, his eyes wide and nostrils flared. She couldn't tell if she'd startled him with her announcement, which had been rather loud, or if he was excited to finally be getting somewhere. "What is it?"

She squinted at the page, trying to make sense of the spidery writing and the old language. "It's an entry from ancient Ireland. It says the gates to Under used to be open permanently. Many people were lost to the mists."

"We knew that," Fen interrupted when she paused to decipher the writing.

"Right. There's more. Apparently, there was a Fae who got trapped on our side of the gates when they closed. He ultimately integrated into Irish society, but he was never really accepted, eventually confessing that he didn't have the knowledge to re-open the gates. No one did."

"What?" Fen leaned forward, hanging on her every word. "How would a Fae not know how to open a gate? Isn't that sort of basic Fae knowledge?"

She shrugged. "I guess not. It says here he told them that the knowledge of how to make certain magic had been lost because of the potion."

"What potion?" Fen interrupted.

She huffed and looked up at him, irritated. "I'm getting to that. The ink is faded in some places and is hard to read."

She bent as close to the book as possible, her eyes nearly crossing in an effort to read the entry. "Something about a potion they drink when they become bored with life. It makes them forget. So they start their lives over or something. According to the Fae, the knowledge had been lost and no one remembered how to open or close the gates because they'd just always been open."

They sat silently, staring at each other for a few moments. "Well, shit," Fen finally said.

"I wonder what it must be like to live so long you get bored enough to want to wipe out your memory," she mused.

Fen shot her a strange look and she raised her hands. "Hey. Vampires live a long time, but we're mortal. We do die eventually."

"So now we know that some magic is lost over time. I guess we need to find more information on the gates."

They went back to poring over the books, pausing only to stretch out their muscles. She was just about to suggest stopping for the day when Fen sucked in a breath. "Got something?" she asked.

"Here's a story about one family who captured a Fae in a cage. They demanded the gates be closed because they'd lost several children. The Fae insisted that the gates were no longer under their control. They were alive and had a tendency to move wherever they wanted."

She shivered, remembering how the mist had seemed to stalk them. As surreptitiously as she could, she glanced around the library, making sure mist wasn't oozing from between books or hovering near the ceiling.

"I wonder why the gates closed then?" Fen said. "If the magic had been lost and they couldn't control the mists."

"And why they opened again," she added. "That has to be how the Fae shifter is getting in and out of our world. And it would explain why it keeps suddenly appearing and disappearing without a trace."

Fen leaned back in his chair, stretching his arms over his head. "The only way to track it is to follow the scent. And even then, it will be hard to follow, seeing as how it tends to appear whenever it wants."

Ara thought back to old Catriona MacDougal and how the woman wished to die before the Fae came back. She remembered the fear in her grandfather's eyes. Perhaps tracking the gates was a bad idea.

And then the image of her mother formed in her mind. The woman had taken so much abuse from her husband for decades until the second he raised a hand to one of her children. She'd put herself between that man and Ara, knowing full well the man would probably kill her for interfering.

After being released from the hospital, Camille had gathered her courage together and made a good life for Ara and Bo.

Ara drew strength at the thought of her mother. If she needed to track down the gates to Hell to keep her mother safe, she would. "You're right. We need to track them somehow. But before we do, we need to have everything set up properly."

CHAPTER TWENTY-FIVE

Colin and the leo greeted each other a little more warmly than the last time they met.

Ara leaned close to Mandy as they watched the two alpha males interact. "Do you think they'll keep in touch once this is over?"

Mandy shrugged. "Probably not. Who knows? The leo is gorgeous. I wouldn't mind seeing more of him around here."

She shot her friend an amused glance. "I thought you liked Josh?"

"Josh is cute but he's not interested. Maybe he's gay."

She didn't bother to answer. Her friend thought any guy who wasn't interested in her was gay. Mandy was a great girl, and the attitude was typical of a female shifter. Which meant she could rub humans the wrong way.

And vampires too, if Ara was honest.

"Where is Josh, anyway? I thought he was staying here."

"He's around. I think I saw Bo showing him his sword."

Fen cleared his throat from his place next to Colin. "If I could have your attention."

The crowd quieted much quicker for him than they would have for Colin. She figured it was because of his role as pack enforcer.

"Most of you know my partner, Paranormal Inspector Ara Classen. And you all know we've been assigned to this case by the human police chief. In the course of our investigation, we've come across some information."

She kept quiet as he explained what they'd read about the gates and how falling through one could result in something very, *very* bad. He told them about their theory of the creature using these gates to enter and leave without a trace. He didn't try to sugar-coat the truth, simply repeating the facts clearly and calmly.

Fen turned to Colin, clearly ready to defer to his decisions once the facts had been put out in the open.

The alpha stepped forward, nodding at Fen. "Thank you both for your efforts." He gestured for the leo to join him. "The leo and I have decided that it's important to meet this creature on our terms. The first time the creature appeared, it attacked Carla's diner, going directly for the booth Josh often sits in."

Ara didn't miss the lack of formality he addressed Josh with. It seemed Josh really had endeared himself to the pack.

Nor did she miss the collective growl that rippled through the crowd of shifters.

She shivered at the sound. Hopefully, she would never be the reason for that kind of reaction.

Colin held up his hands for silence. "It's very important that we try to lure the creature here, which is why Carla and Josh are both here, since it seems one of them is the beast's target."

"Um," Josh said, raising his hand as if he wanted to ask a question in class. "Can I please avoid the panic room?"

Fen frowned in response, and Ara understood the feeling. She wouldn't go into that room willingly, especially knowing what was going on outside, even if it was for her own safety.

Which was the exact argument Fen made. "It's safer for you."

Josh pulled the hem of his loose sweater up a little, showing his pistol. "I have the same ammunition as Ara and Bo, so it should work just fine. Besides, I really should be involved. I'm your official police presence in this case. Fen and Ara don't count anymore because they are involved from the paranormal aspect."

Ara wanted to call Josh on his bullshit. The simple fact that the case had been taken over by the pack and pride as a paranormal investigation didn't negate their legal authority. Besides, the human police had nothing to do with this anymore.

Josh eyed her pleadingly and she relented, shaking her head at Fen when he opened his mouth. The young human was a part of their team now. They'd both have to get over their impulse to try and shield him from any and all danger. There was only so much they could do, and he'd accepted the risk when he'd become a police officer.

Fen stepped forward after a nod from Colin. "After reviewing the evidence, we have decided that the mists we have encountered are probably portals to Under, the Fae Realm."

He glanced around the room, making sure he had everyone's attention. "We've also made the determination, an educated guess really, that the creature we're hunting is entering and exiting our realm through these portals. In the past, they were known as the gates to Under."

He cast a hard look at a group of teenagers at the back of the room. "It is very important that you avoid interacting with the mists at all costs."

"We're wolves," one of the teenagers called with a vicious smile. "We'll just tear anything we meet limb from limb."

Oh, to be a teen again. There was a time when she thought she was invincible too. Or perhaps she had just been reckless.

"You can try," she put in, interrupting whatever Fen was about to say. "But falling through the mists is probably the worst fate you can ever imagine."

"I'm not afraid of dying," the kid said.

"Oh, they won't kill you," Ara replied. She considered telling the teenagers about the horrifying things the stories described but decided against it. Her vague threat would probably work better in the long run.

Fen stepped up next to her. The smile on his face was evil. "Right. You would probably wish they *would* kill you."

He waited for his words to sink in before continuing. "That being said, I do need whoever is willing to volunteer to go out into the woods along with us and hunt for the mist. The more people we have, the better. That way, we can monitor it. We don't exactly know how it appears. We do know it moves. You will phone Alpha Colin if you discover it. You are not to engage with it. Stay a safe distance back. Volunteers who remain in human form will be equipped with guns and ammunition. If the mist begins to move toward you or your group, shoot it. Furthermore, you are not to engage in the creature should you encounter it. Defend yourselves if you have to. Do not to attack first." He didn't bother telling them they wouldn't survive a fight. "Is there anyone willing to volunteer?"

A ripple of sound pushed through the room as nearly every adult wolf in the room raised a hand to indicate they would help. Even some of the teenagers raised their hands, causing Colin to shake his head and glare.

She stepped back as Fen and Colin moved through the crowd, assigning positions and arguing with the teens.

Mandy leaned toward her again. "Do you have Fen's blessing to join us this time?"

Her friend's overly sweet tone had her clicking her tongue. "He doesn't have any say over how I do my job."

"I know. I'm teasing you. Just trying to break the tension."

Ara picked at a fingernail, a nervous habit she just couldn't break. "I know. And thanks for trying. This case really has me nervous. Talking to Mrs. MacDougal didn't help. And the stories in the Old Books…" She shuddered. "I'd forgotten about certain details."

"I know." Mandy rubbed her arm. "I'm sorry I was so flip about it."

She smiled at her friend, though she was pretty sure it looked more like a grimace than anything else. "It's okay. I'm just edgy."

At the front of the room, Colin and Fen were talking again,

something about the safety of the pups.

A sudden inspiration hit her.

Her brother looked at her, and she knew he had the same idea she did. "How about our mother's place?" he said.

The alpha's expression turned thoughtful. "You think?"

"Sure." Bo fished out his cell phone. "The place is huge, so there would be plenty of room. And she'd be thrilled with all the children. Just send some of the teenagers with them to help her out and I promise she'll have every one of those kids eating out of her hand in no time."

"Yeah." She liked the idea even more now that Bo had put it into words. "She'll be like the pack's honorary grandmother."

She waited until everyone was caught up in preparations, then slipped into the kitchen. As always, there was a decent stock of bagged blood in the fridge. She grabbed one and pushed it to her mouth, letting her fangs extend and pop through the plastic. She wasn't hungry but if she was going hunting for Fae, she needed all the strength she could get.

"I was just going to ask if you'd had enough."

She rolled her eyes and continued to empty the bag.

"Sorry," Fen said, wandering over to her. "I *did* promise your grandfather I'd look out for you."

She waited until the blood had completely drained then pulled the bag from her mouth. "I know you did, but I'm perfectly capable of taking care of myself."

"I know," Fen countered, reaching into the fridge and extracting another bag. "I always keep my word though."

"What are you, my babysitter?"

She didn't mean to sound so snappish. Anxiety did that to her.

"No, I think I'm more like a keeper. What's going on, Ara? What's got you so wound up?"

She couldn't answer, not with the second bag of blood attached to her teeth. She held up one finger in a silent request for him to wait.

When she was done, she pulled the bag away and tossed it in the garbage. "It's stupid. We keep running into this thing and it's scary as hell, and part of me is wondering why we're chasing it instead of running away."

The words were so fast she had no idea if Fen actually understood.

"I know," he said. "I get it. That small, wild bit of my brain is telling me to take my pack and move them far away."

She wondered for a second if he would take her with him. "Feeling vulnerable makes me angry," she said. "It makes me twitchy and I hate it. What makes it worse is that I can't see how this can end well."

Fen grabbed her face in both hands and forced her to look at him. "We can't think like that," he rasped. His palms were clammy, and beads of perspiration shimmered on his temples. The roar of his blood rushing through his veins thundered in her ears. "No matter what, we have to think positive, okay? If we don't, we've already lost," he rasped.

He was right. And it was just what she needed to hear.

They stood together silently as they braced for what they were about to do. Finally, she gripped his wrists and nodded. "Ready?"

Fen released his hold on her and rubbed his palms over his face. "Ready."

The plan was to have teams of three or four volunteers, some in their animal form while at least one of them stayed human to use the phone. Shifters were already in wolf form when they made their way back into Colin's huge living room. The teens and children were nowhere in sight. Apparently, her mother had accepted their request and they had been hurried off.

Her partner immediately stripped off his shirt and went to work on his pants button.

As quickly as she could, Ara averted her eyes, searching for and finding her brother.

Bo grinned and swaggered up to her. "So, how many times have you seen your partner naked now?"

A low, threatening growl rippled from beside her. "Inappropriate, Boris," Fen said.

It never failed to amaze her how wolf-like Fen could sound while still in human form.

"Jeez, Fen. Relax." Bo raised his hands, palms out, like he was trying to calm a wild dog. "I'm only teasing. It's what little brothers do."

Fen grunted. "Whatever. Watch out for each other, okay?"

She knew he was really talking to Bo, but she appreciated his wording nonetheless.

A ripple of wild power shimmered in the air. It felt a little like being caught in an electrical storm. The power danced over her skin in tiny shocks, raising the hair on her arms and causing her scalp to tingle.

When she turned toward her partner again, his giant gray wolf stood next to her.

Fen had been among the last to shift and Colin, also in his wolf form, waited patiently by the front door.

All around them, wolves started to pace, prowling the room. Either they were excited for the chase or realizing they'd volunteered for something that might end their lives.

Either way, the energy and nerves in the room were almost too much to handle and she sighed in relief when the leo, still in human form, opened the door.

She followed the pack outside, one hand on the butt of her gun. Bo's heat warmed her back as he followed her out.

The shifters broke into groups and loped into the woods. Fen hung back, clearly making sure she didn't do anything he considered stupid.

The stillness of everything made her jumpy and her muscles twitched. She considered pulling out her gun but didn't want to accidentally shoot anyone, a distinct possibility given how she was vibrating with nervous energy.

A howl, long and low, sounded through the woods. The remaining wolves slowly trotted off.

"They must have scented it," Bo murmured.

"What if they just smelled a rabbit or something? They are wolves, after all. Their instinct is to hunt." She knew she was reaching, but she wasn't as ready to face this thing as she'd thought she was.

"Come on, Ara." Bo pulled his gun from his holster. "You know how this pack hunts. The females always take the lead, cutting off the prey while the males attack from the rear. And they are never slow. Whatever they've scented isn't normal and they are being cautious."

A rustling behind her caught her attention, and the scent of human blood alerted her to Josh's presence. "What are you doing here? You should be inside."

"Inside isn't as safe as you think." Josh readied his own weapon and took a steady stance next to her. "If that thing gets into the house, it's got us cornered."

"Then you should be in the panic room." The exasperation in the leo's voice held no anger. Probably because he would have refused to be locked up as well.

The human snorted. "You can't tell me that room is one hundred percent airtight. Mist can creep in somehow."

Suddenly, she smelled it.

Her heart picked up speed, pounding against her breastbone in an attempt to leap out of her chest. As one, she and Bo trained their weapons at the tree line. The leo drew his gun and followed their example.

"Shit," Josh muttered, whipping out his own weapon. "I would really kill to have some paranormal senses right now."

Wave after wave of ... something ... pushed against her. Tiny shocks crawled up her skin. Her brained seemed to swell, pushing against her skull until she wished it would just explode through the bone to relieve the pressure. Her fangs dropped and her muscles tightened, readying themselves for an attack.

More deep growls ripped through the woods, getting closer and closer until a wolf she recognized as Mandy broke through the tree line.

Her friend was followed closely by a group of wolves, all circled around a young woman. She didn't need anyone to tell her the female was a Fae.

"Oh, thank the stars," the girl exclaimed when she spotted Ara. "Call them off. I'm here to help."

CHAPTER TWENTY-SIX

Slowly, as if she were a vampire of old stalking her prey, Ara descended the porch steps, her grip on her gun firm and steady. "You're here to help? With what?"

"With the chimera. It's not acting as I thought it would."

"What do you mean, it's not acting how you thought?"

The leo's voice vibrated with rage. Ara was grateful he wasn't talking to her.

The young woman stuck out her chin, staring the lion shifter down as if daring him to do something. She was so tiny the alpha towered over her, but what she lacked in stature she more than made up in attitude. It would have been comical if the situation weren't threatening to spiral out of control.

"I mean, the chimera is not acting as expected. I've been trying to track it down to confine it, but it's avoiding me. The gates are not acting as they should either, opening and closing at random points, and it's making it hard to corral the chimera."

Ara kept her gun pointed at the girl. "Leo, why don't you let me question her?"

She was careful to word her statement as a question, a request, instead of an order.

"Question?" the Fae asked. "I was going to ask you questions. Like if you know where my chimera went. I haven't seen him in almost a week."

"By chimera, I'd guess you're talking about the monster that keeps attacking us?" Ara said.

"Attacking you? It's been attacking you? Oh, it wasn't supposed to do that. Oh, Fates, I'm sorry. Did it do much damage? Is everyone okay?"

The young Fae woman wrung her hands as if she actually cared about what might have happened. Her eyes shimmered with moisture. She looked the very picture of concern. If it was all an act, it was convincing.

Very convincing.

Ara hardened her heart. Whatever this Fae had to say, she had unleashed a deadly monster on her territory. "I'll ask the questions. What is a chimera, and why did you release it into our world?"

"A chimera is a shifter that has multiple forms. My chimera has three forms. They are supposed to be excellent trackers. That's all I created him to do, I swear. The magic must have gone wrong. He isn't supposed to attack. He was only supposed to track my mother. I didn't mean for anyone to get hurt, I promise."

Josh joined her. His eyebrows were drawn together, and his skin had taken on an ashy cast. "Who are you?" he asked.

"Annalith." She sniffled.

"What's your last name?"

The girl looked like she would burst into tears any second. "I don't have one. Half Fae are never named. I only have one because my mother named me before she left."

"Do you know her?" Ara asked the human.

He shook his head, though recognition was stamped across his face. "She's the very image of my mother."

The Fae drew in a ragged breath. "*Your* mother? You mean, I have a brother?"

Josh didn't answer. He didn't have time.

A howl tore through the night sky. Ara barely restrained herself from dropping her gun and clapping her hands over her ears.

It sounded like a hunting horn, a lion's roar, and something she couldn't identify all at once.

And it inspired pure fear.

Trees toppled as the creature barreled through. It lunged, passing right by the Fae and the wolves without sparing them a glance.

She didn't stop to think.

She fired, hitting it square in the chest. The wound smoked, like last time. Instead of running away, the beast continued to charge.

Her palms were slick with sweat as she took aim again. Something flew past her and thudded into the beast's shoulder. A bullet.

The wound only slowed it down.

The bullet was rapidly followed by more. Out of habit, Ara counted the shots until they stopped.

Someone had just run out of ammunition and was now a sitting duck. There was no way they would have time to reload before the beast got to them.

A giant lion and Colin's wolf charged the beast as one. They succeeded in pushing the creature back a few feet until it swiped at them.

She fell back, still pointing her gun, trying to remember how many bullets she'd gone through.

Bo's yell startled her as he rushed past. His gun was nowhere in sight though he wielded his sword with the precision of a knight of old.

The steel pierced the creature's gut and it shrieked. It lifted one massive paw and knocked Bo aside, throwing him five feet away.

"It's me," Josh yelled. "It's me it wants. Let me through."

"Like hell I will," she shouted. "Get in the car and go. We'll hold it off."

She hoped.

The sword in the beast's belly seemed to be slowing it down. It shifted from lion, to bear, to wolf and back again. There was no pattern to the shifting.

She risked a quick glance over her shoulder. *Well, hell.*

Josh had not only ignored her order to drive away, he'd advanced with his gun drawn.

Her scream stuck in her throat. The stupid human was going to get himself killed.

She couldn't let that happen. She'd lost too many human friends to age and disease, she wasn't about to lose another to a paranormal monster. Especially if there was something she could do about it.

Out of options, she lunged to the side, throwing herself bodily between the chimera and Josh.

The chimera's eyes were fixed on her, gleaming with malice and maybe a little hunger. She fell back another few feet as it advanced.

Fen's gray wolf cut it off, attacking its vulnerable belly when it shifted to a bear.

It roared again but Fen hung on. It stopped long enough for Ara to aim at its head before shifting back to a wolf.

She swore on a scream. The change put it too close to Fen and she couldn't get a clear shot.

Fen refused to let go, despite how she screamed at him to move.

Another wolf, Colin, she realized, jumped on the beast's back and sank his teeth into the back of its neck.

The creature let out an enraged wail and shifted back to a bear. It stood on his hind legs and shook the wolf off his back, using one paw to push Fen off as well.

Fen didn't go easily and when the creature finally did free itself, a chunk of its abdomen was missing.

In the blink of an eye, the muscles in its hind legs bunched. She knew it was about to lunge before she could raise her gun.

And then it was on her.

Her weapon flew out of her hand at the impact. The beast's weight crushed her into the ground. She raised her arm to fend its jaws away from her throat, managing to push its head away, but barely.

She didn't know how long she would be able to hold out against its superior strength. She shoved the beast with every ounce of effort in her. She pulled her legs up and kicked it in the stomach. It was useless.

Something knocked into her from the side a moment before her left arm went numb. A sharp pain knifed through the back of her head and her vision blurred. She just barely made out the beast's teeth coming closer to her throat with each second.

Blood rushed through her veins as acceptance hit.

This was it.

Her good shoulder stung for a brief second as the chimera's claws tore into it right before its weight fell off her.

Blinking, she somehow focused her fading vision on her savior. Annalith, the creature's creator, stood over her, a six-inch-long dagger gripped in her hand. She dropped it and pulled her hand to her stomach as if she'd been burnt.

"God, Ara." Bo was somehow on his knees next to her.

Her brother was shaking from head to foot and she wanted to reassure him. She didn't have the strength to even open her mouth.

"How bad is it?"

She recognized Fen's voice. She'd never realized how nice his voice was.

"Bad," Bo answered. "She needs to feed now. Bring me all the blood in the fridge."

"No time," Fen said.

She was lifted from the ground until her upper body was propped securely against something hard and warm.

Pain rushed through her, making her eyes roll. Warm liquid dripped down her arm. She could tell from Fen's expression she did not look good.

"Come on, Ara," Fen whispered against her ear. He pressed his wrist firmly to her lips. "You need to drink."

God, he smelled good, like wine and chocolate and something spicier.

No. She couldn't drink from him. It wasn't allowed. Besides, she didn't even know if she could find the veins in his wrist it had been so long since she'd fed from a live donor. She turned her head away.

"She won't do it," Bo said. His voice was high and scared. For a moment, he sounded like he was eight years old again. "It's been drilled into our heads that drinking from a live donor is dangerous and addictive."

"Well, hell. I guess I have to force her then."

Ara wasn't sure how Fen intended to force her to feed. The wrist disappeared and she could breathe comfortably without the tempting smell of blood.

Maybe breathing comfortably was a stretch.

Everything in her hurt. Her chest felt like it had been crushed by a steamroller and her throat burned with every inhalation.

The edges of her vision blurred and darkened. She stared at her brother, hoping he could read the love and apology in her eyes.

"Damn it, Arabella," Fen growled from above. "You are going to feed or I am going to find a way to bring you back to life just so I can kill you again."

This time, his bloody wrist pressed to her mouth.

Temptation gave way to starvation. She tried to resist her instinct, but a small rivulet of Fen's blood leaked between her lips and hit her tongue.

Instead of helping, the small amount of blood left her breathless with pain. It felt like every cell in her body exploded.

The scream that had been frozen in her throat thawed and ripped from her.

"What's wrong with her?" Fen's voice was frantic, "Is it because I'm a shifter?"

A soft breath feathered against her ear. "Ara, it hurts to heal. I know. I've been there. It's a bitch. You need to drink. Colin's gone for the blood in the house. But I don't know if you have that long," her brother whispered.

That's right. She needed to drink to live.

She wanted to live. She really did. Even if it was just long enough for her to chew out her grandfather for making an eight-year-old perform an execution.

Instinct she thought had died years before kicked in. As gently as she could, she pushed her fangs through Fen's skin and right into the delicate vein.

She fought through the pain, careful to take only small sips instead of the gulps her body begged for.

Bo was right. Healing was a bitch. For a brief second, letting herself die seemed like the easiest, most comfortable solution.

Then again, nothing worth having ever came easy or comfortably.

"Don't worry about me," Fen whispered. "Take what you need."

Experimentally, she sucked harder. She wasn't aware enough to monitor him for signs of discomfort, but she trusted Bo not to let her take too much.

When the blood slid down her throat, thick and rich and far more satisfying than anything she'd ever had before, she swallowed faster.

A broken moan sounded over her. She forced her eyes open, searching her brother's face for any sign that she should stop.

Bo didn't look concerned. If anything, he was amused.

She shifted her gaze to Fen, hoping her apology for hurting him showed in her expression.

Except it didn't seem like he was in pain. Exactly the opposite.

Her brain was too foggy, the pain still too intense, to make sense of what he was feeling.

"That's enough, Ara," Bo murmured.

"She's fine," Fen answered.

She vaguely heard her brother speaking to someone and then he was back, his mouth close to her ear. "You've taken enough. Much more will weaken him, not that he will ever admit to it."

Fen growled and pressed his arm more firmly against her mouth. "Fuck you."

"No, thanks." Bo's voice wasn't amused anymore.

She pulled her fangs out of Fen's wrist before they said anything else they might regret.

She slumped against Fen, but Bo looked satisfied. "You'll do. Watch her while I deal with that."

Her brother swivelled until he was face to face with the dead chimera, a terrified Fae and a very angry alpha wolf.

Somehow Fen knew exactly how to move her around until she was comfortable. "Thanks," she whispered. It was all she could manage.

"You didn't have to stop." He offered her his wrist again. "Bo's just being a prissy old prude. I'm fine."

The lure of his blood was strong, so strong she almost gave in. It took all her will to shake her head and focus on what was going on in front of her.

Colin was stroking the dead beast's head. "He was nothing more than an animal operating on instinct. Much like the very first shifters."

The Fae woman flapped her arms in front of her, clearly distressed. "I followed the instructions I found in my father's library perfectly. I didn't realize I didn't have enough magic to control it. I think it realized its purpose was to track down my mother but not that it wasn't supposed to attack people along the way."

The female looked as pitiful as she sounded. Her eyes were large and shiny with tears. She was pale and her expression strained.

Ara's heart went out to her.

Maybe it was the way her muscles softened, or something in her expression, but Fen clearly noticed Ara's mindset.

"Don't," he whispered.

She looked up at him, confused. What was she doing he didn't approve of?

"Don't feel sorry for her. She's the one who unleashed that thing on us."

"All she wanted to do was find her mother." A lump clogged her throat and tears spilled down her cheeks. Everyone should know their mother.

Fen flattened his lips into a flat line. "Ara, stop feeling sorry for her. You saw what happened."

She couldn't help it. Emotions crashed over her and she was helpless to stem the flow of tears.

"Are you Fae-struck or something? Is she using her magic to blind you to what happened?" Fen asked.

"Don't worry," Bo muttered out of the side of his mouth. "She's probably live-drunk. It happens sometimes when vampires ingest blood from a live donor. She'll be fine when it wears off."

Colin apparently had the same feeling as his brother. "What did you expect?" he ground out. "The original shifters were created to hunt down and kill each other, first in the Fae wars and then for entertainment."

"Take it easy." Bo eased between the Fae and the alpha. "She didn't know what would happen."

Colin's face tightened into one of rage. Ara braced her hands on the ground, ready to push to her feet and interfere if the alpha attacked her brother.

Not that she would be much help. The world spun when she pushed away from Fen into a sitting position. She wasn't sure her legs would actually hold her if she did manage to struggle up.

The Fae shrugged and wiped at the tears dripping down her

face. "I didn't know. I'm only eighteen, and I wasn't allowed to read our history tomes. It was only supposed to track the human part of me."

"How would you know your mother even if the chimera found her?" Bo sidled a little closer to the Fae, still shielding her from Colin.

"My father once slipped up and told me her name. I just want to know where she is. I want her to know I exist. Half Fae are treated even worse than shifters or vampires. I just want someone who cares about me."

The woman's voice was so sincere Ara had no trouble believing her.

"Well, what's her name?"

"He called her Viv. Viv Jones."

There was a yelp and a grunt and then Mandy's voice. "Josh?"

"Are you sure?" the young human croaked.

The Fae's eyes widened. "Yes. I've heard that name echoed in my memory ever since my father said it."

"She wasn't crazy," Josh muttered.

Both the leo and Colin grabbed for Josh as his knees buckled. They lowered him to the ground. "Who?"

"My mom. She disappeared for two years when I was a kid. When she finally turned up, she kept babbling about a different world and another baby. She was institutionalized."

The Fae crouched in front of him. "Can I see her? When? Where? Is she okay? Maybe I can heal her mind. I'm decent at healing magic, at least."

Josh shook his head. "She died three years ago."

Ara's heart broke for the both of them.

Colin pushed in front of Josh and growled at Annalith. "Did you open the gates as well?"

Right. The gates to Under. The fog that was out to eat her.

Ara gave her head a tiny shake. Live-drunk was the worst.

"Open them? Me?"

Ara closed her eyes and leaned back against Fen. What little energy she had was quickly draining.

"Yes, you," Colin growled, and Ara knew he was more than likely baring his teeth at the woman. "Who else would open them again?"

"They were never closed."

Her eyes popped open. *Never closed?*

Fen seemed to read her mind. "We've never seen mists like that before."

Ara struggled to keep the woman in focus. "They've just been stationary. They used to open into your Scotland. We're not there?"

The rest of the conversation was lost to her. Fen crooned, low and sweet, in her ear and the pain faded, finally allowing her to rest.

CHAPTER TWENTY-SEVEN

Fen's heart had stuttered when he saw Ara trapped under the chimera. He'd launched himself at the creature's back, tearing into it with vicious force, ripping a chunk of flesh from the back of its neck, but it paused only long enough to shake him off.

He'd felt utterly useless as a mere slip of a woman pushed her way between him and the beast and stabbed it in the neck with a dagger.

The monster had slumped over, no longer trying to bite Ara's arm off. The girl had pushed the creature off his partner.

He'd been wild by the time he'd gotten to her, ready to take Bo's throat out if he tried to stop him from feeding her.

Luckily, Bo had been all for it, and had even helped him slice a cut along his forearm to entice Ara to drink.

He looked down at Ara's pale form where he'd cradled her against his chest. She'd slipped unconscious a few seconds ago. Bo had reassured him that she would be fine. He wasn't so sure.

His wrist tingled where her teeth had broken through his skin. He looked around furtively, wondering if he could get away with pressing his arm back against her mouth and encouraging her to drink. She was just so pale. Faint lines radiated from her pursed mouth.

Damn it. She was in pain even though she was out of it. He could smell it.

"Where the fuck is that blood?" he shouted, not caring that he interrupted the leo's ranting at the Fae girl.

"Mandy's getting it," Colin replied. He hovered over them, his gaze fastened on Ara. "Just hold tight."

"Fuck that." Fen raised his wrist to his mouth, prepared to

bite through the flesh.

"Don't," Bo warned.

"Can't you see she's suffering?" he countered. How could a brother stand to watch his sister in such pain?

Bo dropped to his knees next to him again. "I don't like watching her hurt any more than you do. Trust me. Giving her any more of your blood might do her more harm than good."

"It takes more than a few swallows to get addicted," Fen said, raising his arm again.

Bo seized him and forced his wrist away from his mouth. "Human blood, yes. There's only been a few documented cases of a vampire taking blood from a shifter. Addiction can happen instantly. And I honestly don't know what will happen when she wakes up. She needed the blood so desperately."

Mandy rushed forward, her arms full of bagged blood. "Here. I'll see to the wounded. Colin, you might want to step in before the leo slaughters the Fae. She deserves a chance to defend herself, even if only because she killed the chimera."

"Go," Fen said. "Bo and I will take care of Ara."

He held her still as Bo gently tapped her cheek. "Ara? Come on, you need to wake up and drink."

Her eyelids fluttered. "Bo?"

"Yep. Mandy brought you lots of blood. Just open your mouth and I'll do the rest."

Fen held his breath as her lips parted a little. "You have to open wider than that," he admonished.

"Can't," she whispered. "So tired."

"That's okay," Bo replied. "All you need to do is swallow."

He used the very tip of his sword to cut a slit in the bag and dribbled the blood slowly into her mouth.

"Good girl," Fen praised when she swallowed.

Bo snorted but didn't say anything. He paused the flow of blood every now and then when Ara looked like she had trouble keeping up.

"One bag down," he said, tossing it aside. "You feel up to

using your fangs?"

Ara's eyes popped open and she scrambled to her knees. She heaved, bringing up every drop of blood she'd just swallowed.

"I was afraid of this," Bo said, smoothing his sister's hair back as she continued to retch.

Panic rose through Fen like a wave, threatening to drown him. "Afraid of what?"

"Well, this could be two things. The first is that she's just gorged on too much blood and her body's having trouble processing it all at once."

"Or she's already addicted to live blood?" Fen guessed.

"Specifically, your blood."

He didn't respond, just waited until Ara seemed to have settled down. He tugged her back between his legs. "Better?"

Her pupils were blown so wide she looked stoned. She growled and lunged for his neck, mouth open and fangs completely dropped.

"Well, that answers the question," Bo muttered, grabbing her shoulders and forcing her back. "Arabella, if you bite him, you'll be upset."

She licked her fangs. "He smells so good."

"I know," Bo soothed. "But it's Fen. You don't want to hurt him."

Fen watched as some of the haze cleared from her eyes. "Hurts."

Oh, God, she may as well have just torn his heart out. He had half a mind to tilt his head and offer her his vein. The look on Bo's face stopped him. Instead, he picked up one of the plastic bags of blood and offered it to her. "Why don't you try again?"

The first bag stayed down. So did the second. She gagged a few times after the third and finally turned her head away. "I'm good."

"There is no way you've had enough blood," Fen countered,

holding another bag up to her mouth.

"Just…" She trailed off, as if searching for the right words to explain what she was thinking. "I need to give my body some time to process this. I don't want to throw it up again."

He glanced at Bo, who nodded. "You seem to be doing a little better. Let's take a look at your arm."

The gashes were bleeding sluggishly, but Bo didn't seem to be concerned. "They'll close up completely in a few minutes. I'm more worried about any internal bleeding, broken bones, that kind of thing. We don't want any broken bones healing improperly. That's a bitch and a half to correct."

Bo prodded her abdomen, poked around her ribs, manipulated her legs and hips, until he got to her left shoulder. "I'm pretty sure your shoulder's dislocated. And you probably have a concussion. I'm not a doctor, but I remember how to put your shoulder back in place."

"Shouldn't we find a doctor to do that?" Fen asked, cradling Ara even closer to him now that she wasn't trying to bite his throat out.

"No," Ara croaked. "By the time we find someone, the muscles will have already healed. Just let Bo do it."

It was on the tip of his tongue to argue because, really, how much medical experience could an executioner have?

Bo didn't give him any time to protest. "Grab hold of her good side and hold her still."

"Please, Fen," Ara whispered. She licked her lips and her head lolled back against his shoulder. "I really don't want them to have to dislocate it again."

"On three," Bo said.

Fen grabbed her uninjured shoulder just as Bo jerked her arm. Ara's back arched, her head digging into his shoulder as she let out a grunt.

"Done," Bo said.

Fen swept her sweaty hair off her forehead. "You did good, sweetheart."

She panted, her chest heaving. "I think I'm going to pass out."

"It's okay," Bo said. "Sleep will help."

She blinked up at both of them. "We haven't finished yet. With the Fae, I mean."

Fen carefully shuffled around until he got his feet under him. He lifted her as gently as possible. "Don't worry. We'll take care of everything."

Some of the tightness in his chest eased when she simply closed her eyes, trusting him to uphold his word.

"Where are you going to take her?" Bo asked.

"My room."

He stepped around the carnage and nodded in his brother's direction. He had to force himself not to move too quickly. The last thing he wanted to do was wake Ara up. At least if she was unconscious, she wasn't aware of any pain.

He placed her in his bed, drawing the covers up to her chin. She was dirty and bloody, and the black cotton sheets showed just how pale she really was. He needed to tell her how he felt, about how he would have gone mad if she'd died and how Colin would have had to put him down to stop his rampage.

He should have told her a long time ago. Like a coward, he'd held off, scared of frightening her away.

He folded his long frame into the armchair by the window and settled in for a long wait.

Eventually, a familiar, comforting scent floated under the door mere seconds before it opened. "Hey, Alpha."

"I'm Alpha now, am I?" Colin whispered.

Sometimes, more often than not, Fen was grateful he'd chosen to step aside and let Colin lead. This was one of those times. He slipped from the chair and knelt at his brother's feet, pressing his face into Colin's abdomen and inhaling.

Gentle fingers ruffled his hair. "You held it together pretty well after she was injured. I'm proud of you."

Normally, an alpha's praise would send a shiver of pleasure through a wolf. Contentment did not filter through him, only the sick feeling of uselessness and grief. Fen pressed closer. "Only because she was still alive and needed me," he muttered.

"Doesn't matter. You did well."

Fen counted to ten, allowing himself only that long to wallow in his alpha's comfort before pulling away. "What's going on?"

Colin sat on the edge of the bed and eyed Ara critically. He pushed a strand of hair off her face and sighed. "We gave the chimera the death rites. In the end, he was still a shifter, one of us, even if he wasn't aware of it."

"And the Fae?"

The alpha rubbed the back of his neck. "She's... different. She swears she's only half Fae. And she does smell like some kind of human, and definitely like Josh."

"Do you believe her?"

Colin cracked his knuckles and stood. "Neither the leo nor I could smell any deception in her story. And she willingly went into the panic room."

Rage still flowed through him. "The monster the Fae woman unleashed landed Ara in this bed after almost killing her." He couldn't keep the venom out of his voice.

"I understand, especially given your feelings for her. Maybe you should talk to Annalith."

Though his brother had worded it like a suggestion, the thread of steel running through his tone left no doubt in his mind that it was actually an order.

It was that order that had him rising reluctantly from his chair. He glanced down at Ara. Even in sleep, lines of pain radiated from the corners of her eyes. She was still unnaturally pale and she twitched every once in a while, as if her body just didn't know what to do with itself.

"Don't worry," Colin whispered. He took Fen's place in the chair. "I won't go anywhere."

Out of excuses, Fen dragged himself down the stairs and over to the panic room. Mandy stood guard, her gun at her side, but she looked relaxed. "How's Ara?"

"She'll be fine. I need to talk with the Fae though."

"Don't eat her," Mandy said. Anyone else may have thought his sister was joking, but he knew her well enough to know she was deadly serious. "I know you're pissed, but hear her out."

He raised an eyebrow, a move that always had the pack teenagers scuttling for the safety of their parents. Unfortunately, it didn't work on his sister. "I'll be good," he conceded.

It wasn't exactly a lie. He would listen to the Fae. And then he would rip her throat out for hurting his partner. He was surprised she was still alive. He'd been sure the leo would have killed her in retaliation for the death of his cat.

The girl sat on the floor, picking at the rug. She jumped and scrambled back when he walked in.

"Relax," he said. "I'm not going to hurt you." The *yet* remained unsaid but hung heavily between them.

"I'm sorry," the girl burst out. Tears streaked down her cheeks, and she wrapped her arms around her middle as if afraid she would fly apart. "Truly, I'm sorry. For everything. I just wanted to find my mother."

He'd heard her story the first time, when he'd held Ara's broken, bleeding body. "Tell me about her."

"I never knew her." Annalith's voice broke and her tears picked up pace. "My father was desperate for offspring. Once I was born, my sire sent her back. He was done with her."

Fen breathed deeply, testing the air for any lingering scent of a lie.

Nothing.

"Okay. Tell me why you want to find her so badly. If your father was so desperate for a child that he kidnapped a human, I would expect you had a pretty good life in Under."

The Fae's laughter was tinged with bitterness. "You would

be correct if I'd actually turned out the way he wanted. I took after my mother in more ways than just my appearance. I have barely any magic."

"Barely any magic? You created a monster."

She caught her bottom lip between her teeth and dropped her gaze. "Sometimes I can follow spells," she muttered. "I had enough magic to create my chimera. Just not enough to control him properly."

Fen's urge to rip the Fae's throat out died. She was clearly distraught. But he was still confused. "If we go on that logic, you had to have suspected the creature could be dangerous, even to your own mother. Why would you even release it into our world?"

"I was hopeless. Half Fae who take after their human parent are… reviled in Under. Most of us flicker out before our thirteenth birthday from lack of care. Human food is not provided, and if you can't digest Fae energy, then you starve. And that is the most humane thing that happens to us."

Annalith flushed and Fen could scent her anger. "I overheard my sire discussing plans to sell me. He had the bidders lined up. When he found out I knew about his plans, he took great pleasure in telling me about each of the buyers. Some wanted to use me as a sex slave. Others wanted prey for their warriors. I won't go into details about what some of the others wanted to do with me."

Cold fingers of horror crawled through him. Who could even think to do something so vile to their child? Shifters valued life, and the lives of their young meant everything. He would die for any of the pups in his pack.

"I just wanted somewhere safe. Somewhere I could live without being afraid all the time," Annalith whispered. "And I've always dreamed of meeting my mother. I had to try. I didn't know it would turn out so badly."

His heart ached for the girl and what she must have gone through. He didn't scent any lies, and his nose had never failed him before, but he had to make sure of one thing. "How do I know I'm not Fae-struck?"

"I guess you don't," she admitted. She pulled up her sleeve and showed him an intricate tattoo on the inside of her forearm. "The ink was laced with iron. Not enough to completely override any magical ability, just enough to dampen it in case I was able to use it against my sire."

Bile crawled up his throat. The texts he'd read in the Old Books had described the agony Fae felt when exposed to iron. "Does it hurt?"

"Not so much anymore. It's more like an annoying buzz that's always there. My sire had it etched into my skin on my fifth birthday, when it became apparent I was more like my mother. It's common practice in Under. It helps quell any revolutions."

She held up her other arm. A dull grey bracelet circled her wrist. "I wanted everyone to feel safe, so I asked Josh to find me an iron bracelet. Between this and the tattoo, I have no more magic than an average human."

Fen looked the girl over. She was bedraggled, painfully thin, and defeated. He could be Fae-struck. No one knew how much iron it really took to completely dampen a Fae's magic. But there were times where he had to trust his gut and have faith, and this was one of them.

"I believe you," he said, then knelt at the girl's feet and looked up at her.

"Thank you. You have no idea how much that means to me."

He took her tiny hand in his. "I won't be the one who decides your fate. But I'll stand by you."

CHAPTER TWENTY-EIGHT

Ara threw out the empty blood bag and scowled. Ever since she'd taken from Fen's vein, nothing seemed to satisfy her appetite. She knew it was all in her mind, but telling herself it was psychological never helped.

"You ready?" Josh stuck his head into their shared office.

Running her tongue over her teeth in case there was any stray blood staining them, she nodded.

"You sure? I mean, you were on the brink of death two days ago."

"Vampires heal fast." She didn't mention that she healed a lot faster than she should have. Or that she had her suspicions that Fen's blood was slightly addictive.

"I should be asking you the same thing," she said instead.

Josh shrugged. "Okay, I guess. It's a lot to take in, you know? Having a long-lost sister... a half-Fae sister. And all the times I just brushed my mother's words aside...."

Ara couldn't imagine the guilt Josh felt. She patted his arm and steered him back into the hall. "Have you seen Fen? He was supposed to meet us here before the trial."

Josh looked grateful for the change of topic. "He's already there. He sent me to fetch you. His words, not mine."

The briefing room the chief had grudgingly allowed them was all the way down at the other side of the precinct. An awkward silence settled between them as they made their way there. She just wasn't sure what to say to the young man. "You know, you can always talk to me or Fen. About paranormal stuff. If you want."

He tossed her a strained smile. "Thanks."

She breathed a sigh of relief when they slipped into the room.

The room crackled with nervous energy and barely suppressed emotions. Annalith stood at the front of the room, her hands bound in front of her in iron cuffs. Along a wide table sat a panel of people. Ara's grandfather was there, along with two other vampire Elders. Colin and the leo sat at opposite ends of the table, and she made a mental note to ask Fen about their relationship now that the threat to their packs had ended.

An unfamiliar man sat somewhere in between. The guy was huge, built like a brick wall, and looked bored out of his skull. She'd never met him, but there was no doubt in her mind she was looking at the alpha of the local bear population.

The chief sat in the middle, glowering around the room like he owned it.

She snorted, hiding it in the crook of her elbow to pass it off as a cough. The chief would never believe that he was the least threatening person in the room. "Nice of you to join us, Ms. Classen."

"Well, I'm moving a little slower these days. I'm still recovering from two days ago. You know, when I almost kicked the bucket."

Normally, she would have done her best to keep a civil tongue around the chief, but her intense craving for Fen's blood irritated her, making her snippy.

Luckily for him, the chief kept his mouth shut and stared straight ahead. She plopped down next to her partner and crossed her arms, glaring at anyone who looked at her.

Bo leaned forward from his seat on Fen's other side and smirked. "A little pissy today, are we?"

She opened her mouth to tell him off. Their grandfather cleared his throat before she could and she sat back, mouthing the word *later* at her brother.

"Please, state your name for the panel," her grandfather

said, not unkindly, to the Fae.

"Annalith." The Fae spoke in a whisper.

"Annalith what, my dear?"

She looked up, her eyes full of tears. "Just Annalith."

The bear shifter pushed his chair onto its back legs. Ara wondered if it was specially reinforced, since any normal chair would have collapsed under his weight. "It's my understanding that Fae have family names."

"Yes, they do. My Fae parent does not allow me to use it."

There was silence and some shuffling of paper. Finally, the chief spoke up. "The report I received said you want to stay here, in our dimension." The man choked on the last word. "Why should we let you?"

Ara focused on the panel while Annalith told her story. Fen had relayed it to her when she'd finally come back to herself and wasn't trying to bite his throat every three minutes.

She wanted to take the girl, wrap her in a blanket, sit her by a fireplace and force all the tea and cookies in the world on her.

"I'm confused," her grandfather said when she finished talking. "Why are there half-blood Fae at all?"

"Fae aren't truly immortal. They simply fade from existence after a while. No one knows where they go. They just don't appear one day. The birth rate is dangerously low. The humans who do fall through the gates become breeders."

"If what you say is true, I don't think you will be killed when we send you back. You would be coddled, cherished even." The chief tapped his pencil on the table and Ara could just imagine the smug look on his face. She peeled her lips back and bared her fangs at the back of the chief's head.

"Are you deaf or stupid?" the bear asked. "She just said that she takes after her human parent, not her Fae. Why would they want a child who is mostly human? Chances of her breeding another human-like offspring would be quite high. No offense, sweetheart. I like humans just fine. Except this one." The bear waved his hand at the chief.

Ooohhh, Ara liked him. She wondered if she could talk him into becoming a paranormal inspector.

"Go on, sweetheart," the bear continued. "Ignore the nasty human. Tell me more about your magic."

Annalith blinked at the man, like she wasn't used to anyone standing up for her. "I don't have much magic. Iron suppresses it completely, although it doesn't really hurt me like it does full-blooded Fae. It's just kind of irritating."

One by one, Ara, Josh, and Fen were called to give testimony. The story was told over and over again. "For God's sake," Ara finally snapped. "The woman was looking for her mother. You all have families. Wouldn't you do just about anything to find them if they were missing?"

The room was so quiet Ara could hear the blood rushing through each and every person.

"With all due respect," Fen cut in, "I would like to point out that Annalith defended us from her creature when it came down to it. She killed it even when she thought it was her only chance of finding her mother."

Her grandfather rose from his chair. "We need a few minutes to talk. If the inspectors and Miss Annalith will wait in the hall. I trust the three of you can handle her?"

He didn't wait for a response, turning his back on them as he leaned close to the others gathered at the table.

"Are most humans like the chief?" Annalith whispered once the door had safely closed behind them.

"No, he's a jerk."

Ara whipped around at the voice. "Mom?"

Camille Classen strode down the hall, looking every inch the classy vampire she was. "Hello, Arabella. We have to talk. Why is it that I have to hear from your *grandfather* that you were injured?"

"Mom," Bo intervened. "She was fine. Fen took care of her."

Camille pursed her lips and narrowed her eyes at her son. "I suppose you were too busy to pick up the phone as well."

Bo shrank back, hands in the air.

"Mom, I'm sorry," Ara placated. "It's just—"

"Yes, dear. We'll chat later. You must be Annalith."

The Fae stepped back, her expression caught between terror and fascination. "Yes?" It was more of a question than a statement.

"Well, I just came down to thank you in person for saving my daughter's life. You see, some people do remember to call." She patted Fen's cheek before glaring at Ara again.

Suck up, she mouthed at her partner when her mother turned away.

He simply grinned.

"You are simply stunning." Camille positively cooed when she turned back to Annalith. "My Boris has said some very flattering things about you."

The door opened. "We are finished. You may come back in for the verdict."

That was quick. Maybe too quick. She couldn't tell if it was a good thing or a bad thing.

One by one, they filed into the room. Annalith took her place at the front of the room again. That time, Josh stood next to her. He looked like he was ready to fight to the death if someone tried to hurt his sister.

Ara's soul filled with joy. The young man may not yet be completely comfortable with having a half-Fae sister, but at least he was trying.

The chief glowered down at his stack of papers. Clearly, he wasn't pleased with the decision.

"We won't drag this on," the bear alpha said. "Miss Annalith, we have decided to allow you to remain in our dimension, provided you wear an iron bracelet to mute your magic."

Annalith burst into tears. "Yes, of course. Thank you so

much."

"I would have sent you back," the chief put in. "I was out-voted."

"Yes, well," the bear said easily, "you are here only out of courtesy. Your opinion bears no weight in our decision. Because, as you can see, I'm the only bear shifter here."

Ara cocked a brow and grinned at Fen. Did the bear alpha really just make a joke?

Camille stepped forward and hooked her arm through Annalith's as Bo replaced the clunky iron bracelet Josh had found for her with a slimmer, more discreet one. "Come now, dear. I'm not sure where you've been staying the last few nights, but I would be thrilled if you would spend a few nights with me. After all, I need to get to know the woman who saved my daughter's life."

Wait a minute. Ara crossed her arms. She was grateful to Annalith too, but she wouldn't have needed saving if the girl hadn't created the chimera.

She shut her mouth quickly when she caught sight of her brother shaking his head. Their mother had taken a liking to the young woman. It might turn out to be good for both Camille and Annalith.

Instead, she caught Josh's arm and tugged. "Come on. Let's go get a drink. Unless you want to go with my mother and your sister. Be warned, Mom will probably start looking for a date for you."

He blinked. "I'll see my sister later, I guess. Where do paranormals go to get drunk?"

"We're not getting drunk," Ara said with a laugh. "Shall we head to the diner? I'm pretty sure I heard something about a mean shepherd's pie."

The diner was full when they got there. Carla shooed the group of teenagers out of Josh's regular booth. "What can I get you? It's on the house."

Fen and Josh both ordered lemonade. "You have any blood?" Bo asked.

"Sure do. Started stocking it as soon as I met you guys."

Bo grinned and wagged his eyebrows. "I'll take a bag. With a straw," he said when Ara glared at him.

"Make that two," Fen said. "Put one in a wineglass."

"What? You taken a liking to fresh blood even in your human form?" Bo asked after Carla left with their orders.

"It's for Ara, idiot. Someone needs to take care of her."

Ara rolled her eyes. It looked like she'd just earned herself a new babysitter.

Fen kept up the protective mode the entire night. He even followed her home. "Hey… Are you okay?" he asked as he escorted her to her apartment door. "You've seemed a little off since that night."

She looked him over, about to tell him off for coddling her when she caught sight of the genuine concern on his features.

Maybe having someone care for her wasn't so bad. "Want to come in for some coffee?"

"Sure."

He followed her inside, slipping his shoes off at the front door and lining them up neatly next to hers. She was about to offer him the basic apartment tour when she remembered he'd been there before.

"Have a seat," she said, waving at the kitchen table.

She busied herself with her coffee maker, trying to ignore just how good it seemed to have someone sitting at her table waiting for her.

Not just someone. Fen. *Don't get attached*, she chided herself. *It's already going to break your heart to watch him grow old and die. Don't make it worse by falling for him.*

She glanced over to where he sat. One of the things she liked best about him was the fact that he didn't fill the silence with inane chatter. He was content to sit quietly while she worked through whatever was bugging her.

The problem was there was so much to work through she didn't know where to start.

When the coffee was ready, she slid a steaming mug of the black stuff in front of the wolf at her table and sat across from him.

"Want to talk about what's going on?"

She shrugged. "Honestly, I'm having difficulty with the donor blood. It's been so long since I've taken from a live donor. And your blood was… potent."

"I'm not sorry for saving your life," he said, "I am sorry that you're struggling. Is there anything I can do?"

"No. I just have to get through the next few days."

As much as it sucked to admit she struggled with a slight affinity to his blood, it was the events of the past few days that really had her worried. "Have you seen the mists lately?"

"Ah." Fen cradled his mug in both hands and leaned his elbows on the table. "No, not since Annalith took care of the chimera. No one's really sure if the chimera was somehow manipulating the gates or if they appeared on their own."

She supressed a shiver. "I don't think I'm up for a walk in the woods any time soon."

Her partner frowned, carving lines into his forehead. "If I recall, you're the one who told Josh not to think too hard on what he's seen, that he shouldn't live his life in fear."

The steam swirled over the top of her cup as she stared down into it. "Pretty words. I've ignored so many things over the years. You and I know better than anyone that there are people, *things*, out there, just waiting for someone unsuspecting to stumble into their path."

"We're not unsuspecting, Ara," Fen murmured.

"Exactly," she said, wrapping her hands around her mug. She tried to draw some sense of comfort from the warmth but failed. "I've always been aware of the dangers in the world, both human and paranormal. I've been able to control them, at least to an extent. This… I can't control."

"Is that why you've taken to carrying your gun with you?"

"Yes." Of course he would have noticed. She couldn't deny the heft of the gun gave her some sort of security. "I'm surprised you don't."

He shrugged. "Normally, I prefer to fight in my wolf form. It might be stupid, not carrying my weapon, but I'm just more comfortable knowing I can shift without having to worry about where my gun is."

Fen surged to his feet suddenly, jerking his thumb over his shoulder. "Come on, I have something to show you."

Completely bewildered, she followed him back out the door. "Where are we going?"

He opened the passenger side door of his car and smirked at her. "You trust me, right?"

"You know I do."

"Then get in."

He shot her a bright grin and proceeded to drive them to pack land. When she made for the front door, he shook his head. "This way."

He pointed to the forest.

She swallowed and glared at him. Hadn't he heard a word she'd said?

"Come on," he encouraged. "I promise you'll like this."

Blowing out a breath, she followed him to the tree line. The air smelled fresh and clean, like crisp apples, pine needles and late summer wildflowers. She breathed deep, filling her lungs. There was no hint of the mist or Fae magic floating in the afternoon air.

Fen continued down a path to a wooden shed. "Wait here."

She couldn't completely shake the uneasiness, her hand hovering over the handle of her gun.

Fen huffed when he re-emerged with a red plastic bucket. "Do you really think I'd take you out here if it wasn't safe?"

"I don't understand why you're being so blasé about the

whole thing," she replied.

Suddenly, he was in front of her. He placed the bucket at her feet and cupped her chin in both his palms. "Life is short, Ara. Even for vampires, life is finite. Do I sometimes look out my window at the woods and wonder what might be lurking? Yes. But I don't want to live like that. I can't."

Her eyes fluttered closed. Those strong, warm hands provided so much more security than the weapon strapped to her waistband.

His heart beat, strong and steady. Her gums itched a little and her mouth watered for just a small taste, but the urge wasn't strong enough to worry about.

"Better?" he whispered.

"Yeah."

"Good. Come with me."

He bent over and picked up the bucket, spilling a little of the contents over the side. She raised an eyebrow. "Sunflower seeds?"

"You'll see."

Intrigued, she followed him deeper into the forest. He stopped at a pine tree and cocked his head. "You'll have to be very quiet."

"What, are we hunting for rabbits?" she asked.

"Hey," he said, sounding slightly offended. "Never underestimate a good rabbit hunt."

She snorted but quieted when he raised his eyebrows at her. "Mandy and the kids have the chickadees trained to eat from our hands."

"Really?" The thought of having such a tiny life in her hands thrilled her.

"Yep. Hold your hand like this." He straightened her fingers and pressed her palm flat. He poured a few seeds into her hand and extended her arm. "It might take a few minutes."

She waited, hardly daring to breathe. Finally, one tiny

chickadee appeared at the end of a branch. It stared at her, head tilted, as if deciding whether she was safe or not. The little bird hopped around before fluttering to perch on one of her fingers.

It was only on her hand for a second, just long enough for her to sense its heart hammering a mile a minute, before it scooped a seed from her palm and flew away.

"Cute," she whispered.

Fen crowded next to her, watching the chickadees fly from branch to branch. "That might be the only one that comes down. They don't really need the seed in the summer. They're much more likely to come in the middle of winter."

She held out the seeds a few more minutes. "This was fun," she finally said.

"Just after our fight with the chimera, one of the kids mentioned how the birds had gone away. She was right. We hadn't seen or heard any birds for a week. They're back now."

She let the few seeds left in her hand fall to the ground. "And you're saying I should trust a bunch of birds to tell me when the forest is safe?"

He smiled and gestured for her to walk ahead of him back up the path. "No. I'm saying you should trust me."

A gentle breeze ruffled her hair as they walked. "Trust you to tell me when the forest is safe?" she clarified.

"Just trust me."

She glanced back over her shoulder at the earnest expression on his face. She felt something, deep in her soul, click into place. "I do trust you."

"Really?"

She smiled and punched him in the arm instead of twining her fingers through his, which was what she really wanted to do. "Yes. Really."

"Good." He looked twelve kinds of pleased with himself. "Then, should we go back up to the house? I have it on good authority that Colin just restocked the liquor cabinet."

She rolled her eyes but nodded. "I'm not drinking that much

again."

He shrugged. "That's okay if you do. You're cute when you're drunk."

"Hey!" she protested. "Does that mean I'm not cute when I'm sober."

The look he gave her warmed her to her toes. "Not at all. You're cute all the time."

She should have put her mental wall back up. Maybe she should never have let it fall down. All she knew was that somewhere along the way, her defences crumbled.

"Especially when you're breaking someone's nose," he added with a wink.

"Way to ruin the mood," she muttered.

"Was there a mood to ruin?"

"Maybe," she answered. "Maybe."

ABOUT THE AUTHOR

Lynn lives in Ontario, Canada with her husband and children. She spends her days writing about werewolves and vampires, and longs for a pet unicorn.

You can find Lynn at:
www.lynntylerbooks.com
or find her on
Facebook.

ALSO BY LYNN TYLER

Pack Mates Series
Called to Mate
Micah's Refuge
The Wolf's Tiger
Michael's Heart
Pierce's Choice
Daniel's Mate